WHS

NOVEMBER

November

a novel by

Rolf Schneider

Translated from the
German by

Michael Bullock

Alfred A. Knopf, New York

1 9 8 1

Translation Copyright © 1981 by Hamish Hamilton Limited

All rights reserved under International and
Pan-American Copyright Conventions.
Published in the United States by
Alfred A. Knopf, Inc., New York.
Distributed by Random House, Inc.,
New York. Originally published in Germany
as *November* by Albrecht Knaus Verlag,
Hamburg. Copyright © 1979 by
Albrecht Knaus Verlag, Hamburg

Library of Congress Cataloging in
Publication Data
Schneider, Rolf. (Date)
November.
I. Title.
PT2680.N38N613 1981   833'.914   80–22770
ISBN 0–394–51440–8

Manufactured in the United States of
America
First American Edition

IN NOVEMBER . . . every hour is as long as a day of repentance, as eerie as All Souls' Day, imbued with a positively spiritualistic solemnity, in which we do not merely encounter ghosts, but become ghosts ourselves. The day is not like a day, but like the offspring of night. Between dawn and dusk there lies a wad of compact, wet cottonwool: atmospheric cottonwool. What can you do with it?

—Joseph Roth

Author's Note

*This book makes use, in very free
adaptation, of certain events of recent
history. Precisely for this reason, the
author wishes to state emphatically that
it was not his aim to write a* roman à clef
*or a documentary, but rather a fictional
story with fictional characters. He made
every attempt to avoid any resemblance
to living people. If such resemblances
nevertheless appear to exist, this is
entirely contrary to his intentions.*

—R. S.

NOVEMBER

WHEN HE THOUGHT about it later he felt sure it had all started with the accident. In the house in which he grew up and in the family to which he belonged this accident had become almost a traumatic event, a magical watershed in time. For him personally it became the dividing point between his childhood and what began after childhood. Before it he had been just anyone, a person like other people; after it he was suddenly not like other people any more, but simply himself. The accident happened sixty days after his fifteenth birthday and three days before the end of the month of November.

That morning the garden had been covered in frost, there were mist and twilight in the air, the puddles on the path were covered by a film of ice. He and his little sister wheeled their bicycles out of the garage. His mother was standing by the door of the house; she was wearing a grey-green sweater; she rubbed her bare hands, yawned, smiled; her hair was uncombed; she looked tired out. This scene was interrupted by the arrival of his father, who had to travel that morning to Leipzig, where a scientific conference was just beginning. His father had intended to go by train, but he had missed the streetcar. Now he had hurried back to take the car, despite the dangerous conditions on the roads. This occurrence and the hasty discussion of it between the parents introduced an element of disquiet into a familiar ritual. The children hardly lost any time through it. Nor did the interruption worry them. They lost perhaps two or three minutes on their way to school. It may have been precisely these minutes which caused two paths, originally separated in time, to draw together and intersect at one moment in one place. His father steered the car out of the garage and drove hurriedly away. His mother waved to the children; she yawned again, hunching her shoulders and shivering, he saw that. His sister rode off in front of him. He caught up with her in a minute. The roadway consisted of large, rounded cobblestones, many of which had been lifted up by the increasingly powerful roots of the oak trees growing by the roadside. The hollows between were filled with puddles, which were now frozen over. The whole street was covered with hoarfrost that morning, as though with a thin whitish-grey fur. Other bicycles had impressed their tracks on it, narrow black lines. At the end of the village, in those days, there was a turnpike. The barrier was open, as usual. He saw a light-grey delivery van coming along the straight road from the forest. It was probably exceeding the speed limit, but he didn't think about that. Rather, he looked over his shoulder to make sure that his sister, who was now riding behind him, didn't cross the road too soon in order to turn into the side road that branched off to the left. Because he had turned his head, for one second he didn't look where he was going. Later he could remember that his bicycle suddenly and unexpectedly swerved off towards the middle of the road. He remembered the splintering of thin ice that was conveyed through the bicycle to the palms of his hands as a series of tiny tremors. He could also remember the sensation of losing his balance and the shrill screech of car brakes. He had no visual recollection of this moment.

What happened to him in the next few hours was told to him later, first cautiously, then more and more volubly, faster, more colourfully. It turned into a breath-taking fairy story,

the contents of which were as firmly established as the words
and sentences that had been found to tell it. For a long time
there was no more impressive legend in the family. As he
listened to it he had the impression that the central figure,
who was himself, was in reality someone else, a stranger, if
not an entirely fictitious character, someone he didn't know
and wasn't concerned with.

His father, the moment he arrived in Leipzig by car, was
informed by the conference secretary that his little daughter
had called him up from home. His father was very surprised
at this news. He knew both the children were at school. He
phoned back, and it was indeed Sibylle who answered. She
told him Stefan had had an accident and asked him to come
home at once. No, said Sibylle, it wasn't a particularly serious
accident and Stefan was already in hospital. But even so.
Sibylle spoke very fast. Her voice didn't sound unmistakably
agitated. At least, his father declared later, that had been his
impression. But then, how often had he heard Sibylle's voice
on the telephone, to be able to judge this so precisely? How
well could an eleven-year-old child disguise her voice, so that
an adult with a three-hour drive in front of him shouldn't be
made careless by worry? Such thoughts were running
through this adult's mind as he drove along all kinds of detours on the Leipzig ring road in order to reach what proved
to be the least favourable of all possible exits to the motor-
way. The journey took him over three hours. Afterwards he
told people he had spent all the time listening to light music
and stupid announcements from Radio Luxembourg, simply
to calm his rising anxiety. When he got home he went
straight to the hospital; and that was his, the father's, whole
part in the business.

At that time, he himself—Stefan—was feeling as though he
had left a tangle of evil-smelling curtains behind him and
arrived, exhausted, at a place which, when he opened his eyes,
proved to be a white metal bedstead in a totally unfamiliar

room. The light in the window was pale grey. In the room there was twilight. Someone in a white overall was holding a shallow metal bowl to his chin, into which he vomited. His mouth was wiped with tissue and it gave him a feeling of numbness in his lips. Afterwards—and it cost him a great effort to turn his head and focus his eyes—he caught sight of his parents outside the door of the room. Weren't they displaying an unnatural friendliness, didn't they have unnaturally red blotches on their faces? His mother sat down beside him. His father remained standing. He held his, Stefan's, bare feet and stroked them. Of this, Stefan remembered, he only became aware much later. He listened while his mother told him he had collided with a motor vehicle and had a complex fracture. As though in confirmation, his left arm lay in front of him, bent and wrapped in a white bandage. If he had pains in this arm, the pains in his head were much worse, so bad he felt dizzy, and he was very worried by the fact that in most sections of his field of vision objects appeared double; he saw his mother double and, unless he turned his head, his father appeared so too. It suddenly occurred to him to ask his mother to change the position of his right, uninjured arm. His mother did so. The arm didn't seem to belong to his body. At the same time he clearly felt the hot palms of his mother's hands.

But all this was only the conclusion of what, on the basis of the accounts given him by Billa and his mother, he later pictured to himself thus:

He, Stefan, an incomprehensible if not unknown individual, on his way to school, had suddenly bicycled over a frozen puddle, cracking the ice, which caused him to lose his balance and fall off. At this moment a delivery van coming from the opposite direction and clearly exceeding the speed limit had hit him. Stefan's sister Sibylle, who had also seen the van coming, had vainly shouted a warning to her brother. The van had dragged the jumbled mass that was Stefan's bicycle and Stefan a short way before coming to a stop. In the process one of its wheels had run over Stefan's left arm. In falling, as was evident from a severe abrasion, Stefan had struck his chin on the ground. Billa went on yelling. She turned her bicycle and rode back home. Breathlessly, she told her mother what had happened. She was unable to answer her mother's question as to whether Stefan was still alive. The mother ran out of the house. Somewhere along the way it dawned on her that she didn't even know exactly where the accident had happened. A car pulled up alongside her and a completely unknown man, who nevertheless knew all about what had happened, invited her in and took her to the turnpike. In the meantime, a crowd of people had gathered and was standing around Stefan, lying freezing cold and motionless. Under his back lay a dirty woollen rug; his eyes were closed; a frothy puddle of ice, dirty water and blood was forming alongside him. It was a terrible sight. She could see that Stefan was still alive, but blood was seeping nonstop through the green material of his jacket sleeve from his left arm, which was twisted and projecting away from his body. She squatted down beside him and took his head between her hands. He opened his eyes several times, then muttered a few brief curses. She talked to him encouragingly, still holding his head. They had to wait like this for well over half an hour. At the casualty clinic, only ten minutes on foot from the scene of the accident, the event had been reported three times in all, but the medical staff disagreed as to whose responsibility it was; no vehicle was available; they waited for a laundry delivery and in the meantime made tea. When a woman doctor finally arrived on the scene of the accident, she was horrified at the extent of the injuries. In her confusion she had the unconscious Stefan lifted into her private car, despite the protests of Stefan's mother, who shrilly demanded a stretcher. Then she sat beside her son to support him. As the car drove fast over the uneven surface of the road, Stefan's head was bounced this way and that; at one point he opened his mouth and started to curse again. In the treatment room at the casualty clinic he was placed on a plank bed. A young doctor refused to snip open the fine woollen jacket Stefan was wearing, despite Stefan's mother's almost hysterical insistence. After that things moved very fast. An ambulance took the boy to the hospital, where Stefan's mother was well known. The young patient spent three hours in the operating theatre. During this time, his mother sat on a chair in the corridor, until she was finally informed that they had done everything humanly possible. She took a taxi home. She comforted the weeping Billa; she waited for her husband; she went back to the hospital with him, and before they were allowed in to see Stefan, who was just coming out of the anaesthetic, she was given a cautious description of the situation by the intern. Stefan's arm was broken in five places. One of the fractures was close to the wrist. Moreover the wound had been open and very dirty. She could imagine the consequences for herself: a stiffening of the wrist, and in the worst case amputation. Aware of such possibilities, she entered the ward. For two days and nights she was haunted by a nightmare of amputation of the left forearm, until she learned that the doctors were even more concerned by the fact that Stefan was suffering from hemiplegia, the cause of which could not be ascertained with the diagnostic apparatus available at the hospital.

Stefan, who, when he later inquired about all this, was forced to his bewilderment to see himself as the hero of these events, was finally taken by ambulance to another hospital. He lay with closed eyes. The doctor and the nurse accompanying him seemed to be convinced he was asleep. They were both bad-tempered. It was early on a Sunday morning. They spoke in whispers about people Stefan didn't know and whose description bored him. After that, still in whispers, they discussed the transfer they were carrying out. Thus Stefan learned that he was on the way to a hospital that didn't usually accept cases like his. Stefan learned something about himself that was described by a word he might have heard in the past without understanding it, but which he now understood. The word was "privileged." Stefan had to admit that it obviously did apply to him.

HE WAS THE CHILD of the writer Natasha Roth. One day, much later, he would look up the words "privilege" and "privileged" in the dictionary. He would then read about special rights, and if we may assume that special rights are perhaps based on special circumstances, then Natasha Roth had been privileged by a life over whose beginnings she had had no control. Natasha Roth, born in Odessa, was the daughter of a Socialist driven out by Hitler. Her old mother, who bore the name Sinaida, was living today in Tel Aviv. Everything in this statement was right, and everything wrong.

To begin with, Roth was not the name she was born with but rather her husband's. Similarly, the mistaken idea that she was born with the name of Roth, coupled with the fact that as a young girl she had written a biographical study of the writer Joseph Roth, had given rise to the further mistaken idea that she was the poet's niece. Joseph Roth had been an Austrian, born in the present-day Russian Galicia, a Jew and a Socialist. He had fled from Hitler to France and had died there. Natasha Roth, now a writer, had fled from Hitler to Austria and later to France. How could anyone be made to believe that all this had nothing to do with the writer Joseph Roth?

Her mother, Sinaida, was not her real mother either. Natasha's father was not a Jew. His name was Wilfried Hermann Bleibtreu. He was born the son of a National Conservative grammar school teacher from Magdeburg. Wilfried Hermann Bleibtreu himself was vice-president of the Social Democratic party in the Prussian provincial parliament, and apart from the sensuous music of Richard Wagner his great love was the books of Lev Tolstoi. It was probably on that account that in the summer of 1931 he set out with his pregnant wife, Charlotte, on a trip to Russia and a steamer cruise on the Black Sea. His wife gave birth prematurely. Natasha was a seven-month child, and she owed her name to a sentimental gesture on her father's part towards Lev Tolstoi and the harbour hospital in the Black Sea city of Odessa. What little Russian Natasha spoke she had learned at university when she was eighteen. Joseph Roth, she imagined, had spoken Russian much better.

In spring 1933 the Social Democratic politician Wilfried Hermann Bleibtreu was condemned to seven months in prison, after which he emigrated with his family to Vienna. By then his wife's name was already Sinaida. She had relatives living in the Vienna second district, the Leopoldstadt. Charlotte Bleibtreu had died of a pulmonary embolism shortly after Natasha's birth. Her earliest impressions, Natasha later told her children, related to the Pfeilgasse in the Vienna eighth district, the Josefstadt. The Pfeilgasse is narrow and old, said Natasha, and after a while it suddenly comes to an end in the Lerchengasse, then, just imagine, it starts all over again the other side of a wall; it's a real surprise. At this time her father was a lecturer at the university. In 1938 he went with his family to France, to Strasbourg in Alsace, where he was once again a lecturer at the university. After the German invasion of France, Sinaida Bleibtreu, after many adventures, managed to escape to Switzerland, where she was immediately sent to an internment camp. Wilfried

Hermann Bleibtreu, however, now had a false passport and a new name; he had joined the Resistance. By now Natasha was nine years old. She lived in a little Alsatian village called Wingen-sur-Moder where, apart from old farmhouses and low green hills, there were several trout ponds. She lived with a distant relative of her dead mother's, at an inn. Later, she remembered the smiling German army officers who stretched out their legs in highly-polished boots under the table, ate *quiche lorraine* and steaks with green peppers, drank apple brandy and insisted on having the radio on all the time so they could listen to the popular songs of the day. To her childish eyes, said Natasha Roth, all this seemed like a very peaceful scene. Altogether she spent seven years of her childhood in France, and the circumstances were such that she spoke French little better than Russian. She was never in Paris as a child. In 1946 her father returned to Berlin with his daughter Natasha and a third wife, a Frenchwoman called Jeanne.

The only Jewish thing about Natasha Roth was the man she had married, for Rudolf Roth was the child of a Berlin Jewish coal merchant and a non-Jewish mother, who always refused to be divorced from her husband. As a result, nothing really serious happened to her husband under Hitler. Things like that did occur.

So these were the legends. They were told, sometimes frequently, sometimes less often; in any case, everyone in the family knew them off by heart. Once a year Grandmother Sinaida from Tel Aviv came to visit them. She had thin white hair, a deep voice and very big eyes. Grandmother Roth lived in Düsseldorf and often sent parcels. Grandmother Jeanne lived in Paris; she existed in the Roths' house mainly as a photograph, as a name and as the address and telephone number (TUR 01–29) at which Natasha Roth could be reached when she went to France. This happened at least once a year.

3 H E   W A S   P U S H E D under an X-ray tube. After that the hair
on his temples was greased and he was attached to an apparatus called an electroencephalograph, or EEG for short.
Finally he was taken into a spacious ward; an apparatus was
set up beside his bed, and the cannula for a drip inserted in
a vein on the back of his right hand. Before that, as he was
being wheeled down a long corridor, he thought he caught
sight of his father. He lay on his back looking up at the very
high ceiling. He tried to turn his head so as to make the
annoying double images go away. There was a second bed in
the ward. In it lay a bearded man who from time to time
would suddenly start babbling incoherently or unexpectedly
sit up. All the time there was a nurse sitting on the other side
of a glass wall. She either busied herself with instruments or
read a book.

There were various doctors; there were various nurses.
There was an old woman doctor to whom Stefan took an
immediate liking, because she reminded him vaguely of
Grandmother Sinaida. The doctor didn't seem to like Stefan
all that much, because during one visit she stated audibly that
it was going a bit far to have brought this young man to this
hospital and it could only be because of his special family
background.

A bell button was placed by the fingers of his left hand,
which, in spite of the multiple fractures of the arm belonging to it, was not paralysed. The bearded man in the other
bed, he learned, was a well-known footballer who, following
a traffic accident, had lost his memory and the power of
speech and also control of his bodily functions. He often
dirtied himself. Stefan was requested to ring his bell if he
noticed this happening. A young nurse, a pretty, giggling
girl called Ursula, brought two of Natasha Roth's books to

Stefan's bed and asked him, blushing, if he would get his mother to autograph them.

During the second night Stefan was woken by the bearded footballer falling out of bed and groaning. He immediately rang the bell. The night nurse, a very powerful woman, came and lifted the man, who in her arms looked remarkably frail, back into bed. Stefan was praised for his alertness.

The chief physician was an elegant bald-headed gentleman with big ears and a moustache that reminded Stefan of his father's. The chief physician was very gentle. Stefan learned from Nurse Ursula that he suffered from an advanced chronic illness. She told Stefan that everyone in the hospital idolized the chief physician, who, moreover, was a deeply religious man. Stefan realized on this occasion that there was nothing in the world about which he knew less than about religious matters. The chief physician was gentle and friendly to him. He told Stefan he had gained his most important medical knowledge in a French university clinic, in 1955 in Paris—my God, that was two decades ago! Stefan had to assume that this acount was a cautious reference to the life story of Natasha Roth, although the chief physician did not mention her name. Then she herself appeared, together with his father. She seemed to him as she always did: a bit absent-minded, vigorous, smiling, with strange ideas. She brought him a small Japanese transistor radio with a telescopic aerial and an ultra-shortwave receiving section. The set was so easy to manipulate that Stefan had no difficulty in operating it with the fingers of his left hand. He laid it on his chest, along-side the bellpush. His mother gave him a lively account of her activities. She had immediately written a letter to Grand-mother Roth in Düsseldorf, asking her to buy a loden cape with no sleeves and a hood, because Stefan's injured arm would have to remain bandaged for quite a while. He made no reply to this information. Secretly, he thought his mother odd. Since he was paralysed, it would be a very long time before he could walk, if he ever did. His father said little, but simply kept stroking the fingers of Stefan's left hand, which projected from the bandages and the plaster cast. Stefan noticed this and looked away. He constantly saw people and things, including his parents, double. This was caused, he learned later, by something called abducens paresis. This name didn't make the problem any clearer.

His parents had gone. He was fiddling with his transistor radio. The bearded footballer was tossing about, muttering unintelligibly. The radio picked up broadcasts of pop songs, news. One of the first longer items Stefan heard spoken came from a West German station and included a review of a recently published collection of letters written to various people by an author called Joseph Roth. It was obviously difficult to escape from that name.

4 THE BOOK entitled *Melancholy Reality*, in which a novel called *Radetzky March* was extolled as the Austrian counterpart of Thomas Mann's *Buddenbrooks*, was published many years after it was written. It was originally intended to be the dissertation of the Germanist Natasha Roth, but the professor who was solely responsible for her choice of subject preferred not to return from an international congress. Instead he sent his *"beautiful doctoral candidate"* colourful Christmas cards every year from New York, where for over twenty years he had been supplying other doctoral candidates with other subjects at Columbia University. In any case his departure, as she often said, had freed her from the terrible risk of ruining herself in an academic career. One of her pet

sayings was that German studies was a whore who could turn a profit for even the most stupid pimp. Nevertheless, she had her essay on Joseph Roth published as a book, and if asked her motives she replied that she simply wanted to show up the intellectual pygmies in her field.

She made such statements with her chin up. This made her look condescending, and she knew that as a result she created an impression of intellectual coldness which others might find unpleasant, but this didn't bother her. This, said her husband, was the reason why she didn't have personal friends, but since (unlike her husband) she didn't miss such friends, and since her social milieu placed no reliance on lasting friendships, she decided that coldness was healthier than lukewarmness. Her intellectual malice, said her husband, did damage to her own books, which in themselves were neither particularly malicious nor exaggeratedly intellectual. If her husband, Rudolf, was to be believed, the stories she invented and put on paper acquired exactly what she had chosen as a title for her book on Joseph Roth: a melancholy reality. Were her books not successful? There were editions of them in several countries. Of course she couldn't escape the impression that the newspapers didn't like her books, period, on the strength of what might be called a preconceived idea. In this respect there was little difference between the papers in this German state and the other one. Natasha Roth was angry about this. When she was just too angry, she would sit down and write an article in which she used malicious turns of phrase to poke fun at the errors and stupidities of some reviewer. The article would appear in a weekly magazine and attract attention; but Natasha Roth was made to pay bitterly for the satisfaction this gave her when her next book was published, if not before.

"You're so clever," said her husband, "why aren't you clever enough to see that it's spiritual suicide to try to prove to idiots how stupid they are and how clever you are?"

"Stupidity has to be put to death, that's a moral imperative," she retorted.

The extent to which she was in love with her own infallibility might be very impressive, she was told, but it was also very irritating.

She felt a sense of release only when she travelled to Austria or France, the two countries of her earlier exile. Vienna, she asserted, had developed intrigue and malice to such a noble art through centuries of practice that it always made her, Natasha Roth, feel like a sister of mercy, which did her battered soul good. What she felt for France, however, was not merely love, but total subjugation—because of its landscape, the comical patriotism of its people, the self-confidence of its workers, the strenuous intelligence of its intellectuals. She had said all this in a book dealing with German emigrés in Paris and the houses they occupied, from Heinrich Heine to the alcoholic Joseph Roth.

When she returned from these trips, she immediately filled all the rooms of the house with her voice and her movements. She was then told how calm and peaceful everything had been in her absence. Now her battered suitcases stood in the hall, an invitation to untidiness. Natasha Roth distributed presents, which invariably consisted of soft cheeses and fabrics for the children with the labels of foreign stores still attached. She ripped the airline tags from the handgrips of her luggage and tore them up, giving a rapid, breathless account of her trip as she did so. She was convinced that she was interesting to listen to, though perhaps a bit tiring as well.

She was small. She had jet-black hair and big black eyes. Her shoulders, she claimed, were too powerful. Ever since Billa's birth she had suffered from a change in the pigmentation of her face and after sunbathing she looked as blotchy as Feirefiz in Wolfram's *Parzival*, she said with a giggle. Her voice was constantly hoarse. She refused to wear the glasses she was supposed to wear, except while driving. She loved clothes of raw leather. She drove a French car with a hatchback, painted yellow like a German mailbox.

So she was back. She piled up books around her, smoked cigarettes, made phone calls, quarrelled with people and started to work. She wrote fast. She liked working, although she denied it. She often claimed that she hated literature, but that, as she knew herself, was a lie. It was much the same with her assertion that she hated writers. Her explanation was rather funny. Literary people, she said, were neurotic, vain, uneducated and uncomradely. Only tenors were as bad. The only writer known to her personally of whom she always spoke in friendly terms was Rebecca, who wasn't really a writer at all, but someone who made up songs and sang them herself on records.

Natasha Roth was used to being the centre of all the life in her house. It might seem strange later just how considerately her husband so long respected this state of affairs. Rudolf Roth was an art historian. He had thick glasses and a moustache; his nose was inexpressive, it was too small. He wore tweed jackets and smoked a pipe. He was director of the furniture section of the Museum of Arts and Crafts in Köpenick Castle, and there is not much more to be said about the son of the coal merchant Samuel Roth, except perhaps that he had obtained his doctorate. His professor hadn't run off, like Natasha Roth's, but it would have been better if he had, said Natasha Roth, because he was a complete idiot.

The time came when the suitcases stood in the hall once more packed. Natasha Roth quickly typed a long-overdue letter, while her husband fetched the car from the garage and loaded the cases. The four of them then drove to Berlin city centre. Natasha Roth talked nonstop throughout the journey. The car was left in the car park in front of the Berliner Ensemble. The four of them crossed the Weidendamm Bridge to the big glass front of Friedrichstrasse Station, which served as the entrance for journeys to the other world. She embraced her husband. She embraced each of her two children.

5 STEFAN FELT his mother's dry, cracked lips on his skin. He saw the hand of his sister Sibylle in his father's hand. He saw his mother go through a swing door and beyond the swing door down some steps. He saw her go away among many old people and moustached Turks. He thought of places like Wingen-sur-Moder or the Ile de la Cité, places he knew only by name or from bright-coloured, shiny picture postcards written by his mother, pictures of trout ponds, the cathedral of Notre-Dame at night, and no matter how colourful these pictures were they remained for him flat and incomprehensible, because he had never been able to grasp the things on them. His mother was no longer in sight. The three of them were walking back over the Weidendamm Bridge to the car park outside the Berliner Ensemble, where the yellow car stood.

These were memories. He immersed himself in them, with the cannula of the drip in the back of his left hand and the fingers of the left on the knobs of the little transistor radio. He wondered whether he would ever again be able to walk across the Weidendamm Bridge or anywhere else.

On her next visit to the hospital his mother brought him a box of *suc des Vosges*. These were sweets from Alsace; they were shaped like fir twigs and tasted like the oil of ever-

green needles; the box was bluish-green with old-fashioned
gilt lettering and a picture of mountains, fir trees and a wall.
He turned his head to one side until he ceased to see double.
What did *souvent imités, jamais égalés* mean? He didn't
know any French.

Meanwhile the cannula had been removed from the back of
his hand. Twice a day now a physiotherapist in a white coat
appeared and occupied herself with his paralysed limbs. She
asked him to press his right hand against her hand. His hand
refused to obey him. It was as deaf and without will as a
piece of wood.

He was moved to another ward that was much smaller but
had four beds in it. In one of them lay a fat old man who had
suffered a cerebral haemorrhage and announced in a toneless voice that he was only here to die slowly. This lament
invariably enraged his neighbour, a young man who had a
lot of suppurating ulcers in his face which were treated with
an evil-smelling sulphur preparation. Above all, however,
this young man suffered from constant headaches. He was
afraid of a brain operation. But the third patient already had
been through this, in fact twice. During the removal of a
tumor a motor nerve had been damaged, so that the right
half of his face was paralysed and completely expressionless.
Fluid ran from the corner of his mouth. He had a white
bandage round his head, like a knitted cap that was too small.
This was the headdress of post-operative patients. When the
door of the ward was open, Stefan saw other men with the
same white bandage on their heads shuffling along the corridor. He felt disgusted when he had to use the bedpan and he
was embarrassed when pretty Nurse Ursula helped him
with it.

His father and his mother, and generally also his sister,
Sibylle, visited him every third day. These were the hours
for which he waited with longing and for which he put up

with everything in the meantime. Twice a week a doctor came from the neighbouring hospital for orthopaedic surgery to examine the broken left arm. The doctor was a cheerful, fair-haired man. He praised Stefan's callus formation and talked to him about Natasha Roth's books, which Stefan hadn't read. The quarrels between the corpulent old man and the young lad with the suppurating ulcers in his face grew more intense.

His mother brought Stefan fruit juice from the state foreign-currency shops. She supplied him with a Swiss vitamin preparation of whose overwhelming efficacy she seemed, for some reason, convinced. Probably Grandmother Roth had sent the tablets. He forgot to ask his mother about this.

He lay by the window. He looked out at the strangely shaped metal roof of the hospital building opposite and at the winter sky, which was sometimes grey, sometimes bright with sunshine. The boy who had been operated on began to talk to Stefan haltingly and in a whisper, without demanding an answer, sexual fantasies or experiences, it was impossible to tell which. Listening to them both embarrassed and excited Stefan. The ward was constantly overheated. The fat old man protested when anyone tried to open the window. Stefan had erections. His whirling thoughts pictured what it would be like if he put his hand on pretty Nurse Ursula's breast as she bent over him. He suddenly developed eczema on his face too, a kind of acne. His mother immediately claimed it was an infection caught from the lad with the ulcers. The nurses denied this. All the same, Stefan too was treated with the stinking sulphur preparation. Through the physiotherapy his right hand had become sufficiently strong and mobile to hold a book, not for very long, but at least for half an hour.

Then Dr Erica Roth appeared and caused confusion with her name. She was not related to Rudolf Roth and certainly not to Joseph Roth, of whose existence she hadn't even known for a long time. She had read books by Natasha Roth, because she had been struck by the name when she saw them in shop windows, and now she had learned that Natasha Roth's son was in a hospital she knew because she had once worked there. She would sometimes sit at Stefan's bedside and talk to him. She chatted with the staff. Everyone immediately assumed that Stefan and Erica Roth were related. No one was inclined to contradict this assumption. The relationship with the dead novelist Joseph Roth became ever more legendary.

At Christmas his mother announced that when he came out of hospital he would find a dog waiting for him. This information made him happy. He had wanted a dog for as long as he could think, and so had his sister, Billa. His parents had once kept cats, but he couldn't remember that. Strangely, he could no longer remember past Christmases, or only faintly. Christmas here in hospital was announced by fir branches in retorts hung with tinsel and bright-coloured glass balls. The ward sister distributed cinnamon cakes, chocolate, gingerbread. The other patients in the ward suddenly received more visitors more frequently than usual; the room was filled with the rustle of coloured paper. Stefan turned the station knob on his radio. He kept getting the same songs: "White Christmas," "Rudolf the Red-Nosed Reindeer," "Jingle Bells." In other respects these days passed like an ordinary Sunday. He looked out of the window at the roofs on which there was no snow; the sky behind was mostly grey; the sun shone for only a quarter of an hour at a time.

At the beginning of the new calendar year Grandmother Sinaida came from Tel Aviv, bringing with her an inflatable rubber object the purpose of which was to strengthen the hand muscles by squeezing and kneading it. Stefan had to smile and say thank you. He knew that Grandmother Sinaida expected that. She argued with Natasha Roth, even at Stefan's bedside, about the state in which Natasha lived. Stefan was used to such quarrels. Grandmother Sinaida was old. Yet she didn't seem to grow any older; rather, she gave the impression of having been left aside by time while everything around her had changed. Perhaps Tel Aviv was a city in which time stood still. Stefan, drowsy himself, imagined time in Tel Aviv as a big dark-grey animal sleeping on quaysides or among lemon trees, its head between its paws.

His neighbour, the one who had the two brain operations behind him, was moved to another ward, in another wing of the hospital. Nurse Ursula whispered to Stefan that this was a place from which there was no return. He himself, Stefan, got up for the first time with the help of the physiotherapist. On her arm, he walked across the room and back to his bed. The effort it cost him was close to unbearable. The fat old man, he saw, followed his progress with a contemptuous expression. His mother brought him books about Lorraine, the Côte d'Azur and Languedoc, written in German, with illustrations in colour, and he dreamed that he was walking with a light, springy step along the marina in the little town of Beaulieu-sur-Mer with the sun sparkling on the water. Dr Erica Roth arranged for him to be transferred to the children's ward, as soon as a bed at last came free.

He now shared a room with a fourteen-year-old peasant boy from Oderbruch, a cheeky lad named Gerhard. He seemed perfectly healthy and was only there for observation on account of an insignificant abnormality of the spinal cord.

Before going to sleep they told one another endless stories, comical, obscene, serious, and they threw the remains of fruit out of the window onto the car of a doctor they disliked. After a week Stefan had got so far that he could walk on his own down the corridor of the children's ward.

Late one afternoon his parents came to see him without Billa. He noticed that his father was wearing black trousers and his mother black stockings; her eyes were red. They didn't tell him where they had been and Stefan didn't like to ask. Not until much later would he find out that an old friend of his mother's, a man of forty-three, had died of a heart attack. This was a shock for Natasha Roth. She had been to the funeral in the muddy cemetery of a small town in Mecklenburg. Stefan thought about the fact that for a few months he had been positively surrounded by death and signs of dying, whereas before this death and dying had been no more than empty words for him.

Every day he made his way unaided to the gymnasium, where he had to do an hour's exercises. He had an obvious limp and his body would buckle on the paralysed side. The abducens paresis remained unchanged. He knew now that paresis is the same as paralysis and that the abducens is the external motor nerve of the eye. In these few weeks he had become very thin and grown by a hand's breadth. As he limped along to the gymnasium he had to pass other wards and departments. A baby had recently been put in the infants' ward who screamed every night in a scarcely human, almost animal way. Stefan also got to know other children in the ward. There was a ten-year-old boy who kept throwing himself on the floor and groaning, always without the slightest warning. There was a little girl of one, Anya, a laughing, sweet-natured, very pretty child, who had suffered from birth from transverse paralysis of the spinal cord. One Sunday he was given permission for the first time to go down the steps accompanied by his parents and into the open. His mother really had been sent the loden cape, and she brought it with her. It was a cool, dull early-spring day. For the first time he was able to look at the red-brick buildings of the hospital from all sides. His mother told him that in a funny way it all reminded her of the college buildings of Cambridge University. He had to keep stopping after every few steps. The effort made him break into a sweat.

November

One of the wires holding his broken bones together projected through his skin and caused a suppurating inflammation.
The wire was removed. When he woke from the anaesthetic
he felt so rotten that for two days he couldn't get up. The
surgeon told him the fracture was healing very well. Stefan
went through a series of tests with the resident psychologist,
after which he was declared fit to attend school. He now
went every morning to another hospital, where he received
instruction along with seven other children. After two hours
he was always exhausted. The woman doctor who had reminded him of Grandmother Sinaida told him he could soon
be discharged.

Tests with the electroencephalograph were still being carried
out regularly. Now he only went to bed in the afternoon and
evening. His arm continued to heal well. But he was still
seeing double. The condition of his companion in the ward,
Gerhard, had grown worse during the last days and weeks
in a way that was hard to define, so that he now had to spend
the whole day in bed. And yet the causes of his affliction
remained unknown. Gerhard watched sadly, and rather en-
viously, as Stefan packed his suitcase. A whole pile of things
had accumulated in these four months. Stefan hobbled over
to the veranda, where at this time of day little Anya lay in
bed. She recognized him and raised her head slightly. She
laughed; she waved to him and he waved back. He said
goodbye to all the doctors and all the nurses in the hospital.
His father came with Billa. His father carried the suitcase
down to the car. On the hospital lawn crocuses were in
bloom. As he got into the car, Stefan looked up at the rows
of windows in the two wards he had been in. He wanted to
see whether anyone was watching his departure from behind
the panes of glass, but he could see no one, no face and no
hand. His mother, he knew, had left that day for Paris; it
couldn't be postponed any longer.

SHE WAS COLLECTING material for a book describing 6
events during the Paris Commune of spring 1871. In the
course of a public announcement of her plans she had stated
that she was interested, above all, in the relationship of art
to revolution and to counter-revolution. She also named
names: Verlaine, Courbet, Vermeersch, Rimbaud, the Gon-
court brothers. Gradually the person of the young Rimbaud
had become increasingly important to her and she had decided to write something subjective on the life of the poet.
She had amassed quotations and notes, but the book itself
existed exclusively in her mind and she discovered that she
was beginning to feel afraid to write it down.

This was a fear which she had long known and which
plagued her ever more persistently as the years passed. She
could sit in front of a blank sheet of paper and suddenly find
herself incapable of putting into words something she had
already thought through almost completely. If she tried in
spite of this, she would hesitate at the fourth or fifth word,
because it would seem to her empty, inapt. Then for the same
reason she had to cross out everything she had already
written. She would force herself to start again, only to cross
out the new set of words until the sheet of paper was covered
with the graffiti of her incompetence. Finally she would
destroy the whole sheet, tearing it up, crumpling it into a
ball and throwing it away. Then she would take a fresh sheet
and the whole process would be repeated. Meanwhile the
things she had intended to write about began to seem to her
increasingly insignificant, and why should she write about
something that no longer seemed important to her and hence
was unlikely to be of interest to anyone else? Indeed, why
did she write at all? She was familiar with the details of this

process from countless repetitions. Of course she had always managed to shake it off. But there was no guarantee that she would always be able to do so. Why should the process not suddenly become more obdurate? Perhaps she would really lapse into silence. Perhaps all that was needed for this was some specific cause, either her advancing age or something else. Moreover, she discovered that the poet Rimbaud had become so important to her because he had written his last line of poetry at the age of nineteen and then fallen silent, writing only business reports and commonplace letters to relatives that might have been written by anyone. There must be some explanation for this muteness, she thought. To find the explanation might provide her with the antibody that would suppress her fear, afford her everlasting immunity against being similarly struck dumb.

She thought about this a lot as she found herself, as it were, on the trail of the dead Rimbaud. She was sitting in a plane of the Polish airline on the way from Berlin to Paris. It was a complicated route, since it went via Amsterdam, and the flying time was about two hours. She turned her head towards the window and saw beside her whitish-grey strips of cloud falling away behind. The little window was completely filled by that blue synthetic sky invented exclusively for aeroplane travel. The clouds lay in flocks of raw, dead wool far below her. She turned her head even further. She saw the empty seat-backs drawn up as though on parade; the most lifeless things of all appeared to be the very rare human heads visible between them; at least the smoke from several cigarettes seemed to be alive. Smoking death-mouths, speechless. She tensed up at these words and took the feeling as the long-sought pretext to beckon the stewardess and order a drink. The girl was smiling. Grey eyes in a face with high cheekbones. The drink was set in front of her in a far-too-large beaker of transparent plastic. It smelled of woodruff.

She tried to think of the Polish name for this drink, but could only remember a dark-brown buffalo on the greenish-yellow label of a bottle.

She drank. Her body was soon changed into a capsule that was insensitive to outside influences and filled instead with a crackling indifference. Only in this condition could she bear to feel herself subject to that other fear which, in recent weeks, had plagued her almost as persistently as the fear of becoming mute. Perhaps the two fears were connected by a common root, perhaps they were one and the same and merely wore different faces at different times. She is sitting with her skirt bunched up on a greasy pavement. She sees her bent arms in blue-green wool knitted in a pattern that stands out with excessive clarity. Her hands are folded into a bowl supporting the back of Stefan's head. In the puddle that be-gins directly under her raised knees, splinters of ice are mov-ing almost imperceptibly in a grey liquid through which traces of blood pass and fade away. Beyond and above the puddle she sees people's boots and shoes, knees in wrinkled trousers, gleaming women's knees under the pale mesh of stockings, half-covered by coat hems. Higher still, in the direction of the sky, the faces of humanoid apes, grimaces of lascivious interest and sorrow. She looks at the closed eyes in the face on her lap. Frost is creeping out of the ground into her body, making her limbs lifeless; the cold rises into her pelvis, into her chest, right into her brain. She hears no sound of voices or wind. Merely heartbeats, toneless and without echo, Stefan's heartbeats, her own. She knows they will soon end in the cold. That they are both freezing stiff. They will splinter if anyone takes hold of them. Loss of speech is death.

Death was loss of speech. The memory of this scene was a trauma that again and again froze her limbs stiff. Alcohol usually helped; perhaps running away helped even more effectively. She couldn't have borne seeing Stefan come home from hospital with a white face and a limp. Since Stefan's accident she hadn't been able to get a single sentence down on paper that she could show anyone. Loss of speech was not merely death. The captain's voice announced in mournful French that they were approaching Paris. The stewardess handed out little white forms, *cartes d'embarquement*. On the other side of the aisle sat two young Poles in black suits; at this moment one of them opened his briefcase, in which five bottles of vodka lay side by side. The air bubbles in them slid lethargically along the clear glass walls. She spotted the yellowish-green label with the picture of a buffalo and was able to read the name, *Zubrovka*. Outside, the clouds had caught up once more with the window.

7 THEIR HOUSE stood in a suburb of East Berlin. The area was large and devoid of any special characteristic. What held it together was the trees: oaks, lining most of the streets, or clumps of pines, birches and bush-high locust trees, that had penetrated into the district as outrunners of the forest or been left behind by the forest like islands in the midst of the streets and buildings. Stefan's parents had lived in this house for a long time. They had moved into it when Stefan was two. Sibylle, his sister, had never known any other home. The house, said Stefan's mother, looked like a dilapidated villa in the ribbon development in some English town, because of the tall, thin chimneys. Natasha Roth had once spent several months in Great Britain, mainly in Cambridge, as the result of an invitation from her English translator, who taught at Cambridge.

Now she wasn't in Cambridge, but rather in Paris with her stepmother Jeanne (TUR 01–29) or on the way there. Perhaps by this evening, or at the latest by tomorrow morning, it would be possible to telephone her. There was never any problem phoning Paris in the morning, Stefan recalled, and he thought about such things as he was driven out to their suburb in his mother's yellow car. He was sitting beside his father. Billa sat behind him. They drove along the bumpy street in which their house stood. Stefan had a slight headache and felt generally exhausted. They passed their rusty garden fence; the car turned right and moved through the open gate (the two halves of the metal double gate hung from totally corroded posts) along the open path between the hedge and the lawn and came to a stop, as usual, by the veranda. He thought to himself that during his weeks in hospital he had often pictured this moment of homecoming. The reality was only half as exciting as his imaginings; he felt it to be more commonplace and therefore more tangible, in a word real; he felt absolutely no dismay. In contrast to all his fantasies Natasha Roth was missing.

On account of his return Frau Konjetzki had come, a little sixty-year-old woman, who scrubbed the floors and did the washing-up three mornings a week. Frau Konjetzki came from Silesia and spoke an astonishing German. She had brought Stefan a bottle of tincture of herbs she had grown herself, telling him it would help him to recover faster. As she spoke, a dog began barking outside the glass panes of the veranda. He limped to the front door. His father and Billa had entered the house ahead of him. The dog rushed out and ran excitedly round his knees. It was a long-haired, brownish-white animal with a slender muzzle. He heard his father talking to the dog the way he had talked about it in hospital, when he had visited Stefan with Natasha.

This dog was a present from Ferenc Butterman, Stefan knew that too. For just on two years Ferenc Butterman had

been an occasional unexpected visitor to the house, who conversed for hours on end with Natasha Roth. Ferenc Butterman was the accredited correspondent in the capital of the
German Democratic Republic for a total of fifteen daily and
weekly papers appearing in Switzerland, England and
Canada. They weren't important papers, said Ferenc Butterman; some of them were left-liberal, some of them right-
liberal; his art consisted in writing his articles in such a way
that after changing a few purely decorative terms they had
a distinctly left-liberal or a distinctly right-liberal tone; it was
a lousy job, he said, but a great life. Natasha Roth had met
Ferenc Butterman at a reception in a foreign embassy. She
liked the witty stories he told, and Ferenc Butterman may
have been glad to have made the acquaintance, in what was
to him a foreign country, of a household and a person he
could visit at any time.

Stefan was sitting in an armchair. The dog, a bitch, was
lying beside him. He had to keep petting it; when he tired,
it raised its paw and placed it imperiously in his lap. Stefan's
headache grew worse. The palms of his hands became damp.
He looked at the prints on the walls. They were the work
of famous people, he knew, from France, from Hamburg,
from Vienna. He tried to remember the faces of people in
the hospital he had left an hour ago, where there had been
entirely different thoughts and a different language. His
memory handed him images that were, to him, frighteningly
flat and vague. He realized there was no connection, nothing
in common between the hospital world and the people in it
and the people and things here; he could not establish this
connection or common ground himself, he was the last
person to do so; rather, he felt, the split ran right through
him, it tore his body apart; as though to confirm this, one
half of his body was healthy, the other half partially paralysed. His fatigue increased. His headache grew worse. He
was too exhausted to go on thinking about all this; he only

knew that he might have to do so again later. The dog demanded more affection. Stefan turned his head to the window, where the sky beyond the glass was pale grey; there was no green on the bushes in the garden yet; a single sprig of vine was dancing outside the window; it was still completely black and without buds. He heard his father come into the room and say he had tried to phone Paris but no one had answered at TUR 01–29; evidently neither Jeanne nor Natasha was at home. They were bound to be more successful in the evening, or next morning at the latest.

SHE WAS WOKEN by the hissing of lorry brakes in the 8 Rue St Antoine, while hundreds of private cars roared into life at the Pont-Marie traffic lights in the Quai des Célestines. She got up and groped her way to the window. The net curtains smelled of stale nicotine. The narrow strip of sky above the Rue Charlemagne hesitated between pale grey and a bright, very delicate violet. She looked vacantly at the roof of the lycée whose gates, in two hours, would suck in a multitude of obedient, dark-clad pupils. She still felt numb from the previous evening's alcohol and too little sleep; this produced a sense of having no past, an almost sexual confusion. She walked barefoot to the bathroom. Here all the tiles, basins and fittings were of German origin. From her nine years in Berlin, Jeanne, her stepmother, had come away, above all, with the conviction that technical appliances from Germany were particularly reliable. Jeanne was still asleep, immunized by twenty years' familiarity to the noise of these streets and deadened by pain-killing tablets. Natasha Roth straightened her bedclothes. She smoked a cigarette and waited to be overcome by nausea and to spew out, with tears in her eyes, the dregs of the past night. The sounds outside had now turned into that general, indistinguishable daytime noise that hung like a bell over the whole district and in whose shadow the little Rue Charlemagne would almost become a quiet street again. She sat on the arm of Jeanne's desk chair; she smoked; she hoped for a morning phone call from Berlin, which might or might not come; if it came she would first hear her husband's voice, perhaps also Billa's voice; she was hardly likely to hear the voice of Stefan, who would still be asleep and whom it was inadvisable to wake; on the other hand, most of the telephone conversation would be about him.

She went down into the street. The building had no concierge. The run-down bistro in the Rue Charlemagne no longer existed; it had been given a new front and was now called Chez Kasimir; it was a shop for Polish export goods, hams and vodka, including the one with the brown buffalo, Zubrovka. She walked past St Paul's Church to the Rue St Antoine. She went into a café for breakfast, as she was in the habit of doing when she was in Paris, or at least when she was staying with her stepmother. But the café too had a new owner. The windows had been enlarged and the mirrors removed from the walls. Instead of the dark-blond girl she had known, there was now an Algerian with a moustache behind the espresso machine. Only the espresso machine seemed to be the same, at least it still stood in the same spot. *O saisons, ô châteaux!* She ordered a piece of French bread with ham, orange juice, coffee. Rimbaud had linked the lament for the transience of time and castles with the question of the imperfection of the soul; it was a line from "Mémoire," Rimbaud had been nineteen at the time, it was one of the few lines of his poetry dealing with transience and aging. Soon after that he fell silent. A coincidence? She watched a butcher outside carrying an enormous haunch of beef across the street, white-skinned meat drained of blood. The Algerian switched on the radio. For an instant she felt her own indifference to be a lie, her distance from home as monstrous.

So on the fourteenth of July 1789 the people of Paris had run east from the Hôtel de Ville along this street, this mile of petty-bourgeois business sense, now lined with small shoe shops, wine merchants, butcher shops, low stalls selling seafood, to storm the many-towered Bastille. What was left? Dog shit, spittle, birds' feathers, ashes. Perhaps they had been there then. Nevertheless, she breathed happily as she walked through the smell produced by the moisture on the paving stones; the waste water flowing in the gutter seemed to her clear and virginal. She would walk along this route every morning for as long as she was here: Rue de Rivoli in a westerly direction, past the Châtelet, the Louvre, twice she had to negotiate a chaotically busy crossroads, where she had ample opportunity to watch the helpless choreography of a traffic policeman. She approached the Palais Royal and passed the entrance. The trees in the garden looked mortally ill. Beneath the brightly lit galleries moved ghosts reeking of musk, age and wealth. She entered the Rue de Richelieu. She went into the Bibliothèque Nationale. She sat down at her place in the reading room, casually arranged around her the books she had ordered and studied the arrogant faces of the supervisory staff; she tried repeatedly to impress on her memory the frescoes on the ceiling, knowing that she would have forgotten them by the time she got home. Was Rimbaud in Paris immediately after 1 May? The only one to state this categorically was Ernest Delahaye, who was, after all, a personal friend of Rimbaud's and the recipient of letters from him. Delahaye knew that Rimbaud was in Paris until it was taken by Thiers' troops, but at least this must be wrong, since the "bloody week" began on 21 May and Rimbaud was back with his mother on 13 May. I shall return. With iron limbs. With dusky skin. With wild eyes! And yet it was an irresistible idea to imagine the young poet among the defenders of the Fort d'Issy. Fire on me! I throw myself before the horses' hooves! She looked at a drawing on which she could make out a walled bridge near Issy and soldiers marching towards each other; the smoke from the gun barrels looked like cottonwool. *Les autres avancent.* Arthur Rimbaud wrote his first poem at fifteen. In her imagination the young man from Charleville bore the features of her fifteen-year-old son Stefan.

She sat for nine hours in the Bibliothèque Nationale. Around noon she bought a sandwich and a beer at a tiny bistro in the Rue Réaumur. She asked for a *jeton* and from a public call box telephoned the Rothschild Hospital in the XXth Arrondissement, where an eye doctor who had been recommended to her was a consultant. She was told that the doctor was away. At five o'clock she walked as far as the Opéra, now revolted by the stench of bodies and half-burned petrol; after the brooding quiet of the reading room the din in the street seemed to her obscene. She went down the steps to the Métro; she looked for inscriptions on the walls and found nothing; eight years ago the walls of the underground tunnels had been living newspapers. She missed the sleepy Africans who had sat behind the grilles, in dark uniforms, with a ticket punch in the right hand and a thriller or a textbook of electrophysics in the left; in their place were automatic machines that swallowed the ticket and in return raised a metal barrier. Insignia of change, of crude, earsplitting modernity. The old, clattering Métro trains, Jeanne had told her, now ran only on the line between Porte Dauphine and Place de la Nation, and they too would undoubtedly soon be replaced; a crime, oh what a loss! She travelled in over-full carriages to St Michel. At least the groaning cast-iron lift that took her up to street level still existed. She went out. She expected that the sight of the fountain and the big bookshop in the Rue de la Huchette would induce a feeling of sensual delight, but nothing happened. She walked down the Rue St André-des-Arts to the Carrefour Buci and then along the Rue Dauphine to the Quai de Conti. Everywhere Greek snack bars had been installed; in the windows huge balls of grey meat were turning on electric spits; the fat dripped onto the slices of meat like brine in a salt refinery; it was revolting; from time to time a brown-handed shop assistant would cut a thin slice from these balls and sandwich it in part of a French loaf. These streets had become noisy, bare and mercenary. There was nothing left of the old multi-coloured bustle she had so loved. She felt like sitting down in the pigeon droppings in a doorway and lamenting.

Was there a threshold beyond which the years were no longer counted, where old age was simply an absolute condition? Natasha Roth, immersed in contemplation of the backs of her hands, on which the veins pressed thick and blue against the skin, had reason for such thoughts, for her stepmother, Jeanne, chattered on incessantly in a jumble of German and French about old age, *la vieillesse*. Jeanne was laying the table. When she walked, did things with her hands or talked, she kept a lighted cigarette in her mouth, an ability only the French possess. Between Natasha and Jeanne there was an age difference of nine years, and when Natasha looked at Jeanne's fair-complexioned horse's face, the skinny breasts under her jumper, the senile discolorations on her arms, which no amount of jingling silver jewellery could hide, Natasha saw her as an older sister whom life had quite rightly spewed out in rejection. But sisters are subject to the same biological laws. Her secret contempt for Jeanne included herself. She broke into a sweat at this realization and clutched at the white, fleshy hand of the visitor as though it were a lifebuoy. The visitor's name was Henri. He was a plump man with reddish-brown hair and freckles. Jeanne had fried scallops in garlic. Henri spoke very fast. Natasha had several attacks of coughing while smoking. She made

up her mind to switch to light cigarettes. Jeanne said Henri
was a Communist Party member. Henri said he was working
as a German teacher at a lycée in St Denis. He had studied
for five semesters in Frankfurt-am-Main, at the Johann Wolf-
gang Goethe University. There was a possibility that Natasha's monograph on Joseph Roth would appear in France.
It was by no means certain, but someone was interested in it
at a publishing house in the Rue Jacob for which Jeanne
edited translations. Natasha, Jeanne and Henri talked about
Germany. Their opinions generally differed, and Natasha had
the impression that, despite words and names that sounded
the same, the people and things they were discussing were
not identical. Henri was a gifted essayist, said Jeanne. She
obviously wanted to push the translation of Natasha's book
Henri's way. After coffee, Henri talked about a jazz cellar
in the Latin Quarter. Natasha Roth said apologetically that
she had no control over the translations of her books or the
choice of translators. Jeanne laughed shrilly; she was now
tipsy. Henri drove with Jeanne and Natasha in his Deux-
Chevaux to the Quai de Montebello, where, incredibly, he
found a parking place. The cellar was cold and damp; the
audience sat on chairs, on crates, their hands clasped round
their knees, their eyes almost closed. The musicians consisted of a slim Negro and three whites. Pianist, drummer,
trumpeter, saxophonist. Their music sounded melancholy
and rather cool. Natasha studied her drunken stepmother,
who, with her fur stole over her shoulders and her skinny
backside on a wooden crate, was a grotesque sight. She stood
up and got herself a glass of *piquette* from the bar. The other
listeners were bobbing their heads or their feet up and down
in time to the blues beat. They were all very young, students
or foreigners. Did Henri sleep with Jeanne? She tried to
imagine it. She drank some of the *piquette* and listened to the
muffled saxophone chorus. She felt shabby. She felt exactly
how old she was.

STEFAN HAD TO LEARN to walk without assistance. He
continued to find the exercises extremely strenuous. Several
times a day he walked from the front door to the garden gate
and back. Later, he tried to get as far as the nearest crossroads. This distance exhausted him and the last few steps
were such an effort that once again his hands turned damp;
the knee and ankle joint on his paralysed right side went
numb and he lost control of his movements. At least he would
have liked to take the dog with him. He had quickly made
friends with the animal. The bitch was friendly, affectionate
and good-tempered. His father forbade him to take the animal
out in the street on the leash. It would pull so hard on the
leash, said his father, that Stefan wouldn't be able to hold it.
Stefan had to admit this, in silence, impressed by the un-
mistakable note of worry in his father's voice. To make up
for this, they all of them—his father, Billa, he, the dog—
went for a walk together in the forest one Sunday afternoon.
The animal was let off the leash. It dashed into the young
plantations. It barked twice. After that, Stefan saw it a long
way off racing along a path and across a clearing. Billa blew
vigorously into a whistle and this signal called the dog back.
It threw itself down on the ground at their feet, panting,
with its muzzle open and its tongue hanging out to one side,
a long, bluish piece of trembling flesh. This was the chief
thing that stuck in Stefan's memory, together with the fact
that he himself had to keep sitting down on boundary stones
and the trunks of felled pines. In the end all strength and
vigour had seeped out of his muscles, all alertness from his
head as though from a damaged vessel. Indifferently he
looked at the ground, at roots, at the waves in the grey sand.
In this state he remained behind with Billa at the edge of the
forest, while his father went off to fetch the car. The bitch

lay on the floor in front of the passenger seat with its back to the windscreen. For Stefan it was not so much a relief as a different kind of indifference when he was finally sitting in his place. Just as they drove off, he suddenly discovered that the tops of the pines and birches outside the window were all bent in the same direction and were constantly trying to straighten up out of this position. From this he had to conclude that there was a strong wind blowing outside. He hadn't noticed this before.

Twice a week he had to go to the hospital for gymnastic exercises under the supervision of a therapist, using wall bars, a medicine ball, or a bench or else lying on a mat. He was taken to these exercises by car. Eventually this stretch of the Berlin ring road would become boringly familiar to him with all its exits, bridges, uneven patches, all the houses the other side of the embankments, until it finally led to the brick buildings of the hospital, which he hated. Its smell of sweat, carbolic acid and stale food disgusted him, as though he felt entitled to blame the building and the people in it for his condition and its consequences. And yet he made this trip punctually and took care that it was never forgotten. He carried out the prescribed exercises without protest, as fully and as often as he could within the space of one hour. On the instructions of one of the hospital doctors, who examined him regularly, he now wore a black patch over his sound eye. This was supposed to stimulate the nerves of the other eye. The lids became damp and sticky under the covering and an itch developed where the edges of the patch rested on the skin. When he took it off, he saw the familiar double images again. No one seemed seriously to expect that this injury would ever be cured.

They drove to Schönefeld, his father, Billa, he himself and also the dog, which would remain in the car. In Schönefeld a new airport building had been erected, which Stefan had not yet seen. It made him feel he wanted to go looking for mortar that was still wet, for scaffolding that had not yet been taken down. They had to wait a long time. Either his mother's flight was not delayed or no announcement to this effect was made over the loudspeaker. Finally his mother came into view in the opening behind the customs counters. She dropped her luggage, opened her mouth into something like a cry, came running over to Stefan and took him in her arms. As a result, this reunion suddenly became burdensome to Stefan. He felt as though he were on a stage or the reluctant participant in some exhibition. He could only rid himself of this reluctance by shrugging his shoulders so that his mother's wrists slipped away from his neck. Back home it was like any other return from a trip. The suitcases stood open in the hall. Natasha Roth had brought her son various things to wear, from shops in the Boul' Mich', she told him, and also from big stores on the right bank of the Seine. Stefan had grown so much in hospital! None of his previous clothing fitted him any more. While piles of blue jeans gathered round his feet, Stefan had the feeling that his mother was trying to buy his approval and understanding for something to which he could give no precise name but to which he discovered in himself a certain resistance, if not aversion. At the same time any affectionate contact with his mother would have remained embarrassing. He would have tried to avoid it, just as he had at the airport. And yet he was angry that she didn't make the slightest attempt to establish any such contact, but just went on talking. He followed the hoarse sound of her voice with scorn. Was she glad to be back? In her ruined castle? The familiar words. After every return. He would have liked now to do something completely uncontrolled, to yell or piss on the carpet. Indeed (if he forced himself to look at it with her eyes), the house in which they lived was a fifty-miserable-years-old building. The yellow-ochre plaster on the outside had patches of mould and in some places had crumbled away. The rain had washed all the paint from the timber frames of the mansard windows and the roof. Some individual battens had fallen off. The beams and floorboards of the ground floor were no longer very solid either. They creaked and you could jump up and down on the floor in his mother's study as if on a trampoline. Everyday processes, dreary events. From time to time Natasha Roth wrote furious letters to the state administrative department to which the house belonged, but she was too absent-minded to follow up her demands with sufficient determination, so all she got were promises from the authorities that were never kept. Natasha Roth much preferred writing books and travelling abroad. The house grew ever more dilapidated with the years.

Stefan was now sitting in the dining-room. He knew that he was surrounded by crumbling and gradual collapse. He enjoyed this knowledge more than he hated it. He suppressed it. His parents were sitting in the next room. The door between was shut. He heard their voices. They were talking animatedly, not very loudly. Perhaps they had forgotten his presence next door. He heard them talking about him. His mother said she had spent several days in Paris looking for a specialist; France had narrow streets with an extraordinary amount of traffic; consequently there were more traffic accidents with certain characteristic injuries and hence greater therapeutic experience. She said that with the help of Jeanne, especially Jeanne, she had found a specialist; she had been to see him; she had told him all the details of Stefan's accident and Stefan's paresis, with Jeanne's help, because her own French wasn't up to that. She said the doctor had reassured her. He had promised to help. Provided it was necessary. Wasn't that amazing? Stefan heard his father say it was no longer necessary, the abducens paresis was decreasing, Stefan hardly saw double any more; he had watched him, and the doctors at the hospital had confirmed it as well. Here Stefan started with fright. He felt as though his parents were talking about someone who had his name, his appearance, his skin, his illnesses, but who wasn't him. They were saying unbelievable things, weren't they? Several times he passed his hand to and fro in front of his eyes. His hand remained single in its outline; there was no double image. He almost forgot to breathe with amazement. How could the improvement have taken place without his noticing it? He ought now, he thought, to feel uncontrollable joy and relief, but he felt no such thing, at most a kind of satisfaction mixed with apathy. He also deduced from the conversation that there were facts about him of which he knew nothing, which he could at best find out about secretly or by chance. He suddenly saw himself surrounded by observations, conversations, suspicions, judgements as if by metal walls. He shivered. He made up his mind to watch out for double truths or hidden feelings in the conversations his parents had with him; but where was certainty and how could he confirm his suspicions? Such thoughts came back to occupy him again and again, for days and weeks.

WITH THE AID of the notes and photocopies she had brought with her, Natasha Roth now tried to write the very first sentences of a portrait of the young Rimbaud in the spring of 1871. She hoped to create a scene whose terrible lucidity would light up everything in the biography which came before or after it. Poetry answers revolution. Revolution answers poetry. Revolution is poetry. If such equations were correct it must be possible to obtain from them an answer to the question, is non-revolution silence? In what times was she herself living at the moment? Her thoughts ended unexpectedly in the futility of all writing and the parasitical life of the poet. Rimbaud had been a dirty, brutal streetwalker who peddled his skinny boy's behind around the Café du Théâtre du Bobino. But this happened at a time when the Commune had long since been wiped out by the firing squad and was perhaps the physical answer to this, while the mind was still seeking final metaphors for falling silent. She discovered, now that she was no longer sitting under the milky light of the Ile de France, that all names of people, places and streets were losing substance. She tested out the idea that a sudden prohibition would prevent her from ever going to France again. She looked out of her study window into the garden. Close to the house stood a morello cherry tree. The blossoms had fallen. The fruits were lewd nipples of chlorophyll. There were stinging nettles growing within eye range. Rust was flaking away from the wire netting of the fence. The sight caused her physical pain. Further away, in a neighbour's garden, a small child was running to and fro. She herself would never again be able to bear a child. She opened a bottle of red wine and began to drink. Two relatives of her husband's were visiting; they wanted to stay overnight. They were sitting in the living-room talking, smoking stinking cigarettes and gulping down vast quantities of brown liquor, without getting drunk. Experiences from the provinces, self-satisfied, fusty stories. Listening to them, Natasha had the same feeling aroused in her by Russian short stories from the nineteenth century, by Kirilenko or Leskov. When she was alone with her husband she cried out in exasperation that she couldn't stand these two happy conformists any longer. Her husband told her it was good for her to meet people like this, what else did she ever get to know about reality here apart from brief stays between two trips abroad? She yelled that she didn't give a shit for all that; and a strange, hurtful quarrel arose, at the end of which she was completely out of breath. All reality now appeared to her flawed and threatened by death. She wondered when she had last slept with her husband, counting the days with dismay. *Reconnais ce tour/Si gai, si facile.* Non-revolution was speechlessness? She locked away her material for a biography of Arthur Rimbaud during the Paris Commune. She dug up out of the wastepaper basket the invitation to participate in an anthology, which she had already thrown away. She decided to write a story for children.

She went to Berlin to visit Rebecca, who lived at the back of a building near the Oranienburger Tor. To get to her, you had to go through a gate and across a yard of grotesque ugliness. Rebecca lived in vast rooms full of twilight, disorder, smells and brightly coloured cushions. As she embraced Rebecca's soft little body in greeting, Natasha was overcome by a rush of tenderness. Rebecca seemed to her like a ruined mirror-image of her own existence. But what did "ruined" mean? You could take it, thought Natasha Roth, as the logical consequence of inescapable personal unhappiness; whereas she herself, thanks to her outwardly intact family, her reasonably successful work, her life of packed suitcases in a crumbling house, was merely running away from the danger of being reduced simply to herself. Rebecca was not alone. As she stepped from the sooty corridor into the room, Natasha saw the poet Bodakov. Natasha harboured secret reservations about Bodakov, which were perhaps due to the fact that Bodakov was responsible for periods of evident unhappiness in Rebecca's life. Natasha had wondered whether to write up the tragic tale of Rebecca and Bodakov together with the life story of each of them.

Something like this: In the town of Czernowitz, which must be considered the home of a number of sensitive talents in the German language in this century, in October 1937 a daughter, Yaidl, is born to the wine merchant Salomon Moszkovich, his fourth child. She grows up alongside Turks, Greeks, Serbs, Croats, Montenegrins and ever-changing gypsies. She is allowed to play with horses and goats, with beetles, with little snakes, with the dog. She is four when the disaster of war falls upon the town, and she is five, almost six, when she sees all her relatives from the town packed into big cars, Uncle Moishe, Aunt Thamar, Uncle Nathan, Uncle Loeb. Finally her father, Shloime Moszkovich, as well. She herself has to go with her mother to Theresienstadt in Bohemia, where there is a high fence and where, of all the neighbours from Czernowitz, she finds only the gypsies, and how much more disreputable they look and how tormented by hunger for bacon and cheese. But she, Yaidl, is shown into one of several filthy wooden houses and allowed to sing, paint, run around and play leapfrog with other children. The stories of the adults creep away on bloody bones and at night, as they fart in their beds, the Jewish poltergeist, the Dybbuk, leaps through the darkness and seizes the people by the throat, so that they groan and many of them scream or choke. One night Yaidl's mother is among them. One must say that the ashes, to which her body is reduced in the interests of hygiene, are light. After three years of a more or less animal existence, in the course of which she learns fragments of various languages, but chiefly a horrible German, the fence is opened up and the orphan Yaidl Moszkovich, small, with no neck and pudgy because of disordered glands, comes north, that is to Germany, with a transport of former inmates. The many inquiries by international committees produce no reply, so that Yaidl is allowed to stay in children's homes, with adequate meals upon which Djugashvili grins down from the wall and where tablets and liquids, mostly from Canada, help her glands to heal. She grows only hesitantly. Many others beside her can flail around and scream at night. All the pity of the world stretches out its hands to her, seeking to make amends, which can be thoroughly troublesome and not always helpful. She can do what she likes and confidently expect to be exonerated. Since she had a deep voice and played a bit of piano, violin and guitar at home, and since she didn't particularly take to university studies on Slavic linguistics or philosophy from Theocritus to Hegel, she started to write and sing her own songs, about the gypsies' god or brimstone butterflies sitting on gleaming barbed wire. People are touched. The songs are broadcast on the radio or recorded on black discs. She makes a living. Because she had discovered that the name Yaidl Moszkovich conjures up garlic, mutton fat and sweet wine, she had assumed the name Rebecca, because it was her mother's first name and also the name of the wife of the famous biblical Issac or Itzak; he came upon Rebecca, daughter of Bethuel, by the well; she was carrying a jug on her shoulders from which Itzak's camels drank.

The time has come to speak of Bodakov. Who is Bodakov? Born three years earlier than Yaidl Moszkovich, of whom—tragically—he will for too long know nothing, he comes from a town far to the north of Czernowitz but with a similar, because Slavic-sounding, name: Myslowitz. This town has black iron towers, with wheels on top continually busy with their own affairs. Eight Bodakov brothers spend six days out of seven travelling down into the soil of Upper Silesia cutting coal and developing pneumoconiosis. At times Arnold Bodakov wears the white gown of an acolyte and stands reverently before the black-faced Mary of Czestochowa; at other times, he carries a torch high above his black-haired head and wears a brown Hitler shirt and finally, at an angle because he is hanging on with both outstretched hands to the rear end of a wagon, moves off westward from Myslowitz, ahead of him a dun-coloured hinny led by Anna Bodakov. In Thuringia, where there are bright-coloured houses, all the talents Arnold Budakov possesses are fostered, thanks to his demonstrably proletarian origins. Gratefully, he writes poems to Djugashvili. He listens incredulously to the long report on transportations to the Gulag. Later a fault line will open up in him and never heal. Bodakov marries. He makes two children. The stories he writes come slowly, appear difficult, say difficult things and therefore create difficulties. Gloomily, with all the lethargy and unerring perception he has inherited from generations of Catholic Upper Silesian underground workers, he moves away not merely from Djugashvili but from everything for which, for a long time, Djugashvili stood. He meets Rebecca. The poet who looks like a miner. The camp child grown older, who is almost deformed and writes sad songs. The religious fantasies of the acolyte Arnold Bodakov naturally contained bloody hatred of Caiaphas and Iscariot, Jewish Christ-murderers, whose crimes must be avenged on their Jewish posterity. In his passion for Yaidl Moszkovich, Bodakov now does penance, we may suppose, for his past hatred of the Jews and at the same time his past submission to Djugashvili. A substitute, perhaps, for Catholic confession, to which he has long since ceased to go, or perhaps not yet returned? Bodakov lies with Rebecca. Bodakov writes ballads for Rebecca, twenty-eight altogether. Rebecca shows Bodakov the Bohemian plain, the Tatras and the Zips. Bodakov doesn't break free from his marriage; perhaps he is still influenced, or reinfluenced, by convictions relating to the sacraments and deadly sins. Rebecca gives birth to a child by Bodakov that immediately dies. Bodakov, a poet from Catholic Upper Silesia, groans at the horrifying thought that he might be refused benediction. He buys a vacant farmstead in the district of Schwerin, Mecklenburg, half an hour's drive from the nearest market town: Plau am See. Bodakov makes his wife two more children, which live and are healthy. The publication of his stories meets with resistance, since they deal with spirits, nightmares, prison and death at the frontier. So Bodakov sends his stories to the other country, where they attract attention. Thereupon the newspapers in his own country print abuse of Bodakov.

This is what anyone seriously interested in the story of Bodakov and Rebecca would have had to write about. Now, instead of being on his Mecklenburg farm, Bodakov was with Rebecca in Berlin, Auguststrasse. Hesitantly, accompanied by violent movements of his broad miner's shoulders, he announced his intention of publishing a new volume of stories and ballads. He raised his powerful shoulders and said: On the other side. Natasha Roth asked few questions and secretly wondered whether she should admire Bodakov's ruthlessness and be ashamed of her own conflict-free life or not. Was Bodakov possessed? A fool? A saint? Rebecca filled cups from a copper pot and talked trivialities in a soft voice.

STEFAN BEGAN to go to school again. He had missed a 11 great deal, which he would somehow have to make up. In the beginning he was completely exhausted after the first two lessons of the day; later, after the first three; later still, after the fourth. His parents had forbidden him to cycle to school. In fact he didn't even have a bicycle any more, and the way to school was for him a very considerable walk that took him almost half an hour, twice a day. Among his old schoolfellows he realized how much he had changed. This was true even outwardly. He was now the tallest of the thirty pupils; he had the feeling he was an old man among a lot of children. His fellow pupils treated him with kid gloves. He imagined that if he tyrannised or tormented them they wouldn't put up the slightest resistance. He was absolutely convinced of this. He was excused sport and also technical classes. Neither of these worried him. The Stefan Roth who had enjoyed swimming and was a fast runner over long distances bore little resemblance to him and had been as childish as the rest of the pupils in this class. Sometimes Billa would give up her bicycle and walk to school with him. Sometimes one of his classmates would accompany him, taking his satchel from him and placing it on the luggage carrier of his bicycle, which on this occasion he pushed. This had to be repaid by carrying on a conversation. Endlessly patient, Stefan listened to the sentences full of childish words and empty of conclusion or logical transitions. Rather than paying attention to the contents of the words and sentences he concentrated on the voices, which the beginning of sexual maturity caused to break with a kind of croak, or to the other boys' red hands with their dirty nails and tattered quicks, which occasionally oozed pus. He was very arrogant.

Twice a week he went to do gymnastic exercises at the hospital, and now it was generally his mother who took him by car: from Highway One onto the autobahn at Vogelsdorf, past the Seeberg, Blumberg and Weissensee exits, then onto the branch leading to Potsdam and Rostock, immediately afterwards turning off into the Schwanebeck exit. Through the village. Behind the railway crossing the gleaming roofs of the hospital. The car radio was switched on to news or else a commercial channel. Insects smashed against the windscreen and immediately disintegrated into green or colourless bubbles. His mother had to wait an hour for him outside the hospital, while he got through his orthopaedic exercises. Sometimes she went into the waiting room or to Erica Roth's living quarters. At other times she leaned a hard board against the steering wheel, resting on her thighs, so as to create a comfortable writing surface. She left the car radio on while she wrote. She seemed to enjoy this unusual manner of writing, since she never complained of these time-consuming trips. On one of these trips she told Stefan she was writing a children's story with the following plot: After some future mutation the dolphins had become rulers of the completely flooded earth. Specially privileged dolphins presented their children with living human beings whom they kept in artificial air bubbles so the children could watch their strange antics. His mother intended to call this story *The Aerarium*.

Once he asked her: "Do you still believe that everything is going to turn out all right?"

"Are you talking about yourself?"

"I'm not just talking about myself, but I'm talking about myself as well."

"What else, then?"

"I mean everything else."

"What else? Life?"

"Yes."

"Life with us?"

"Yes."

"Do you doubt it?"

"I don't know."

"Then why do you ask?"

"We live differently from other people, and the others live differently from us. The two things have nothing to do with each other."

"Yes? Well? What's the problem?"

She obviously didn't understand him, perhaps because of the clumsy way he expressed himself. Or perhaps she didn't want to understand him, or perhaps it wasn't the right moment for such a discussion. His mother, short-sighted behind the glasses which she always wore now when she was driving, stared at the concrete roadway in order to avoid any possible obstacle in good time; she had to devote her whole attention to the route and the roadway, but when else did he have an opportunity like this to talk to her? At home she was preoccupied; she would sit in her room, lock herself in her room and be angry if anyone knocked at her door or disturbed her in any other way. At such times he preferred to go for a walk in the forest alone with the dog, which he now did about every second day. Incredulously, he remembered a time when he wasn't allowed to hold the animal on his own and the path between the pine trees had been a very great effort for him.

12 HER PUBLISHER in Leipzig sent her the proofs of her new book, which was to appear in early autumn, almost simultaneously in the two Germanies. She broke off her other work, or she convinced herself she was breaking off her other work, because her children's story was finished and she was grateful—as she unwillingly admitted—for any excuse to delay the writing of her biography of Rimbaud. She read the report, which she had started two years ago and finished one year ago, on a worker in the youth department of the social services in the most heavily populated area of the city. The laborious struggle against crime, prostitution, refusal to work, alcoholism. A landscape of antisocial life, with countless children, with incest, with songs full of strange symbolic words that were almost incomprehensible to an outsider. Natasha Roth had described four weeks in the life of this young woman, giving her a fictitious name, Lisbeth P. For more than five months she had paid regular visits to the woman she called Lisbeth P, had accompanied her on her rounds, had read through files and documents with her, had taken part in discussions with her, had helped her to write

final reports, had sat in the young woman's kitchen-living-room, which it was impossible to rid of the smell of coffee, potato peel and stale cigarette smoke, the hub of the world which continually produced fresh clients for the office this woman exercised. She had taped the conversation of the woman Lisbeth P, who was divorced and had three children of her own to look after. Things she had said about disappointments, lack of leisure, limited success, relapses, lack of recognition and her own sexual frustration. Said in a tone of mingled apathy and high spirits. From all the documentary material she had assembled, Natasha Roth had had to create a fictional world in which the names of people and streets had been changed and life stories mixed up.

This had been a year ago. She herself had become a year older. She read statements she had made such as: Nature is cruel. The beauty of old age is a lie. The feeling that is never disappointed is disgust. Life is indifference. There was no limit to the number of such sentences it was possible to set down. They betrayed a cynicism that was purely external. Secretly, such observations made her suffer as though from an infected tooth. She was suddenly seized by an incomprehensible rage; the sweat burst out from her pores and made her scalp itch. She ran out of the house, jumped into her car and drove off, with no purpose other than to erase some of her agitation in the noisy action of the internal-combustion engine. She drove by a roundabout route to Woltersdorf, parked the car in a public car park and then walked to the lock. The bridge was raised. In the lock-basin a barge was being slowly lowered to the level of the Flakensee. Children were watching the performance. They were licking away noisily at soft ice cream cones and had a blackish scum round their mouths. She watched them with a feeling of relief, almost of lust. The barge in the lock-basin was carrying broken coal; she couldn't help thinking of Bodakov. The barge floated out of the lock-basin. The bridge was lowered again. The children rode over to the other side with a shrill tinkle of bicycle bells. She herself walked with steps that grew ever slower to the east bank of the Flakensee. The wind fluttered the proof sheets she was carrying with her in an open basket. She sat down on a bench in order to carry on reading under these changed circumstances. The ground under her feet was muddy. Beside her among the reeds stood an angler wearing a speckled canvas jacket with his broad back to her. *Je me crois en enfer, donc j'y suis.* I believe myself to be in hell, therefore I am. When she was writing the book about Lisbeth P she had long since begun her study of Rimbaud. Were there similarities between the Rue Nicolet in Montmartre and the Stargarder Strasse on the Prenzlauer Berg? Where did these similarities lie? She saw two old men walk past along the path by the bank. The angler shifted his weight from one leg to the other. The water lapped against the bank, smelling of tar and excrement. Suddenly she had a vision of an occasion late one evening when her husband stood naked in the bedroom carefully folding his clothes. His back was bent in an ugly curve; the flesh over his hips showed the slack folds of old age; his flaccid penis was a ridiculous monstrosity.

She packed the proofs together, went back to the car, got in and drove off. On the way it occurred to her that she could think of no reason for her agitation. It did not arise simply from the blatant dogmatism of what she had written, which now that she looked back on it no longer caused her any anger. Ten months ago she had gone to visit again the woman who served as the original for Lisbeth P. Once again she had passed through the smells of decay and human living that filled the hall. She had mounted the worn wooden steps to the third floor. On the door of the flat she found a plate with an unfamiliar name. The nameplate of the model

for Lisbeth P had been removed, leaving only a roundish
hollow in the dark-brown paint and two holes for the screws.
She rang the bell but no one answered. She didn't want to
ask other occupants of the house, so she went next morning
to the youth service office. Her inquiries of other employees
were answered vaguely and with obvious embarrassment.
From replies and hints she finally discovered the truth. The
person she was looking for was under arrest and awaiting
trial. For what offence? She was found with her three children in a sealed lorry with Bavarian registration plates, and
arrested for attempting to leave the Republic. One could
only hope that the reason for this action had been a dark-
skinned man who several evenings a month had crossed the
Friedrichstrasse check-point, close to Leipziger Strasse, with
an alien's permit and carrying a bright-coloured plastic bag
containing sweets and articles of clothing for the three children on the Prenzlauer Berg. One could imagine hurried
embraces. One could picture anticipation, despair and weakness. The motives might have been more complex, or more
commonplace, or more terrible. Natasha Roth didn't try to
go as a visitor to the remand prison. She wouldn't have got
to see Lisbeth P in any case, she thought, her well-known
name notwithstanding. She didn't try. Lisbeth P had broken
away from her original and become a purely fictitious character, as untrue to life as any other literary invention. While
Natasha Roth corrected the proofs through to the end, she
thought to herself that Bodakov would have continued the
story of Lisbeth P on into Niederschönhausen prison. But
would Bodakov have been willing to tell the other story of
Lisbeth P? Without this ending, which could not have been
foreseen? Would she herself have written, would she have
been willing to write this story, if she had had to reckon with
an ending like this? Full of doubts, she put the proofs in an
envelope and took them to the post.

13 WHEN THE SUMMER HOLIDAYS were over, Stefan
was to go to another school, which was in Berlin-Köpenick.
There he would be able to learn three foreign languages,
among them French. Out of curiosity, and because one particular afternoon he had nothing to do, he took the streetcar
to Oberspreestrasse to look at the building which, from
autumn on, he would enter every day for four years and in
which he would spend thousands of hours of his life. Stefan
found the building. He liked it. His father had told him that
its construction was described in various books as an example
to be followed. The architect's name had also been mentioned, but Stefan had forgotten it. The building had light-
coloured walls with very wide windows. The outer walls
were supposed to have been clad with ceramic tiles and perhaps still would be, when sufficient funds were available. He
went up the steps and through the open door. In a glass
cubicle sat a woman porter in a flowered apron. She was
eating a piece of cake and had a coffee pot, some knitting
and a daily paper on the table in front of her. Still chewing,
she looked up at Stefan and at once turned back to her interrupted reading. He went up the hall steps. He saw announcements painted on the walls in various colours. He tried to
imagine what it would be like to come in every morning
through this entrance, to go up the stairs and then through
one of the many doors in the very long corridors. He
imagined it without effort. After this, he went down the steps
again, past the porter and out into the street. He felt relieved
as he walked back to the streetcar stop. It was a sunny day.
He yawned. As he did so, he looked across at Köpenick
Castle, the museum in which his father worked. There things
were collected and put on exhibition that could immediately
be forgotten, and no one demanded that you should have

looked at them and be able to describe them. He saw his father walking across the wooden bridge leading from the gates of the castle over a moat to the street. Beside his father was a young woman. His father, Stefan noticed, had put his arm round the young woman's shoulders. Stefan immediately left the island in the middle of the street. The streets in the old part of Köpenick were all narrow; traffic jams were constantly forming in them; the narrow pavements were crowded with people carrying shopping bags. By the time Stefan reached the Grünstrasse he could no longer see his father, but only, across the distance of perhaps twenty paces, the blond hair of the young woman like a signal. He tried, amid the lethargic movements of the bodies around him, to move faster. Perhaps it was the weakness of his side damaged by paralysis that prevented him. He remembered a dream he had often dreamed in the past: someone he could easily escape was pursuing him, but all of a sudden he could no longer run, it was as if his feet had grown one with the ground, the path beneath him moved along with extreme lethargy, suddenly he heard quite close behind him the scornful panting of his pursuer. (Stefan couldn't remember any dreams from the last few months. Perhaps this was strange, considering what lay behind him?) He turned into the Kirchstrasse. There he succeeded in overtaking several people. He saw the young woman's blond hair again. She seemed about to get into a waiting streetcar, but first, Stefan saw, she hastily embraced his father. His father remained standing in the street, waiting for the streetcar to move off. He waved to the streetcar window. Stefan too had come to a stop. It would have been easy for him now to cover the distance to his father. But he wouldn't have known how to greet him, what words to say, what questions to ask about what. He saw his father slowly lower his waving hand. At this moment the streetcar was already crossing the embankment bridge. His father crossed the tramlines and walked quickly and without looking up to the Köpenick Town Hall. Stefan tried to convince himself that the man he had seen was not his father, but simply someone who looked like his father. Soon afterwards, as he himself was travelling on a streetcar out of Köpenick, he really began to believe that he had been the victim of an illusion. There were so many imponderables, so infinitely many possible mistakes!

In the evening—they were lying in bed reading—he asked his sister Sibylle through the open door between the rooms what she would say, how she would behave, if their parents were to separate? Billa refused to be distracted from her reading by such a question. She merely muttered that she had no opinion about it. He wanted to know which one of them Billa would choose, their father or their mother. Billa repeated that she had no opinion on the subject and, without looking up from her book, stuffed her mouth with sweets with her left hand. Then he said to himself: I made a mistake. The man I saw at the streetcar stop wasn't my father. He looked at his bare arm, which was lying bent on the bedspread. The skin on his right forearm bore three thin scars, made by a scalpel. The skin here was smooth and in the slanting rays of the lamplight it shimmered as if it were greasy.

14 FROM VARIOUS MEETINGS and conversations the life story of Erica Roth had pieced itself together in Natasha's head. It seemed a possible, indeed sensible plan to put down on paper the sentences that remained in her memory, preserving the abrupt transitions. Of course there would be some loss, due to the fact that it would be impossible to capture

the high-pitched, almost childish voice in which these sentences were spoken. In such notes this could be indicated only superficially.

As a child I seriously wanted to become a nun. Or a deaconess. Or a missionary. Never a teacher.

The anaesthetic used in our hospitals is called Halutan. It is used in surgery not only here but all over the world. Constant contact with Halutan obviously causes lasting damage. You can recognize anaesthetists by the fact that they look emaciated, thin, fleshless, with transparent skin on their head, neck and hands, and a face that looks as though it is shrivelling up.

I met my husband while I was a student, during the last vacation before examination year. My parents had given me the money for a trip to Prague, because I looked to them as though I had been overworking. Baroque as a cure for intellectual strain. Well, anyhow, we went by bus. The usual programme. The Old Town. The Little Quarter. The Hradcany Palace. The old "Kelch" tavern. Beer and fritters. The bus was packed solid and the weather was warm anyway.

That was when I took this flat in the hospital grounds, because it was close to the ward. Even now, when I hear the ambulance with its siren sounding, especially at night, I still start to jump up and reach for my coat.

My parents were religious.

As regards Stalin—I mean the revelations of 'fifty-six—what I felt, even more than horror, was the fear that everything might disintegrate, so that all the effort would have been in vain.

I put several photographs side by side on the table. The various figures or faces they show are always Erica Roth. I'm a pretty young girl with dark hair and small teeth and without glasses. I'm a child with plaits and thick glasses, very plain. I'm a plump young woman among a group of people in old-fashioned clothes. I'm standing on the tip of a granite rock behind a dark iron railing that is supposed to stop people from falling.

Even before I had to give up the post of hospital director because of my ruined health, and again afterwards, I was offered the position of Deputy Minister of Health.

In 1944 I was ten. We were sent out of the city, several hundred children within a certain age group. We lived in a village in Thuringia, in various houses, farms or public buildings. Among vineyards, by a small river; its valley caught and held the warmth. From our window we saw an old castle which, we knew, was used as a boarding school for future leaders. The pupils, all boys, were mostly fair-haired and tall. We watched them as they walked through the village in their Hitler uniforms on their way to swim. Then came 20 July, the day of the attempt on Hitler's life. The next day but one we were all summoned to the castle courtyard. This was the very first time we had been there. We had to form ranks. Then someone called out the names of individual pupils of the school and they had to step forward. All their braids, piping and epaulettes were torn off. I can still remember the names: Schulenburg, Trott, Witzleben. All names of the families involved in the Stauffenberg conspiracy. I know that at this sight I sobbed with pity.

My brother has been a pastor in a village in Central Franconia for the last ten years.

After I had to give up the directorship of the hospital I founded, I began to work as a dermatologist. It took me four years to get the necessary specialist qualifications.

One patient, a Jew, told me how as a child she used to play in the Jewish Cemetery in the Schönhauser Allee. During the last three years of the war. Together with her friends. They were all little Jews. There are many famous people buried in that cemetery. My patient told me that playing among the graves and gravestones, where they were neither molested nor forbidden, was a pleasant memory for her.

At the present time, injury from Halutan is being investigated in many institutions throughout the world. My application for its recognition as an occupational disease was turned down by the authorities.

My husband completed training as a foundry engineer. He worked in his profession for ten years. Now he is a proofreader for a technical publisher and translates specialist texts from Russian and English.

If I have to do something merely for its own sake or to my own advantage, I can't produce much energy.

My father was a cabinet-maker. We lived in a poor street on the edge of a wealthy district, in which most of my father's customers had their houses. My father was a specialist in the repair of old furniture; he might have done better as a restorer in a museum. His pride was his professional and financial independence, as he always said. We had certain regular customers. They often used to come to our workshop. I remember how amiable my father always had to be on such occasions. It was a completely false amiability. These people had a lot of money, but they were stupid and crass. When I asked my mother about it, she told me to be quiet and didn't answer.

For a long time, Leon Feuchtwanger was my favourite author.

The collision between our private car and a small bus took place on Highway 2 1. My husband was taken to the hospital at Merseburg. Doctors understand each other fast. I had only to look at the X-rays.

I keep up a correspondence with my brother.

The rooms in my flat are dim. If the sky is at all cloudy I have to switch on the lights in order to read.

I built up this specialist clinic simply with a commission from the state and the knowledge of a few specialist publications. Later visitors came to us for information, even from abroad.

I believe it permissible to compare a nation with a human organism. For eighty years we have known which psychic energies spring from repressions. I think we skimmed too quickly over the revelations in Khrushchev's secret speech.

As a child it bothered me that in the cemetery there were rich graves and poor. So I used to take flowers from particularly expensive graves and put them on poor ones. I simply didn't understand why I was punished when someone saw me and reported me to my parents.

I would like to see the Irish islands.

My parents lived in a street that ended against the long wall of a cemetery. It was a quiet street. The sound of the cemetery orchestra was almost the loudest noise in it. We lived in an apartment house, on the second floor. My father had his workshop out in the yard at the back. From our kitchen window, if I leaned out, I could see his outline though the half-dark windows of the workshop. I could see him moving about. My father was a quiet and very correct man. There was no need to feel afraid of him. The street outside was asphalted and smooth. I used to rollerskate on it. Often people went by in black mourning clothes. Sometimes I used to actually skate in and out among them. They didn't even notice me. They kept their eyes fixed on the wreaths and their own feet.

I like listening to chamber music. For instance Brahms. Schubert too. I only have time for gramophone records.

We keep this flat on because here my husband can get out into the open without help and because there isn't much traffic in the hospital grounds. The big meadows and the little forest glades are an advantage. Since electrically driven self-propelled vehicles have become available, people suffering from tranverse paralysis of the spinal cord have greater mobility.

AT THE BEGINNING of the summer holidays they went 15
to Frau Babendererde, who lived on a Baltic island in Lübeck
Bay. Frau Babendererde was an old, fat peasant woman. She
owned a farmhouse and a barn. She lived in the farmhouse
surrounded by hundreds of old things: baroque chests, Empire and Biedermeyer chairs; on the walls of the rooms hung
views of the island, of Lübeck, Rostock, Stralsund and
Greifswald and places all over Swedish Pomerania. Frau Babendererde had big black eyes. The sky beyond her living-
room window was a very bright blue; the curtains were
snow-white tulle and swelled in the wind. Frau Babendererde's house stood at the edge of the island, facing east,
where there was only a narrow strip of water between the
shore and the mainland, with ooze, small fish and flocks of
seagulls. But Frau Babendererde's barn was three hundred
years old, the oldest building on the island. The reed roof
had sunk in. The walls were half-timbered with mud in between. Pigeons nested in the gables. At night, pine martens
scuttled about in the granary, obviously on good terms with
the pigeons. This was the building Natasha Roth wanted to
buy from Frau Babendererde, in order to have it rebuilt and
then live in it for long weeks during the summer, among
bushes, brackish water, cattle paddocks and boggy pastures,
on the flat land, the only place, according to her, on which
the thick books she wanted to write could flourish. His
father, Stefan knew, couldn't stand Frau Babendererde. His
mother had constantly to pacify him. She wanted the barn
and the barn belonged to Frau Babendererde; moreover
Natasha Roth considered Frau Babendererde to be a fascinat-
ing fossil, the kind of person it would be impossible to invent.
Finally, his father merely breathed heavily. He no longer
contradicted. He had to find thatchers, carpenters, brick-

layers, plumbers and electricians who would undertake the repairs. Meanwhile Natasha Roth went with her children to the beach, where the dog immediately ran off into the maize fields on the landward side. The beach was stony. In the water, pebbles washed round dug into the soles of the feet. The swimming did Stefan a lot of good. Outside a wooden shed stinking of herrings in the summer heat sat two fishermen, spitting brown tobacco juice on the ground beside them and mending nets.

Frau Babendererde had once been the richest woman on the island and Herr Babendererde, who was already lying in the island cemetery, had owned the largest fields here. After the war, Frau Babendererde had suddenly turned out to be half gypsy, racially speaking. Consequently the land reform hadn't taken a single acre away from her and for fifteen years the Babendererde land had been leased for a total of fifty years to a state undertaking for the cultivation of cattle fodder. "I get what I want," said Frau Babendererde, blinking her black eyes. Natasha Roth murmured something that sounded like *fantastic*, while Rudolf shifted about in his Empire chair with a disgusted expression, but said nothing.

Then Billa fell ill. She developed a rash, first on her arms, later on her face. Natasha Roth brought Billa to the hospital on the mainland, where she was painted with a dark-blue liquid that made her look as if she had smeared ink on herself. Billa screeched and stamped her feet. In the barn there was no possibility yet of washing thoroughly. So Natasha Roth had to put her dark-blue daughter in the mailbox-yellow car with the hatchback and return with her to Berlin. Stefan remained alone with his father in the barn. He waited for his father to tell him something, perhaps about a woman with blond hair who visited the museum in Köpenick Castle or, who knows, perhaps even worked there. His father merely busied himself with buying cement. Sometimes builders came along, looked phlegmatically at the damage to the barn and sucked on tobacco pipes. Stefan's father had to talk to them and drink gin with them.

Behind a wooden partition in the barn stood the black four-in-hand in which, Frau Babendererde told them proudly, she had driven around the island until twelve years ago. Frau Babendererde possessed a fine big garden. People came to her regularly from the state cattle farm, elderly women, who tended the garden, pulled up weeds and trimmed the lawns and hedges. Frau Babendererde merely cut flowers and looked after the bees. When she was working at the beehives with her head wrapped up in white, Stefan thought she looked like a monster. Frau Babendererde put the combs in a centrifuge. Since she was peacefully inclined at this time, she often gave Stefan a jar of honey. Then Natasha Roth came back with Sibylle, now cured. Stefan saw that his sister's face and arms were chequered, with patches of white skin next to patches of brown skin. This made her very specially the daughter of Natasha Roth. Two Lady Feirefizes, said Natasha Roth, and took the two children back to the beach again, where Billa's white patches turned red, which did not stand out so much but caused Billa some pain. The dog raced around the cattle paddocks, chasing fieldmice, rolling on the ground and stinking of liquid manure.

Then Stefan suddenly fell ill. It began with a feverish catarrh. The fever gradually rose. It rose continuously until it was so high the doctor had to be called. He diagnosed pneumonia in one lung. Stefan immediately imagined he would be taken to hospital. He had the smell of the Berlin hospital clearly in his memory. Fortunately his mother opposed his transfer to hospital so vigorously that the doctor relented. But in his condition there could be no question of Stefan being taken back to Berlin. Frau Babendererde, who was still kind and compassionate, cleared a room on the first

floor of her farmhouse, where Stefan lay in a wooden bed
with posts turned on a lathe. On the walls hung framed
landscapes with brown patches of mildew under the grass.
There were a few other pieces of furniture in the room, all
of them attacked by woodworm. The floorboards were also
gnawed by woodworm. The window had no curtains and
was often open. Stefan could hear the swifts crying in flight
or see their shadows. He had to swallow antibiotics, and
Frau Babendererde brought him fruit juice. His mother sat
at his bedside, reading, writing or crocheting. Stefan himself was too tired to read, so the transistor radio was on a
great deal. It picked up a Danish station, and a few times
every day a French woman's voice kept moaning the same
song: *Un, deux, trois, l'amour n'est pas pour moi comme un
roman de Kafka*. One, two, three, love is not for me like a
novel by Kafka. What was Kafka? A Jewish writer from
Prague, his mother told him. What was love? Outside, the
first craftsmen had come. They were putting up a scaffold
round the barn. They hammered; you could count the blows.
Then the weather changed; it turned windy; rain lashed the
windowpanes. Frau Babendererde slept badly at night. She
walked about in the darkness over the creaking floorboards of
the house, sometimes half the night, coughing, muttering or
singing in a thick voice. The doctor, who came every day,
told Natasha Roth to beware of Frau Babendererde, who
was unpredictable whenever the weather changed. At night,
too, Stefan could hear the dog barking in the barn. It probably smelled pine martens. During the day Frau Babendererde no longer brought fruit juice or honey either. During
the day his mother sat at his bedside, reading, writing, crocheting, listening to the radio or talking to him. Outside,
the rain fell. Listening to the sound of the rain on the zinc
covering the window-sill, Natasha Roth told him about the
time when she was the same age as Stefan. Wingen-sur-

Moder and the inn, which, according to circumstances, was called Zum roten Ross or Au Cheval Rouge. "Did I ever tell you about Lorraine? It's like the sea, like dunes that aren't sand, you know; just on the outer edge, in the east, there are blast furnaces; they belch out smoke and colour the air grey; in the west the earth becomes black, with humus, with rotting flesh; it is where the battles of Verdun and Douaumont took place, legions of grave crosses like a low, sparse wood, between them the blessed hills, Sion-Vaudémont, places sacred to the Virgin, places of pilgrimage, Celtic shrines; the goddess Rosmerta ruled here and the earth yielded up salt." In Stefan's mind all this merged with the rain falling outside on the island. The Maas and the Moselle flowed into Lübeck Bay. The island was called Bar-le-Duc and was ruled by the famous stone skeleton by the sculptor Ligier Richier. That was why he, Stefan, was consistently ill, again and again. His heart pounded. The fever rustled in his ears.

Once he asked his mother: "Would you rather be in Lorraine than here?"

"Not particularly in Lorraine," she said. "Lorraine makes one sad. I don't like being sad."

"Would you rather be somewhere else?"

"Perhaps I'd rather be somewhere else."

"Then why aren't you there?"

"Because there's you, for example. Where could I leave you?"

Soon after his fever reached its highest point again, Stefan had a vision. His father was marrying a woman with fair hair. His mother took him and Billa to France and rented a house in the Ile de France, in a place that was perhaps called St-Germain-en-Laye, to which the east wind blew the exhaust gas and the explosions of Paris. This dream meant good luck.

Another day, the radio reported that an Italian lorry driver, a Communist, had been shot by GDR soldiers on the frontier with Bavaria. Natasha Roth was very upset by this news. She strode up and down the room, smoking one cigarette after the other. Even in his sleep, Stefan heard the vehement whispering of his parents. The radio was on in the background, repeating the same news over and over again. The rain had stopped outside, but it was still dull and cool. "Ah, Stefan," he heard her say as though through a curtain of fever sounds, "I learned part of my convictions from an old Jew, who convinced us of the power of Utopia—that's another word for hope—and that Utopia changes reality, even if it remains Utopia. Sometimes I detest the reality we have created. But I can't break free from it. It's like with a religion. And I don't want to be an apostate, a heretic. I want to be like a child taking Communion, but of course I grew up long ago. It's horrible to be grown up, Stefan, you aren't grown up yet." He listened to her through his fever, hardly understood what she was saying, didn't care. He had the impression that his mother was talking entirely to herself. She seemed to him childish; he felt ancient.

A few days later the fever was finally gone. The doctor let him get up. Two suitcases were put in the yellow car and Natasha Roth drove back with her son to Berlin, where the air was not as damp and where you could take hot baths. Before leaving, Stefan had said goodbye to Frau Babendererde, who had gleaming black eyes and hollow cheeks and in general didn't look well. Stefan's father was to stay on the island with Billa and supervise the repairs to the barn, which were going very slowly.

Really, Stefan had hoped to go back to the island after ten days or so. Instead, three days later, his father and Billa came home. Their luggage was following them by train; they could expect a card notifying them it was at the station within a few days. Immediately after Stefan and his mother left, the police had been to see Frau Babendererde. They had questioned her about smuggling some of her antique furniture into West Germany to be auctioned and then giving the proceeds to her children, who were living in Hamburg. Frau Babendererde had raised both hands in horror and denied everything, swearing in both Low and High German. The police left empty-handed, but Frau Babendererde went in a fury to her bees. Afterwards, she accused Dr Roth of sending the police to her house. Why? Dr Roth knew about antique furniture, he had told her so himself; he was an expert with a degree. The peasants on the island knew nothing about furniture. They were as stupid as geese. Dr Roth denied the accusation. But Frau Babendererde had gone on to say she suspected Dr Roth of wanting to have her arrested so that he could get hold of the farmhouse she lived in and the antique furniture it contained, in addition to the barn. Thereupon Dr Roth had called Frau Babendererde a miserable kulak, and Frau Babendererde had called Dr Roth a damned foreigner who had no business on their Swedish island. Then she hinted that the proper place for Dr Roth was Jerusalem; and when Dr Roth reminded her of her gypsy ancestors, Frau Babendererde laughed her head off and screeched that her grandfather came from the Hungarian province of Banate, his name was Brustellin and he could trace his baptized Swabian forefathers through parish registers back to the fifteenth century, all the young male Brustellins had been in the Waffen-SS during the war, she had only invented the gypsy blood to dodge the land reform: "I get what I want."

Thereupon Dr Roth had paid off his workmen and taken the train to Berlin with his daughter. The writer Natasha Roth had to admit that her plan to rebuild the old barn had come to nothing. Her husband had always predicted that. Natasha Roth drew a deep breath, sighed noisily and shrugged her shoulders. His father was still furious, Stefan saw. Now

Natasha Roth became hilarious, picturing her husband, with a doctorate in art history, and a crazy old kulak hissing and yelling at each other on a Baltic island. This made Stefan's father all the madder. He counted up the hours he had wasted to no purpose on the workmen. At this Stefan's mother became serious and agitated again and counted up the hours she had sacrificed nursing her sick children. Stefan watched his parents blaming each other for the failure of the holiday. They swore at one another, striking each other with words. It was as though they had their claws in one another. The quarrel grew noisy and tedious. Stefan himself looked back to the days on the island with regret. He couldn't remember any time during the last few years when he had been able to talk with his mother so often and at such length. He came across something she had evidently written during his illness:

EPITAPH

he had done the trip with the 20-ton refrigerator truck several times before. berlin/gdr to milan. in between spending the night in an autobahn lay-by.

the checkpoints behind him, already in the other country with the same language, he knew he would be called back, because his papers had been accidentally held. he went on foot. because, for reasons that were later not clear, he didn't stop when called upon to do so: there were shots.

he left behind a family and a membership card of the pci.

his body was handed over on the plane. his refrigerator truck was towed into the gdr. it was carrying pigs disembowelled in slaughterhouses belonging to the people.

He would have liked to talk to his mother about why she wrote differently from the way she spoke, why she wrote for herself differently from how she wrote for publication, why she talked to him differently than to other people. He couldn't ask her, because then he would have had to tell her what made him ask: the piece of writing he had read. And he knew she would have forbidden him to read her private writings.

SHE WAS SITTING at her writing-desk again. From here 16 she could see over the top of the pile of books and papers into the garden. Through the window she saw that the fruit on the morello cherry tree was overripe; it had turned black. A blackbird was hopping about on the branches pecking at it. The bird looked sideways out of fixed yellow eyes. Its attitude was one of natural arrogance. This time the nettles reached halfway up the windowpanes. The rust on the fence was completely covered by greenery. In the next garden a metal pole for the washing line was leaning at an angle. The overturned bucket in the grass was coated with dully shimmering enamel. On the zinc covering her windowsill a brown moth had alighted to die. The sky seemed covered with a whitish-grey powder. The oaks in the street were moving in the wind. She leeched onto all these things with her eyes. She felt that she was sucking these things dry. The tears that ran tickling into the corners of her eyes were the overflowing blood of things. She shook her head. Outside, midsummer heat had reigned for several days. They should have got into the car and driven to some bathing beach; but none of them, neither she nor the children, had the energy for that. Stefan and Billa were in bed in their rooms with the radio on, arguing about a book. She could hear indistinct voices from the upper floor. Her children were talking in electronic sounds, produced by dark-brown tapes lying on dully gleaming metal plates in a sound-proof studio. She got up and walked into the kitchen to pour coffee from a pot standing on the hotplate. On her desk, received at last through the mailing service of the State Library, lay *Etude sur le mouvement communaliste à Paris en 1871*. The author's name was Gustave Lefrançais. The book was published in Neuchâtel. The printed pages were crinkled and brown. The binding smelled musty. She read a section, made notes and wrote down a sentence that seemed important to her, in German translation. Twice she had to look up a word in Langenscheidt's dictionary. A yellow dust-jacket over a dark-blue cover. By no means for the first time, she had the feeling she was pursuing a completely useless activity. She doubled up with helplessness. Then she heard the dog run panting through the ground floor of the house. Someone had opened the door to the veranda, where the animal was usually kept. She heard Stefan's voice; she heard Stefan calling the dog back. Stefan had come downstairs without her noticing. Through the closed door of her study she asked him if he wanted anything to eat? No. Wasn't he hungry? No. Wasn't Billa hungry either? No. Dead hours, Pan's hours, but Pan had become a hump-backed Brandenburg forestry labourer who got drunk after sunset on stinking corn-liquor. Stefan's footsteps moved away in the direction of the veranda door. When she listened carefully, she could hear that he walked unevenly. The old, paralysing picture of herself sitting with her child's head in her lap beside a puddle in which blood and pieces of ice mingled.

Gustave Lefrançais came from Angers and had been a teacher. In 1851, because of his socialist leanings, he was forbidden to teach. He fled to England. Two years later he returned and worked at various jobs. He was a popular speaker, was several times arrested and finally became mayor of the XXth Arrondissement. On 26 March 1871 the IVth Arrondissement elected him to the Council of the Commune, of which he became president. The Fourth District included the Place des Vosges, the Rue St Antoine and the Rue Charlemagne, where her stepmother Jeanne lived, where she herself lived when she was in Paris. During the summer weeks the city was abandoned by its inhabitants. Paris was entirely taken over by foreign visitors, who tried to make themselves understood in all the dialects of late capitalism. The chairs of the street cafés in the Boulevard St Germain were filled by Alemani with two or three Lebanese among them in bright-coloured shirts, with thick gemstone rings on their dark-skinned hands. For five weeks Jeanne lived in Dieppe, where she stumbled about on the pebbles of the beach in transparent plastic bathing-shoes. Was the plump Communist German teacher with her? Gustave Lefrançais had founded a union of socialist teachers with Pérod and Pauline Roland. In 1871 he was condemned to death in his absence during the trials of the Communards, having escaped in time to Switzerland. He did not die until 1901. A life story made up of flights. What drove a teacher to a foreign country where they spoke a foreign language? Teachers were the brothers of poets: silence ruined them. Throughout his life Gustave Lefrançais was a convinced anarchist. Jean Arthur Rimbaud, if his poetic cosmos was translated into a political system, could only be described as a follower of Blanqui and Bakunin. His dreary end also illustrated the melancholy decline of aging extremists. *J'ai eu raison dans tous mes dédains: puisque je m'évade!* A series of little dull thuds told her that Stefan was going back upstairs. Evidently he wasn't wearing shoes. A bluebottle whirred through the room and banged several times into the windowpane. She looked at the gleaming insect's body. *Corset velu des mouches éclatantes.* Blowfly. Rimbaud fly. In the Charleville poet's theory of vowels they symbolized the letter A. She remembered having read some-

where that the wonderful surrealism of "Voyelles," this key
poem of poetic modernism, this object of so many explanations of a psychoanalytical or cabbalist nature, was no more
than a memory from the poet's schooldays. The reader used
at that time in French elementary schools, which Jean Arthur
Rimbaud must have studied just like, for example, the teacher
Gustave Lefrançais, showed the vowels in exactly the colours
repeated by Rimbaud. *A noir, E blanc, I rouge.* The natural
well-spring of all *belles lettres* was childhood. She stared at
the sun-flecked leaves outside her window and the word *midsummer* drew from her memory as the oldest, earliest image
a smooth, glittering mountain lake in the Austrian Alps. A
path ran alongside this lake. She was walking along it. The
path was mostly dry, but muddy in some places. It led past
crumbling rocks, for the most part through a tall forest of
gigantic pines. Twice she passed a cabin of dark-stained
wood. A painted sign invited visitors in for snacks. On the
verandas in front of these cabins stood only empty chairs,
no people. On the other hand, she met people on the path.
She was five years old and stared at the fleshy, hairy knees
of grown men who, because it was summer and because they
were on holiday, wore leather shorts. How dependable were
the cloth-encircled legs of her father, who walked beside her
and whose hand she could hold when she felt like it. Her
mother—that was Sinaida with the blue-black hair tied in a
gleaming knot at the back of her head—beckoned to her. She
was sitting on a large stone jutting out over the water. Little
waves were running over gravel, threads of waterweed drifting, snailshells rolling to and fro. Her mother unwrapped
chocolate from crinkling foil. Above the opposite bank stood
a steep ochre-coloured wall of rock rising to a broad peak
like a barrel, behind which fuzzy clouds drifted past, fore-
runners of a change in the weather, said her father. In the
mountains you had to be afraid of storms. That season eight
people had already died while climbing during the thaw.

Two young men had even drowned in the lake above which she was dangling her scrawny bare legs. The water had remained clear. The water ran over the gravel, hissing a little. She counted twelve boats drifting with the wind. What was death? *Blue green black white red. We'll beat the Jews until they're dead.* The counting rhyme that at home in Vienna the children from the Pfeilgasse recited. When she herself sang this rhyme in the house, Sinaida had taken her head and pressed her mouth into a cushion until she could no longer breathe and began to choke and kick. But these were things that no longer had anything to do with midsummer.

To make something happen, she swivelled round on her desk chair to the telephone, lifted the receiver and dialled Erica Roth's number. She let the instrument ring for a long time. If Erica was on duty at the hospital at this time, her husband would have to come along the corridor from his room in a wheelchair, first switching on the light. Natasha waited a long time. No one answered the phone. She felt a desperate need to talk to Erica. In spite of the unbearable heat outside, she would have been prepared to get into her car and drive to the hospital grounds. She now dialled Rebecca's number. Here too she had to wait for a long time, but then—and at first she was grateful for this response—she heard Rebecca's hoarse voice enunciating one word at a time. In the background there were sounds of a twanging string instrument, perhaps on a record. Rebecca kept talking as though under the influence of some narcotic; consonants turned to lead in her mouth; she had to pause before every fresh word. Are you drunk? Instead of an answer, laughter; after the laughter the line went dead; Rebecca had hung up. There was no point in trying to talk to Rebecca now. She dialled Erica Roth's number again. Contemporary life was interwoven with telephone cables, caught up in them as in a net. Beware the moment when the net went rotten and broke. There was no answer to her call. Now Natasha Roth began to have doubts whether the number she had in her head was really Erica Roth's number. Her memory might have failed, might be fooling her with contorted mirror images. What was the correct order? She no longer knew. She looked among the writing pads, notebooks and scraps of paper scattered round the telephone. She couldn't find anything. She didn't know whom to ask. She found a scrap of paper with a seven-digit number written on it: unknown, meaningless, ir-relevant, a code for conversations in which she would never take part, sentences from the arid mouth of a minor civil servant, the chirping of a child's voice belonging to a friend of her daughter's. She dialled seven digits. To make something happen. She intended to put the receiver down immediately. Quicker than she could there came a woman's voice giving a name that was unknown to her. Natasha suddenly pictured breaking into an entirely alien existence. She wondered what words she could use to lead from an apology to questions that would provide her with information. In the midst of the silence the woman's voice uttered her husband's first name in a questioning tone. Now it was as though a small vein had burst in the back of her head. No pain. Only a strange dry sound. She could hear the woman at the other end of the line breathing. Then the receiver was replaced. Natasha picked up the sheet of paper with the seven figures on it. She recognized her husband's handwriting. Why hadn't she realized that immediately? But she had had no need to real-ize it, there was no cause to do so. She saw the skin on her bare arm begin to pucker. She would be able to play down the discovery she had just made with any number of sensible explanations. She knew that. But she also knew that it would leave behind a poison. A small, indestructible ferment of putrefaction. It would eat away her ingenuousness. She would look for further signs. She would feel fear and tri-umph when she found something. Nothing would remain as it had been before.

OCCASIONALLY he travelled in the city railway during the evening rush hour. The compartments were full to overflowing. The weather was hot. People stood crushed together, red-faced, glued together by their own and other people's perspiration. Once he found himself staring at a young woman whose dress was clinging as tightly to her body as a second skin, so that every protuberance was visible, shameless and irresistible. Only when the train stopped at a station was he set free from this close contact. He gazed lustfully after the departing body: to the obscene contours were added the almost equally obscene movements of a walk. What finally stayed with him was a sense of relief, interwoven with a feeling of nameless disappointment, even bitterness. He went to his father's bookcase, took out one of the volumes with colour reproductions of Greek vases and opened it. He looked at the red figures with erect penises, the casually bent figures of the women, whose nakedness struck him as completely unsensual. Only the choreography was important. He studied the various forms of human copulation. He tried to read out of the two-dimensional vase paintings the intensity of a pleasure which he didn't know, which couldn't be imagined. He tried to picture himself in these positions. These images turned his thoughts to the bitch he owned, which, when she was in heat, swelled, bled and ran about whining until a pack of male dogs surrounded the house and dirtied all the doors. He shut the book. The excitement gradually seeped out of him in a patch of sticky dampness on his skin. With his lame foot, he thought, he was condemned to be like one of those goat-footed satyrs, ugly, with a goat's beard and a huge sexual organ. But all this wasn't true; he was his parents' son, endowed with this appearance, burdened with these defects; all his thoughts about himself ended in his parents' library, in illustrations, in black-and-white printed pages; he was afflicted by art, by artificiality; he hated it; he wanted to get away from it; it encircled him; it walled him in; he hated it. He thought of ways of escape. He thought of flight. From one day to the next he rejected all demands of the world around him and merely satisfied the most pressing needs of his body. Activities like working and learning he abandoned completely. Inevitably, his changed attitude showed. His parents, in particular, were so worried by it that they talked to him earnestly and at length. He replied that he didn't want to upset or anger anyone, least of all his parents; he merely demanded the right to follow his own inclinations and feelings. When his parents' reproachful speeches continued, he left the house. He slept on park benches and to begin with he lived on the money he got from the sale of his watch, a valuable object which he considered he no longer needed. He lay on the grass in public gardens. He sat on the stone steps of large doorways. For a time he lived with a man who was only a little older than he and whose feelings and thoughts were similar to his own. This man lived in two shabby rooms in an old apartment house. The most important item of furniture was an open coffin, in the lower half of which the young man slept. He was constantly preoccupied with death and for a long time he had been plagued by the fear that, because of a shortage of coffins, there would be nothing available at the moment of his death but a paper bag. He let Stefan sleep for several nights in the lid of the coffin and in general struck up a friendship with him. But his endless chatter began to irritate Stefan, who had meanwhile discovered that he had no need of speech. Listening became bothersome to him. Speaking disgusted him. Some days later, exactly how many he didn't know, since he made no effort to count them, Stefan left the shabby flat. Once more he spent his nights on park benches. He lay on the grass. More and more, he rejoiced in doing nothing, thinking nothing, being nothing. When he needed money, having nothing left to sell, he sat down at the edge of a busy street and put a tin plate in front of him that he had found in a dustbin. By now he looked so seedy that in the course of a few hours there were always enough people who threw coins into his tin plate. So he was able to buy himself something to eat before the shops shut in the evening. Not infrequently he was sworn at by passers-by, because of his appearance. In view of his youth, his inactivity was seen as a provocation. Stefan didn't reply to these attacks. He looked the people in the eye, with astonishment and sorrow, until they left him alone. By this time he had stopped speaking altogether. One day, when he was sitting at the edge of a wide main street, several dark cars drove past. Soon afterwards four plain-clothes policemen came up to him, showed him their identification cards and ordered him to come with them. He was taken to an office. He was asked questions to which he didn't reply. He took very little notice of anything that was said. Much of what he heard the often excited voices say remained unintelligible to him. He refused to give his name and allowed himself to be searched without resistance, but there was nothing on him to reveal his identity. He was put in a cell overnight and taken out again next day to be asked more questions, to which he again gave no answer. He was admonished to give up his delinquent way of life. He was told in any case to stop begging, because next time he would be severely punished. Although he didn't want even to think about it, he was forced to realize that his release was solely due to the fact that his was an unusual case for which no rules or regulations existed. When he was set free he sat down again at a street crossing. During the time of his arrest it hadn't occurred to anyone to feed him. He had grown thin. His appearance scared the passers-by. He was soon arrested again. Again there were one-sided conversations in which he was merely a mute participant. Again he was put in a cell. Later he had to lie down in a hospital bed, after his stinking and rotting clothing had been removed and he had been washed and medically examined. He put up with all this without resistance but also without helping. More than once he was threatened with violence if he didn't talk, but it never happened. Finally a group of people of very varied professions occupied themselves with this person, whose only wish was to be nothing and no one. This wish was so strong in him that no words were needed to communicate it. By now he had reached a point where he took no further notice of words, which no longer meant anything to him, which he no longer understood. He grew weaker. He fell ill because of his weakness. People constantly forgot to give him food. Probably all he had to do was to ask for it, but he no longer had the necessary words at his disposal. After almost a month of trying to talk to him, to examine him, of trying to find out at least his name and origins through various official departments, a committee of experts was set up. The committee met for several days. Detailed reports were read and then debated. In the meantime, he himself had died as a result of his general debility, still without uttering a word. It wasn't until considerably later that the committee members heard of his death. For some of them this fact was disappointing, for others a relief. Later it was rumoured that his mother had been a member of the committee, as an expert on imagination and a sense of the possible. It was said that she had no idea the subject of their discussions was her own son. It was also said that she knew perfectly well, but had remained silent out of shame and regard for her public reputation. In any case, she secretly attended his funeral. Since there happened to be a shortage of coffins at the time, his mortal remains were placed in a paper bag and buried without any ceremony in a municipal cemetery.

SHE NOW FOUND herself playing a role whose gestures 18
and actions were completely predetermined. As though she
were driving her car in a rut worn by hundreds of other
wheels. Even if she had wanted to, it would have been impossible to turn off. A mechanism almost independent of her
consciousness was in operation. She watched it open-mouthed,
with secret terror and soundless laughter. She had to listen
with redoubled attention when people spoke. Perhaps the unexpected intonation of a word would reveal something. A
sentence would be started and then broken off. Perhaps the
explanation she sought was to be found in the rest of the
sentence, which she had to imagine. She had to slip her hand
into the pockets of jackets hung carelessly over the back of
a chair or on a wardrobe hook. She had to do this surreptitiously or she would have given herself away. But if she found
what she was looking for—perhaps a photograph or a note
scribbled in an unfamiliar handwriting—this would have
justified her action. Every word might contain a trapdoor.
Every familiar gesture proved its opposite and every assertion denounced itself. Sometimes she groaned under the
effort, under the banality of the most hackneyed movements.
She found herself giggling as she watched the performance of
a situation comedy at the Mermaid Theatre near Piccadilly,
in an auditorium two-thirds filled with people in grey Lon-
don business suits. Gesticulating at the footlights was a man
who couldn't decide among several women. A well-known
actor who had made his name during the period of the
angry young men. Now he had grown older, grown fatter.
He hammed his part, putting his jokes over crudely and without subtlety. The period of the angry young men had been
the time of her own youth. In the actor's fat face she could
read the passage of twenty years. The woman who, accord-

ing to the plot, was being betrayed should have been called Natasha, instead of Jane, or was it Cecily? Jane or Cecily was banished from the stage. In the living-room, which according to the actors was in a house in Hampstead, the nymphomaniac girl pulled the shirt off a civil servant and bared her own breasts. Laughter broke out all around her. She had missed the joke and didn't know why people were laughing. Much later she would discover that it was she they were laughing at. Jane or Cecily was really called Natasha. At this moment there was an explosion near the theatre. Shock waves ran crackling through the walls and the stucco ceiling. Next morning the newspapers would report another bombing by the IRA. Autotype photographs would show a blackened hole in the wall of a house, splintered glass on curbstones, two damaged cars. The men in grey business suits continued unimpressed to make rustling sounds with sweet wrappers. Approving laughter as the intended embrace on stage was disturbed by a telephone call. She laughed too. She had made several calls to the number she had found scribbled on a scrap of paper in her husband's handwriting, in order to hear some insignificant phrase or her husband's name or merely the breathing that might betray more than words. Her calls had remained unanswered. In an attack of self-torment she had torn up the note, but the figures stuck ineradicably in her memory. She looked at the cherry tree outside her study window, from which all the fruit had now vanished. The leaves on the branches turned yellow and were filled with holes. The stalks of the nettles had snapped. She telephoned Erica Roth. It had all started with a call like this. This time she got through to Erica Roth. Why couldn't she get through then? She made a date for a talk with Erica Roth, got in her car and drove to Berlin. The city stank, spluttered and choked from the blue exhaust gas of two-stroke engine mixture. She met Erica Roth in the Alexanderplatz, in a café that formed part of the airlines building. She watched Erica carefully insert between her lips a spoon with which she had first scooped up flakes of whipped cream. The skin over Erica's cheekbones was taut, yellow and transparent. Perhaps the telephone number on the slip of paper was a different, secret number for Erica. For an instant she saw the doctor's narrow skull between her husband's hands. Erica pushed the glass plate away. A damp mark remained on the table top. A radio was turned on and delivered an excited report on the preparations for the harvest in the Socialist countries. Natasha smoked, blew out the poisonous fumes to one side and dirtied herself with cigarette ash. Erica was talking didactically about an innovation in health care that cost a lot of money and was being introduced far too slowly. Natasha tried to think of nothing else.

Back home Ferenc Butterman was waiting for her. He had just spent five weeks' holiday in Canada. His face was tanned; he had become thin; two teeth were missing from his upper jaw. Natasha discovered that she was irritated by her children. She yelled at them on the slightest pretext, especially Billa, who reacted by sulking and once with tears. Ferenc Butterman had brought foreign newspapers with him and a bottle of Canadian whisky. She didn't even try to sit down at her desk and work. She would have liked to get drunk. She saw herself lying among down-and-outs, at the foot of a wall, unconscious, in a pool of her own vomit. After Ferenc Butterman had left, the rooms stank of his black cigarettes. She had to open the windows and wait for the smell to go. She phoned Rebecca. This time Rebecca didn't answer. Then it occurred to her that Rebecca was away in the Riesengebirge and she wondered whether Bodakov had secretly gone after her, away from his Mecklenburg farm to Rebecca's fleshy white body, to confusion and sin. She heard Stefan's uneven footsteps going upstairs and down. A draught passing through the room whirled around balls of white dog's hair. Her husband was talking about a collection of articles on ikon painting to which he was to contribute, about an exhibition of Marc Chagall's graphic works to be shown in the Old Museum during the winter, for which she ought to lend the Chagall drawings she owned. The exhibition organizer was a friend of her husband's. She nodded, shrugged her shoulders, answered indifferently. She saw herself nodding, shrugging her shoulders, and heard herself answering indifferently. The Natasha Roth she was observing was absent-minded, trying to trick her husband, with whom she was talking across the corner of the breakfast table, into rash replies that would not escape the Natasha Roth who was watching intently. He stroked his moustache several times with the tip of his right middle finger, from his nose down to the corner of his mouth. The skin under his chin was red, slack and full of small wrinkles. In the face confronting her across the light-brown table, showing the damage wrought by age, she sought the still beardless face of the student of art history called Roth, whose friends abbreviated his name not to Rudi, as might have been expected, but to Rudo, which seemed to her pretentious. She had seen him first in the corridors and lecture halls of the university building that bore the name Melancthonianum. Her father had had strong objections to his daughter studying at the university in which he was a professor. He wanted to avoid any suspicion of personal influence. So his daughter studied in the central German industrial town of Halle an der Saale, where the dirt fell from the air in flakes. All open water stank of phenol. Against all the dams seethed a poisonous white scum. Gradually she succeeded in seeing behind the face of the man with whom she had lived for twenty years a white young face with strands of hair falling over the ears. A painting in impasto. It was two-dimensional. It was lifeless. A pipe-smoker

even then, he burned pale-coloured shreds of tobacco, sweet
as fig juice, taking the tobacco from big, rectangular gilded
tins. No one else had anything like that. She lived in a spacious room in the house of a pastor's widow that looked out
on the Botanical Garden. Victoria regia, banana plants, a
ginkgo tree. She was better dressed than other girls. In her
memory she saw herself as frigid. He got the gleaming tobacco tins from his father or from relatives of his father in
West Berlin; the wall didn't exist yet. In the cinema across
from Neukölln Station she saw *The Third Man* during the
vacation. In a cinema in the Kurfürstendamm, between
Joachimsthaler Strasse and Meineckestrasse, she saw Jean
Cocteau's *Orphée*. The black-clad, black-haired messenger of
death resembled her stepmother Jeanne. But of course her
stepmother Jeanne had fair hair. At that time Jeanne was
still living in the large flat in the Stalinallee, between Straussberger Platz and Koppenstrasse. A short distance from the
Dornburg Castles, which took almost two hours to reach by
train from the town of Halle, one Sunday afternoon with the
chatter of hikers on the woodland paths in the background
and moving flecks of light on the pages of their books, she
managed by dint of determined and aggressive caresses to get
her future husband to go down on his knees and draw her
to him among the ferns. Apart from a vague recollection of
pleasure and amusement, what remained in her memory was
the taste of earth and moss between the teeth. She spat both
of them out afterwards in some surprise, while listening to her
friend's heavy breathing. The three Dornburg castles were
a mixture of Romanesque, late Renaissance and rococo elements. In 1824 they were acquired by Goethe's Duke Karl
August, secular buildings of Thuringian gaiety.

Stefan had many of his father's features. Rudolf Roth said
that in two days he was going to a colloquium to be held at
Halle an der Saale. Was this colloquium really taking place?

What happened in the evenings at this colloquium? At night? In one of those concrete overnight caves whose soundless beds offered space for one body or two? The place name Halle an der Saale did not provoke in her husband the slightest reference to shared memories. A town with objects and institutes. The Moritzburg. Feininger had painted the Market Church, the Cathedral and St Ulrich's Church. During the conversation she had not detected a single revealing remark by her husband. Through the open window two wasps sailed in. They circled the greasy remains of breakfast. She felt pains in her head. The children took the dog out into the street. She would go to her room, pretend to be working and secretly drink. In the evening Ferenc Butterman would come to dinner.

Four days later her husband had long since gone to his colloquium. She knew the address of his hotel. He had phoned her twice; she had phoned him twice; as he had told her, he had spoken twice during the colloquium, which was concerned with the long-overdue official recognition of non-figurative art. On the university circle everything was different. The *Stations of the Cross*, which used to be in the Franconian Institute, had been moved to the circle. Did she remember? Separated by distance and electronics, he dared to speak of the past. This might be revealing or it might not. She walked slowly down the garden path to the letter box. She picked up the newspapers and two letters. The lawn needed mowing; the grass was too long; in many places it had been burned in the summer heat. On days like that you weren't allowed to water the garden or only in secret or only at night. She didn't feel like doing either. The letters were a bank statement and a request to give a public reading in the municipal library at Greifswald. She threw them away.

That afternoon the poet Holger Musäus was sitting in her room. He wanted to put together an anthology of new works by East German authors. It was intended to be an audacious book. Utterly relentless, he said. She said, yes, yes, she'd think about it; she hadn't been listening very carefully. The poet Musäus smoked black cigarettes that could be bought only with foreign currency, the same brand as Ferenc Butterman's. She would have to open the windows afterwards. The poet Musäus smoked nonstop and went on talking. He was a few years younger than she and was said to have written a few good books, though she hadn't read any of them. The poet Musäus was talking about the Revolution, about Latin America. He quoted sayings from memory and clenched his right fist in the Communist salute. Most of his sentences were badly constructed. Marxlenintrotskygramsci. She could feel herself gradually becoming irritated. The voice of the poet Holger Musäus had an unpleasant whining tone in her ears; it sounded like a tape being played backwards. A leptosome with a receding hairline and long strands of fair hair hanging down on either side. His full beard was probably shot through with white hairs, but with his hair colour you couldn't see this clearly. Secretly, she felt repelled by this forced youthfulness, this bohemianism smelling of kitchen waste and artificiality. The poet Musäus was saying now that he was afraid of the police, of spies. He felt surrounded by secret agents whose only aim in life was to ferret out the most guarded secrets of his private life. Perhaps he was heading direct for an accusation of high treason, the evidence was piling up. Pens were scratching away on the documents of the case. At this point Natasha Roth felt it was time to answer. She said amiably that she had rarely heard so much nonsense on one afternoon and she strictly forbade him ever to talk such rubbish in her house again. She couldn't stand it when Kautsky and Gramsci were constantly confused with one another just because their names sounded alike. She added that if the poet Musäus wanted to be a revolutionary again he would do better to go to a café, where there were more chairs for listeners and for secret agents. The poet Musäus lowered his head and strands of hair fell over his face. His colleague Roth's remarks were utterly arrogant, he said. After all, he was the child of working-class parents. "Rubbish," said Natasha Roth, "you're merely uneducated. You're always discussing things you know nothing about, Musäus. And how do you come to be called Musäus? I bet you've never read a line by Johann Karl August Musäus. You hardly know who he is. In fact, your name is Hans Maus." At this point the poet Musäus rose to his feet. He was white in the face. He left the house without saying goodbye and not another word was said about the audacious anthology of new prose.

That evening Rudolf Roth called from a public telephone at the main station of Halle an der Saale. His train was leaving in ten minutes. An hour and a quarter later she started the car, to meet her husband at Schöneweide Station. He would be exhausted; he wouldn't draw her to him in the crowd of other passengers on the platform; he wouldn't even put his arm round her; he never did, hadn't done so for a long time; that wasn't a sign.

19 SEPTEMBER CAME; school began again. Stefan had to get up very early now and travel by one streetcar, from which he either transferred to another streetcar or else took the city railway and then another streetcar. This latter procedure was more complicated but saved almost ten minutes. Later, his father would take him by car. For his father this

meant a loss of time, of sleep and of comfort. In exchange he got tired and bored in a room that was not yet warm in a museum devoid of people. By now early autumn was colouring the front gardens yellow. On the first day of school (all the pupils wore blue uniform shirts, a flag was hoisted, solemnly resolute words were spoken by various mouths), Stefan found himself amidst two hundred total strangers of his own age, to whom he was presumably as much of a stranger as they were to him. He greatly enjoyed the feeling of almost total anonymity. He hoped he would be able to preserve it for a long time. Only his limp made him conspicuous, so he tried to conceal it. In the general bustle he hoped it would not be noticed.

He made friends with a pupil in his class called Thomas. He was a skinny boy, taller than Stefan, with shoulder-length blond hair that hung down loose. He moved with a light, bouncing step and raised shoulders, as though walking over a sprung floor or trying to make as little sound as possible. Thomas's parents lived only ten minutes' walk from the school. He often invited Stefan home when they had a free hour or there was only a short break between the end of school and the beginning of the evening activities. Thomas's father worked as a toolmaker in Oberschöneweide. His mother was a buyer in a pastry shop. Everything was clear, simple and normal. Thomas's parents were the same age as Rudolf and Natasha Roth, but they looked much older, or at least more worn-out. Stefan wondered if it was fair that some people became worn-out quicker than others. Then he didn't know what to do with the verdict if he came up with one.

Thomas's mother was fat. She was very friendly. When he came home to lunch with Thomas, she was often there. She had brought fresh bread or fresh cakes from her place of work. The warm, sweet smell greeted them as soon as they opened the front door. To Stefan this was a pleasant, everyday smell. He was very fond of it. The three of them would sit eating on hard wooden chairs in the kitchen-parlour. They chewed, talked, drank, didn't often laugh. The view from the kitchen window was a high grey fire wall, with cracks, with ivy that pulled itself up on the dirty corners and scars in the plaster. Far down below in the yard stood dustbins the colour of anthracite. Children banged a ball up against them as they played. Sometimes they would drum rhythmically on the lids with the flat of their hands or with sticks. Stefan listened. It was all unfamiliar to him. He enjoyed it, almost with defiance. He didn't want to think about the reasons.

Thomas's parents, for example, possessed almost no books. Was that it? Their living-room was full of dark furniture, including a cupboard with a glass front behind which, alongside vases and crockery, stood a dozen books, a mere dozen. On the walls hung brownish family photographs. There was also a painting of an Alpine lake. Then there were several framed athletics diplomas bearing the name of Thomas's father. Bulgarian carpets, Kelims, of the kind displayed in the windows of the craft shops. Everything in this flat was small; it was simpler, more everyday, more inconspicuous than in the Roths' house. Stefan enjoyed this difference; the difference did him good. He liked being here and could imagine what it would be like if his parents were not called Rudolf and Natasha Roth or at any rate were not a writer and an art historian by profession.

Always with Thomas and only to please him, Stefan now watched sports programmes on the television again. He really hated them, since he could no longer take part in competitive sports. To begin with, he watched the panting, sweating athletes full of furious contempt. Their self-satisfaction when they flexed their muscles was revolting. So was the claptrap with which they replied to the servile questions of reporters. He shook himself. Thomas laughed. Thomas taught him that they were non-material heroes, even if the sweat was pour-

ing off them. They were figures from a colourful world of
myth, two-dimensional like Asterix and Barbarella. People
needed them in order to recover from the other heroes,
whose names were immediately associated with effort and
school. They needed gods who could be quoted by putting
two fingers in your mouth and whistling. The world would
be different, easier and better, if it had only gods like these
and if all heroes were made of plastic. You could admire
them without scruples, since they consisted merely of an
easily inflammable hydrochloric acid compound. Thomas
didn't put things like this, but Stefan translated his remarks
into these terms. To please Thomas he watched, at first obediently and later even with interest, the ten-minute replays
of the most important scenes from important football
matches. Stupid or quite commonplace names. Beckenbauer
or Sparwasser or, again and again, Müller. He watched the
films along with Thomas, in Thomas's home, on an old-
fashioned black-and-white set. He could have watched a
coloured and much larger picture at home, but it was more
important to be here, to sit beside Thomas and not to think
about home. Oddly enough, Thomas didn't express much desire to visit Stefan out in his suburb. Stefan invited him two
or three times, but Thomas hedged. His curiosity obviously
wasn't very great. Perhaps he found the long journey a
nuisance. He and Thomas preferred to walk along the banks
of the Spree, behind the villas and the sports ground in
Spindlersfeld or in the little park. Thomas found inconspicuous plants, picked them or dug them up, rubbed the leaves
between his fingers, smelled them. He knew strange names,
vulgar stories, what was good against what or a symbol of
something or other. The movements and murmured sentences
of an Indian medicine man might be like this. Stefan fell in
love with this comparison. He loved going on these walks
with Thomas.

Thomas was crazy about progressive rock music and whenever he went into his parents' flat with Stefan, his first act was to put a cassette on his tape recorder, switch it on and play one of his favourite pieces, "Santana" or Mike Oldfield or "Yes" or even, as he put it, poor old Hendrix, that washed-up freak. He gradually turned up the volume until the regulator was pulsating and the decibel level could be physically felt. Thomas had put his equipment together himself out of miscellaneous parts. They were only fifteen-watt speakers, said Thomas, just enough for this small room, though naturally he would have preferred decent double speakers. Incomprehensible magic formulae. You couldn't help shaking your head as you listened. Thomas sat amid the bellowing of the synthesizer sounds with a sort of bleached smile, almost motionless, completely "relaxed." This was his form of participation. He watched the football matches on TV in exactly the same attitude. "Close to the edge, down by the river, down at the end, round by the corner." Thomas slowly rolled a cigarette, slowly licked the paper, gummed the cigarette together, inhaled the smoke, leaned back. And all these movements on the part of his friend seemed to Stefan simple, meaningful, like those of an animal. The music boomed against your forehead and on every surface touched with your hand. The echo became a living body. Here too Stefan had to make a great effort to get used to it. It was like the televised football matches. As a child he had learnt piano for three years, with old Fräulein Nilius, the only, the last piano teacher in his neighbourhood, an extraordinary woman, thin, with a screeching bird's voice. He had got as far as the third volume of *The Young Pianist*, then had given up. His mother used to listen to light music on the radio while she worked, from the West Berlin military stations, for example. The notes seeped insipid and irritating as they emerged through the cracks of her study door along with the smoke from the cigarettes she smoked. After half an hour beside Thomas and after pieces like *Eclipse* or *Abraxas* he felt dizzy and empty. It was a shallow, satisfying feeling. He didn't think about anything much. It was a pleasant state. He enjoyed sitting like this beside Thomas.

Sometimes they talked at the same time, about girls, school, sex, the future, politics, sport, not so much about experiences, more about dreams. Thus, for example, they sketched out dream trips, perhaps in parts of the Arctic Circle, Siberia, Alaska or Greenland, where in summer the sun rotated low down on the horizon without ever disappearing. Stefan never uttered the words Vosges or Wingen-sur-Moder or Ile de France. Afterwards, he couldn't help thinking that perhaps Thomas was keeping as much back as he was. For some reason he wouldn't admit to himself, he didn't really believe this. Thomas didn't lie; Thomas didn't lie to him; Thomas really wanted nothing but to walk with long springy strides over a flat tundra inhabited by gnats. This was his most ardent wish. "River running over my head." Stefan finally had to tell himself it was arrogance to deny Thomas the ability to have a secret from anyone, even from him. Stefan didn't want to be arrogant towards Thomas.

He considered it perfectly in order for Thomas to stand outside the school with a girl. Thomas had a right to it, more than others, more than he himself. Only they were often brainless, inhibited geese, in Stefan's opinion not worth Thomas's time and breath. It enraged him. He tried to talk Thomas out of it. Perhaps he went about it clumsily. Thomas listened, didn't nod, hardly answered. He looked at the granite slabs of the pavement, as though there might be a magic plant growing in the cracks. After such conversations, Stefan saw Thomas putting his arm round the shoulders of precisely one of the girls Stefan had ruled out and walking off with her with long, springy strides. Stefan felt tears of helplessness come into his eyes. But then they turned into tears of pride that in his decisions Thomas remained independent and unshakeable. He admired Thomas. If he thought of himself in Thomas's place, he saw himself limping. This fact and his awareness of it decided so much.

Thomas's father was a grumpy, taciturn, grey-faced man. He was powerful, but he walked stooped, a tired athlete, marked by the rigours of a three-shift factory. Once when Stefan was having supper with Thomas's parents the conversation turned to the state foreign-currency shops, the things on sale there, the prices of these things, the foreign currency needed to buy them. Thomas's father suddenly looked up, stared at Stefan and said sullenly, almost with hostility: "That's no obstacle to your parents." Stefan was startled. He now realized that everyone at the table knew who he was, where he came from, who his parents were, how they lived. And yet he had felt so safe; he had been convinced that at least in this home, at this table, among these people he was just anyone. From the words of Thomas's father he heard the unspoken word that he had first heard applied to himself while he was being taken to the hospital. The stretcher on which he lay was being shaken by the bumping of an ambulance with poor suspension. The word was "privileged." It never left him again, since the fact did not leave him, since it could not be hidden. Stefan would rather Thomas's father had told him he limped. Later they would appear to him to be two words for the same concept, two expressions of the same fact.

20 REBECCA HAD COME back from the Riesengebirge later than planned. Her face was sunburned. Instead of Yaidl or Rebecca, she ought now to have been called Sinte or Dunya,

gypsy names which figured in some of her songs and which
at the moment would have suited her perfectly. No, Bodakov
hadn't been to see her. Not once. You could believe her or
not. Rebecca had a few new verses in her head and was trying them out. Bodakov wasn't mentioned again that day.

He was sitting in Rebecca's room when Natasha came back
a few days later, an even gloomier Bodakov, his head sunk
even deeper, even more finally, between his powerful
shoulders. For a second Natasha thought with a shock: The
man's mad! But Bodakov was only a bit drunk, like Rebecca.
Bodakov had a small pile of books in front of him. They were
all the same book; that's why he had been drinking; they
were the first copies of Bodakov's latest book, published in
Munich and sent to its author in Berlin by an unknown but
undoubtedly tortuous and bizarre route. While Rebecca
looked with closed eyes for mutual compatible notes on the
guitar, Bodakov wrote a few words in one of the books; then
with angular movements he shut it and handed it over to
Natasha. Since she was there. She read: Truth cannot be
broken, even if it breaks those who proclaim it. Delicate
letters, as though written with an engraver, incomprehensible
in view of Bodakov's huge miner's hands. There was no trace
now of his drunkenness, at most in his choice of words,
which struck her as too sentimental, in any case silly. Bodakov
was engaged in a monologue: things were getting worse, time
was getting short, it was night. Natasha didn't want to contradict him in his drunken state. In secret she compared him
with her own husband. Rebecca poured plum brandy she had
brought back with her into tiny, colourless glasses. When
she got home, Natasha read Bodakov's book, which had a
fiery red cover, a small book containing ten stories, fifteen
ballads and a total of one hundred and eight pages.

She was horrified by the expression of such utter hatred of
the country in which Bodakov lived, in which she herself
lived, in which, according to Bodakov, there was nothing

but brutality. She wouldn't have liked to write such things herself. She felt admiration for Bodakov's ruthlessness and radicality. She read through various pieces again. She came across verbal ineptitudes that gave her a feeling of relief. When her husband came home he immediately asked her what had upset her. So he still noticed such things? It brought back into her mind certain thoughts which she had temporarily repressed. She gave him the book. He read it quickly, scraping the mouthpiece of his pipe against his front teeth and shaking his head as he read. He didn't like it? No. Why not? He found the book gloomy and lachrymose. His reaction reassured her as far as her own book was concerned, but at the same time drove her into an idiotic solidarity. She said: "I wouldn't have wanted to write that myself, but I must stand up for the freedom to write it." He said: "I must ask you to consider whether anyone would speak like that in your defence. This Bodakov, for example?" "I'm not him and I don't write like him," she said. "The book is simply a pack of lies," he said. "May I be burnt at the stake if every word in it isn't true!" "Oh sure," he said and laughed. "One can perfectly well lie by telling the truth. Bodakov isn't right, but he is determined to be right, you see. That's his lie. He was a Stalinist, now's he's a Stalinist in reverse. To me, the one is as intolerable as the other." She wondered how her husband came to know Bodakov. He had met him once at Rebecca's and hadn't exchanged a word with him. She said with hostility: "If we don't constantly push for more elbow-room, I mean our elbow-room as writers or simply as intellectuals, it will shrivel up again." "That's not what he's after," said her husband. "He always wants to be outside. That also reduces one's space." She continued to contradict, repeating what she had said before. He shrugged his shoulders and said: "I'm not a writer and I admit that for those of us in the visual arts things are easier now, just as they were more difficult for us before."

The discussion had exhausted her more than it should have. She switched on the late political news on West German television. The dog barked, and because the children were already in bed she took it on the leash through the garden, out into the street and there, in the light of the single far too dim street lamp, as far as the crossroads and back.

She went indoors. The lights were still on in all the ground-floor rooms. She found her husband upstairs in the bedroom, sitting on the edge of the bed with his head in his hands and his back so bent it looked as if he had some painful disease. It occurred to her that she still hadn't found any proof and would perhaps have to abandon her suspicions as groundless and stop thinking about them. She had made a mistake. As they undressed, they faced away from each other. For a long time they had done this by an unspoken mutual agreement. As though by this means they could hide their disfigurements from each other. She was ready before him; she was already in bed and watched as he walked to and fro with only his pyjama jacket on and no trousers yet. She saw his spindly thighs and the ugly black hair that grew increasingly dense towards the edge of his pyjama jacket. He lay down beside her. He sat up again to take off his glasses. With his naked eyes he looked like an amphibian.

She recalled that in the morning, before going to Rebecca, she had looked in an old crate in the attic: in order to look for something, not in order to find something. The motions of looking had become so ingrained through all the practice she had had during recent weeks. She had found a few sheets of paper, photographs and notes in a folder that still had a lot of room in it and was made to expand. All the materials related to a Polish woman painter, a naive artist, Krystyna Borowska, whom they had got to know on a trip they had made together—first through an exhibition and later personally because they had wanted to meet her. They had decided to write a book together about this painter. This was at a time when in their own country deviations from a specific canon of painting had been obsolete and even a naive painter was considered a formalist. But since then naive painting had forced its way into exhibitions and even abstract art was officially recognized. Hence the folder on Krystyna Borowska had been forgotten. Her husband switched off his bedside light. She would lend her Chagall drawings for the exhibition. She had brought these drawings from Vienna herself, as contraband. She remembered wrapping them in a thin roll of paper and slipping them into her suitcase among her dirty linen. She thought of her husband's remark that things were easier now in the visual arts but that in the past they had been more difficult. This was undoubtedly true, but perhaps literature would gain an advance on painting again. She pictured a cat moving cautiously forward, one paw after the other. She thought over all the things her husband had said and was astonished by the decisiveness with which he expressed his opinion, including his agreement with the general view. In the past he had expressed himself with much more indifference or caution.

She suddenly knew that this was what she had been looking for so hard. This was it. She had to clench her teeth to prevent them from chattering.

"There's another woman," she said, "isn't there? You're sleeping with her, aren't you?"

"How do you know?" he asked.

"I don't know anything," she said.

"Yes."

Tonsillectomy. She remembered a brief pain, the stink of hot metal. Afterwards she felt exhausted and slightly nauseated. She heard him say: "Let's not dramatize it, eh? That was what we always planned if this happened."

"Is it so serious?"

"Yes."

That was all. And when the exhaustion had gone, which could only be explained by the sudden ending of a very long period of tension, she would begin to form a rough picture of the time to come. It would evolve this way or that. Her professional association had rented two flats in a block in Unter den Linden for recently divorced writers which were constantly occupied. What would they do about the children? She would often be reminded of Jeanne, her stepmother in the Rue Charlemagne, who was growing old without echoes between her bookcases and her wardrobe mirrors. She would have to beg someone to satisfy the sometimes inescapable need for another warm body. With the years this someone would become ever more random, even more whore-like, prostitution for lonely old women. This too would wither away. She would become an old woman amidst the reek of urine and acetone and wouldn't notice it, because it came from her. Now the tears began to flow as if a knob had been pressed on a machine. Indifferently, she smeared the salty fluid on her face with the backs of her hands.

STEFAN DISCOVERED that he was starting to become negligent. He suddenly stopped doing certain things he had done regularly as far back as he could remember, things that had been as self-evident and compelling as the alternation of night and day, like the progression of time and life. Now he neglected these things, while night followed day, life and time did not stand still. This was a remarkable discovery. Apathy gnawed away inside him. It was wonderful to discover how many activities could remain unperformed. For a week, for example, he did not clean his teeth and there was no one to tell him that his mouth stank like a cesspit, that his teeth had become yellow, his gums and his tongue black, mouldy, slimy. Not a word, nothing. He rested in his body, he felt, as in an old, comfortable, unaired bed that stood somewhere out of the way, to which no one paid any attention, in which he lay until his vision grew hazy.

All this may have had something to do with the fact that during these weeks he often went with his friend Thomas, and at Thomas's suggestion, by train to the centre of the city, Jannowitz Bridge Station. There they crossed the bridge over the Spree directly behind the station and walked as far as the Ohmstrasse. Thomas knew people there. Thomas knew countless people. He rarely mentioned where he had got to know them, but it was not surprising in view of his easy, smiling gift for making contact. The district they walked through was fantastically dilapidated. Little old-fashioned shops with boarded-up doors and windows. You could have scratched out the crumbling mortar with your finger nails. In one of these houses lived Thomas's friends.

Perhaps there was really just one friend who was always letting other people stay in his room and consequently was never to be found alone. An extraordinarily lofty room. After a quick glance Thomas estimated its height at about thirteen feet, if not more. The walls were covered with bookshelves displaying grubby book backs or grubby steel engravings in frames. All the furniture came from junk shops, worn-out, damaged stuff. There were always about a dozen people in the room. At this time Thomas and Stefan were by far the youngest. When anyone spoke, most of the talking was done by a small, bearded fellow wearing nickel-rimmed glasses. He had studied theology or wanted to study theology or was just studying it. They talked, for example, about literature, about a writer called Hans Henny Jahnn, his mysticism, his absolutely pagan sexuality. Jahnn's books, all of them out of print, were passed around. Stefan was recognized as the son of Natasha Roth and treated with smiling indulgence. In this group the stories and ballads of Arnold Bodakov were common reading. The name was unknown to Stefan. There was a hi-fi set in the room that was weaker and less efficient than Thomas's, and there were usually tapes and records playing. Once they talked about Sylvia Plath, about Charles Bukowski and Anaïs Nin, names that meant nothing to Stefan. The tapes and records emitted the music of Oriental string instruments, or of Pink Floyd or Emerson, Lake & Palmer. Stefan's favourite was a recording made by Alan Parsons and Eric Woolfson. Alan Parsons had started as a sound engineer with the Beatles.

Tea was poured in tiny cups without handles. The tea tasted of jasmine and after three or four cups it made Stefan dizzy, but this might just as well have been due to the stubborn booming of the strings in the loudspeakers. Many visitors smoked. There was always a sweetish smell in the air. Like a perfumed intensive care unit. There were also girls in the room, never more than three or four. Their outward appearance was slovenly, if not positively sluttish. They were thin and had anaemic faces, dangling hair and a harassed look, as if they were looking at something terribly painful. The record made by Parsons and Woolfson consisted of compositions to words by Edgar Allan Poe. This time Stefan at least knew from his English lessons who that was. "The Raven" and "To One in Paradise." One of the young men present, Thomas whispered to him triumphantly, was a minister's son. Stefan scrutinized him. The minister's son looked just like all the others, smoked cigarettes he had rolled himself and drank tea. "Is there—*is* there balm in Gilead?—tell me—tell me, I implore! Quoth the Raven 'Nevermore.' " Stefan enjoyed all this for a time and went to the Ohmstrasse frequently. But he refused to read the obligatory books. Gradually it all began to bore him, and he was glad that Thomas evidently felt the same.

Around this time, his mother made a trip to West Germany, where her latest book, *Days from the Life of Lisbeth P*, had just been published. He knew that for three weeks his mother would be travelling from one town to the other, from one bookshop to the next, giving readings, answering questions, autographing her book and talking to journalists. From time to time she telephoned her family. Once his father said that this evening Natasha Roth was appearing on West German television. Stefan and Billa immediately decided to wait up for this and in the evening sat down in front of the television set. But after a while Billa fell asleep. She lay in the dark-brown upholstered armchair curled up tight, her mouth half open, while someone on the screen reviewed an experimental ballet performance. Only when this was over did the interview start with Natasha Roth, a writer from East Berlin.

She was standing by a wrought-iron gate. Her left arm was resting on the top of the gate with the hand dangling. Behind her was a wide, grey, turbulent stretch of water, the Rhine. From time to time, at a particular camera angle, a bridge came into the picture with small, brightly-coloured cars crossing it. Natasha Roth's voice sounded hoarser than usual; wind was blowing through her hair; she blinked frequently, her pupils darting this way and that. Otherwise she was Natasha Roth as Stefan knew her, and yet she wasn't. Stefan saw a highly-strung, contemptuous woman who reacted to questions with quick replies, one of those figures who live out their electronic existence between five o'clock and midnight. There were hundreds of them every day. A procession of figures without depth bound to real life only by the imitation of sounds and movements, like this one, the figure of Natasha

Roth from Berlin in the GDR. This woman, thought Stefan, couldn't be his mother. She hadn't carried and given birth to him. She hadn't, as he had been credibly informed, held his head as he lay injured and bleeding in a frozen puddle. This woman had given birth to a brightly-coloured two-dimensional child. She had held its two-dimensional head during various incidents suitable for the screen. Stefan felt an urgent desire for the real Natasha Roth. He couldn't explain why he felt this. As he turned these impressions over in his mind, he almost missed his mother's answers to her questioner. She was talking about her book, denying that it was written with the intention to appease, an accusation that had evidently been made against the book and its author. "The description of antisocial behaviour is disturbing. I describe the steps being taken against it, but I don't say they are sufficient. I write about a lot of things that haven't been written about before." The reporter smiled ambiguously, displaying teeth that were far too white. Now Natasha Roth was being questioned about a book of which she was not the author. She said she knew the author and his new book. Her impressions? When the name Arnold Bodakov was mentioned, Stefan had to rack his brains to recall where he had heard that name before, until a high-ceilinged room by Jannowitz Bridge Station came to his mind. Bodakov described a reality to which she had to react, said Natasha Roth, since she was part of it. That was quite true. She added that in her eyes audacity was not necessarily a sign of literary quality. The questioner nodded his head and once again displayed his white teeth. The Rhine flowed on. To conclude the broadcast, the camera swung away from the speakers onto the traffic crossing the bridge and beyond. "She's crazy," yelled his father. "She's determined to create difficulties for herself, and on account of that madman, of all people." The cry woke Billa, who swore because she hadn't been woken in time. She would have liked to see her mother on television, it would have been so exciting for her, but she was always forgotten, it was always Stefan who mattered, never anyone else. Screaming and crying, she went out and slammed the door.

Next day, at school, it seemed to Stefan as though faces were constantly being turned to him, unknown, inquisitive, prurient faces. It was hard to guess the reason for this attention, and the faces belonged to both pupils and teachers. Thomas told him the class was talking about Stefan's mother's appearing on West German television the previous evening. Stefan lied, saying he didn't know anything about it and wasn't interested. The curiosity flickered for a day, through to the next, but after four days it died down. The reason for this curiosity became a thing of the past. It had been wiped from people's memory, thrust aside by other matters.

22 SHE HAD FLOWN to Cologne, where her West German publisher was based, on an Air France plane from the West Berlin airport of Tegel. The junior partner of the publishing company had met her at Wahn airport with his sports car and taken her on to Cologne along the autobahn. In the afternoon she had done a recording for radio and after that a television recording, by the banks of the Rhine, near the Hohenzollern Bridge. In the evening her publisher had given a reception for her. She hadn't had to read much from her book, just a quarter of an hour. Champagne, wine, Campari and sandwiches had been provided. She had had to autograph about forty copies of her book. A hundred and fifty people had attended the reception. She knew many of the

names: they were the names of famous industrial families—charming people, only she couldn't imagine what information these people would derive from a book like *Days from the Life of Lisbeth P.*

Next morning a woman photographer with a Fiat 500 fetched her from the hotel and drove her to the main station. Before the express arrived she let herself be photographed several times. Once with a lighted cigarette. The train carried her up the Rhine. The well-known panorama of the left bank with its vineyards and castles. In Frankfurt she pushed her baggage on a metal trolley to another station and bought an evening paper. She travelled to Darmstadt.

In the evening she read in the foyer of the Municipal Theatre. About one hundred and twenty people had turned up. The bookseller, who had hired the foyer, a man who perspired a lot, told Natasha Roth he had met her personally eleven years ago. He was sure she wouldn't remember. She did indeed remember. Her memory was very accurate in such matters. She was able to tell the bookseller a few details of their meeting and he felt very flattered. She drank three bottles of wine with him at a restaurant.

Next morning she travelled to Frankfurt. The weather was sultry that day. The city was plastered with posters relating to the Federal elections, which were to take place in exactly a week and a half. She took a taxi to the radio station, where she recorded a forty-five-minute-long extract from *Lisbeth P* on tape. Immediately after this she gave an interview. She was asked about Bodakov. She said the same things as in her television interview. The radio producer who was looking after her squinted noticeably and looked like a forest goblin. In the evening she read in the company library of a vast chemical undertaking on the edge of the city. While she was going there by taxi a heavy storm came down. She was rather drunk. There were eighty people in the room. She was asked again about Bodakov. In the audience was a Pole who was working for six months on a grant at a university institute and whom she knew from Warsaw, because he had translated several pieces by her into Polish. He now had a full beard. He took her to a friend's place for beer and canapés. She stayed till long after midnight. In the end she was completely drunk with exhaustion.

Next day, Saarbrücken. On the way she read a review of *Days from the Life of Lisbeth P* in a major daily paper. It tore the book to pieces, as a piece of calculated opportunism that had only to be compared with Bodakov's latest book. Natasha Roth, it said, was cold and calculating and no credit to her famous uncle Joseph Roth. To calm herself, she drank half a litre of red wine in the dining car. In Saarbrücken she had an interview with a newspaper reporter. At her reading, in a left-wing bookshop, she was confronted by a crowd of young people in washed-out jeans. Again and again the same two extracts; the sentences came into her mouth automatically and she let them out again faultlessly. Question time was mainly taken up by a debate about Bodakov. Most of the audience had seen Natasha Roth's television interview. The bookseller attacked her for her friendly opinion of Bodakov, and yet he had several piles of Bodakov's book in his shop. He had to have them, he said, for the sake of the sales. Afterwards she drank beer with a few people in a workers' pub.

Next morning she picked up a rental car. The city looked shabby to her; the various elements in it didn't seem to go particularly well together. She had never been here before. She kept coming across election propaganda, but it was almost all for the Conservatives. She drove with the car, a VW 1300, towards the frontier in the direction of Forbach. She still held a French visa. The French border official waved her on without looking at her papers. In a hut directly over the frontier she changed her money into francs.

She drove on along the N61 in a south-easterly direction, via Phalsbourg and Saverne to Strasbourg. Gradually she calmed down. She parked her car on the banks of the Ill and walked into the Old City. She recognized a lot of it. She hadn't been in Strasbourg since her childhood. Now it was because of her childhood that she had driven to Strasbourg instead of to Metz or Nancy. The streets filled up; it was the weekend, and on top of that the vintage was just being gathered in. When she was there, the Rue des Grandes Arcades had been called Gewerbslauben. During the two years between leaving Vienna and the German takeover of Alsace she had lived in the south of the city, in Neudorf, Rue Jean Jaurès, where her father had rented a furnished house. Sinaida used to take her stepdaughter Natasha's hand and walk with her to St Urban's Cemetery on the Kromme Rijn.

She ate in a large restaurant by the cathedral, La Brasserie du Dauphin, a meal that was far too heavy: duck roasted in garlic, with haricot beans. She tried to telephone Berlin, but as she failed to get through, she sent a telegram. She slept at a hotel by the station. For many hours, without waking, without dreaming. She woke around noon. It was a sunny day. She drove in her hired car into the Vosges. There she couldn't bring herself to drive to Wingen and went towards the Col du Donon instead. Three thousand and twenty-seven feet high. A military cemetery from the last war. Two thousand years ago a pagan holy place. She looked down into a deep valley. On a felled tree trunk a young woman lay with closed eyes in the sun. Otherwise no one. She sat down on the blood-red forest soil. She wept a little and thought about nothing. Next day she drove a little way down the Rhine and crossed the frontier at Sarreguemines. This time her passport was checked. In Saarbrücken she returned the rented car.

Three days later she travelled in various trains as far as

Recklinghausen. She had never been in the Ruhr. She kept seeing school children wearing T-shirts or carrying canvas bags with Conservative election slogans printed on them. It was astonishing how few pit-head towers, blast furnaces or heaps of industrial waste were to be seen. She stayed in a hotel that was a converted castle. She had the impression of being in flat, black-earthed farming country with endless enclosed pastures. The bookseller gave a dinner for her with three journalists. Photographs were taken. About fifty people came to her reading. She was asked about Bodakov again. She thought to herself that if the numbers continued to go down like this, in the end she would be left alone with the bookseller.

At the next reading there were over a hundred in the audience. This was in Kiel. The bookseller said that if it wasn't for the elections he would have had a bigger audience to offer. She gave one interview on the radio, another on television. She was in a good mood that day. After the reading, the bookseller took her to a cellar restaurant. She wanted to see the Kiel Fjord. A drunken journalist took her in his car to the Olympic Stadium, where all she could see in the darkness were lights reflected in the water.

It was very cold. Next morning she saw grey vapour in front of her mouth. She walked to the station. In her compartment two friendly elderly women were discussing the forthcoming election. Outside, dusk was slowly disappearing. Through the window she could see lakes with smooth grey water, green banks and red-brick houses. She hadn't had nearly enough sleep. She would have liked to show her children something like the view outside. When she remembered her children she strictly forbade herself to pursue these thoughts. The two friendly elderly women were agreed that only the sturdy politician from Bavaria could save their private incomes and keep down taxes. When a waiter passed down the train selling drinks she bought a vodka and Coca-Cola.

By the time they reached Stuttgart it was afternoon. (Her publisher's publicity manager apologized for the complicated travel arrangements: it was the only way to fit in all the dates.) She drove up the Königstrasse with a young taxi driver who told her, unasked, he would prefer to vote for Hitler. Then the streets would become safe again, the currency stable. She read in a small left-wing bookshop in the Inner City before an audience of fifty. A casually dressed young woman related that in the district where she lived all cars bearing Social Democratic stickers had been damaged, their windscreens daubed with black paint, their tyres slashed. The Conservatives were hiring unemployed youths for this at fifty marks a night. The young woman looked very much like a militant Socialist and probably was, but her name was Lobkowitz and she actually came from the aristocratic Viennese family.

Next day, Nuremberg. She hated this city. She knew it from a previous visit: witch hunts and Nazi trials, Nazi Party Congresses and Wagnerian opera. Her reading was to be given in a university extension building. This time only twenty people turned up in a vast room with a hundred and fifty seats. The organizer was a man with white hair. They moved into a smaller room. The election battle was now at its height, said the white-haired man apologetically. Then he complained about the general lack of interest in cultural matters. Next morning she drove along a street lined with dozens of gigantic posters showing a picture of the leading Social Democratic candidate, the chancellor, laughing with a display of white teeth. On every poster the eyes had been scratched out.

The daily speculations as to who would win the election had gradually brought her to a state of tension and excitement. As though her own personal fate would be decided by this election. In a certain sense this was true: she didn't live in a world of her own and the country she lived in was not just anywhere. She was on the way to Cologne again. Her publisher had got her an invitation to an election party to be held in the evening of election Sunday at the radio station in the Wallrafplatz, for selected guests. Presumably he saw some possible advantage in having a well-known authoress from the other German state there among the journalists. Any comment she might make would be helpful to sales. In her Cologne hotel she took a Valium and slept through to the following morning. The publisher's junior partner called for her, so that she could watch him cast his vote. They drove to a school. The junior partner was given a slip of paper and disappeared into a booth. Groups of petty bourgeois in their Sunday best came straight from High Mass. They would vote as God had ordered them half an hour before through the mouth of their priest. On the way back she was handed a folder containing all the reviews of her book that had appeared up to then. All the major newspapers had torn it to shreds. Lisbeth P, the reviews said, was a show figure, the sort of meretricious character Communist writers true to the party line could suck out of their fingertips.

In the evening she drove to the radio station. Her publisher was waiting for her at the entrance and gave her a badge. A studio was fitted out with long tables and television cameras. On the tables stood name cards and bottles of lemonade; microphones were hanging everywhere and journalists were running around in their shirtsleeves. The TV screens showed the results of the latest poll. It predicted not a neck-and-neck race, but a clear lead for the Coalition. The poll was not considered to be accurate; its election predictions contained enormous margins of error. A newscaster said there had been a very high turn-out. Single results came in and were noted in chalk on the big blackboards in the studio.

Natasha Roth went to the bar to get herself a drink. There, to her surprise, she found Ferenc Butterman. He kissed her demonstratively on both cheeks and she could feel that he hadn't shaved. He had just come from Bonn, where he had to stand in for a sick colleague. He had come to Cologne solely on Natasha's account, after hearing that she was here at Broadcasting House. She had to give two other journalists her personal prediction. She said truthfully that during her two weeks of travelling to and fro she had come across far more propaganda for the Conservatives than for the Coalition. Precisely in districts governed by the Coalition. She foresaw a close victory for the Christian Democrats. The effect on Eastern Europe would be considerable. Her listeners nodded with concern at each of her replies. Natasha Roth's opinion seemed to be identical with their own.

Ferenc Butterman went with her to an Italian restaurant in the Ring. She was so preoccupied by the failure of her book and by political excitement that for the moment there was no room in her head for any other thoughts. They ate *calamari fritti* and drank dry Soave. Ferenc Butterman said that back home there was an odd mood, like in a hothouse, at least among intellectuals; it reminded him of Prague in summer '68, where he had been as a correspondent. Something would explode at any moment, he felt it in his bones.

They went back to Broadcasting House. Ferenc Butterman returned to Bonn. The first computerized predictions had come in. They gave the Coalition a slight lead. One computer gave the lead as much slighter than the other. Natasha Roth suddenly found herself sitting on an upper floor, in the office of a radio producer who was directing several studios with the aid of telephones and intercoms. A television set was on. For a time it looked as though the Coalition's lead would be so small as to make real government impossible. Ferenc Butterman appeared briefly before the camera and talked rubbish. People ran through the office shouting out information that five minutes later was worthless. The Coalition's lead was obviously going to be big enough. The commentators expressed doubts about the reliability of the Liberals. By two in the morning it was all over. The commentators met to discuss tactics with expressions that said they had known all along. She herself, without quite realizing it, had drunk almost the whole of a two-litre bottle of Chianti during the last few hours. This must be the way people would feel after the happy ending of a great threat. The world had once more been saved—assuming it had actually been in danger.

There were two more cities left in her reading tour: Giessen and Braunschweig. She left Cologne at noon. Again the left bank of the Rhine; behind the tinted windowpanes of the express compartment a film in bad color was running that showed the aggressive blue of the nets stretched over the not-yet-harvested vineyards. In Giessen she found a letter waiting for her at her hotel. A writer she had met about fifteen years before at a meeting of the Evangelical Academy wanted to see her. At that time the writer had been a resolute anti-Socialist. She had argued with him bitterly.

She met him now at a Spanish restaurant with bull-fight posters on the white-washed walls and fandangos constantly playing on the tape-deck. She looked into an old face and knew that at this second the writer was thinking exactly the same as she. He said he had wanted to write to her before, in Berlin. He hadn't done so for various reasons. They had a few mutual acquaintances, about whom they now talked. Six months ago the writer had been in Moscow, for the first time in his life. He had felt lonely and vulnerable. They both spoke of their impression of alienation, gained in opposing parts of the globe. Their words made no contact with each other, even if they sometimes seemed to. The writer described his environment: it was now cold, coarse, violent, lazy, possessed, a neon world in whose shadow drainpipe trousers sprouted out of boot-legs. For this reason he owned a small house in Tuscany, where people were simple and friendly. He also talked about Bodakov, whose book seemed to him snivelling. Bodakov struck him as a grumbler who was obviously out to cause controversy.

By now it was time for her reading. Outside it was already dark. The writer now related that he had once been friendly with Ulrike Marie Meinhof. They walked through the streets into a green belt. Suddenly they didn't know where they were. Only cars passed. They didn't meet a single pedestrian. It was getting late. The writer was lapsing into a Swabian accent. They walked faster and faster and the route became more and more complicated. Finally they found themselves at a crossroads they had passed before. The time for the reading to start was long past. She giggled. She found consolation in the thought that by tomorrow she would be out of this city and in three days out of this world. Then they met someone, a drunk, who despite his condition was able to give them directions. At the door of the room in which the reading was to take place they met the worried bookseller, standing behind his colourful improvised book counter. Ten people had left already. The room was draped in black, a small experimental theatre. During the reading a powerful spotlight was on her. It remained on her during question time. She could see no faces, only grey outlines with several spectral colours around the silhouettes carved into the black background. There might have been twenty people or only five.

During her whole tour she had never come up against such massive rejection. The questions were not questions at all, but semantically disguised expressions of hostility. As though she had built the wall all by herself with her own hands, as though she had laid every mine herself. At one point someone shouted: "I hate you, even though you give me no reason to; that's just why I hate you." Twice the writer voiced a favourable opinion. From further back in the room a woman's voice made a friendly comment. The voice seemed familiar to her, but she didn't know where she had heard it before. When the reading was over the spotlight was switched off. She could hear the bookseller fold up his table and run, as though from a crime.

The woman whose voice she thought she recognized now rose from the darkness. She saw before her, with a different hairstyle and also somewhat changed features, the person who had served as model for Lisbeth P, the heroine of her book, from which she had been reading here and all the other days. Now Lisbeth P had finally become a synthetic character, created at will, untrue to life, at least not justified by reality. The contemptuous reviews were all correct. The woman and the writer and she went back to the Spanish restaurant, which was quite close. The woman said she had spent ten months in Hoheneck women's prison. She had been released before completion of her sentence. The writer wanted to know if Natasha Roth had differences with the poet Musäus. No? But she knew him? Slightly? The woman told them that the man on whose account she had fled the country and been arrested, a widower who owned a large service station in Giessen, had died of a heart attack a few days before she crossed the frontier. She hadn't known anything about it. He hadn't known she was coming. She could make no claim on his estate. It occurred to Natasha Roth that the name Musäus had been mentioned several times during her trip, even if not nearly so often as Bodakov's. Musäus was engaged in a similar reading tour. He had also been in Giessen, said the woman, in the black-draped experimental theatre. She herself always went to any such events that concerned the country she had come from. Not from homesickness; purely out of curiosity. Or something like that. She had to build a new life. She didn't want to go back because of her rotten experiences. She then said, twisting her fingers, that people were saying that Natasha Roth—the writer immediately confirmed this, in fact it turned out that this was why he had sought a meeting with Natasha Roth, but the woman wanted to be the one to tell her, because she knew Natasha Roth personally and because she couldn't believe this of her—after his reading in an experimental theatre the poet Musäus had told a few people—and things like that stick, as she knew herself—that Natasha Roth was really an agent in one of the East German secret services. Outwardly Natasha Roth laughed and shook her head. She thought bitterly that now things couldn't get any worse.

WHEN HIS MOTHER got back, it was more than three hours later than she had told her family that same day in a phone call from the West Berlin airport. In the end all three of them, including Stefan's father, had begun to get worried. When they heard the taxi stop outside the garden gate, Stefan and Billa had run from the house to meet their mother. This was a way of coping with their sudden feeling of relief. Stefan's father was furious, because of the delay and the worry it had caused. Natasha Roth explained that at the last moment she had mislaid one of the documents, the yellow census paper. The loss of this document had caused unusual and unforeseeable delay at the border crossing. She had been taken aside into a special room in a hut, where she had first had to wait and then undergo extensive questioning, interrupted by several telephone calls. Finally a senior official had taken a detailed deposition. Natasha Roth laughed. She was unnaturally red in the face. She smelled of tobacco, eau de Cologne and her own sweetish perspiration. Stefan's father gradually calmed down. Stefan's mother unpacked the gifts. They were the usual things: a pullover, a pair of jeans, records of rock music. In the evening Stefan's parents drank French apple brandy and talked. The radio was on. The news reported that the poet Arnold Bodakov, living in the GDR, had been awarded a major West German literary prize for his latest book, the Friedrich Hölderlin Prize presented by the city of Tübingen.

Soon after this—it was in the second half of October, the autumn school holidays had begun—all four of them went for a week to the Mittelgebirge. They stayed in a big hotel on a mountainside, whose outer walls were completely covered with dark-brown shingles. During the whole of this holiday the dog had to sleep in the car. They had brought tins of dog food for it. The animal was fed in the evening around five o'clock, while Stefan and Billa held it on the lead to prevent it from going after cats that crouched under the parked car. The autumn had remained very warm. They went for walks along paths that were often very steep and found yellow boletus mushrooms, which they cut into thin slices in the evening and laid on the radiator to dry. In this way they gradually filled a transparent plastic bag with dried mushrooms, brownish, wrinkled slivers that made Stefan think of leather, of shreds of skin, of death. Most of the woodland paths ended in turnpikes or yellow signboards with printed lettering imperiously forbidding anyone to go any further. Beyond them lay the bare strips of no-man's-land. Sometimes soldiers would pass by. Their dogs always started barking and running towards them and had to be whistled back by the soldiers. From the hotel they could see a mountain with a ski jump on the other side of the valley. There was also a high tower of bone-white concrete, reminiscent of

an observatory. Something military, the hotel barber told
Stefan as he worked. The mountain with its buildings lay on
the other side of the frontier.

One evening during dinner Natasha Roth told her children
that she had been on this mountain during her last reading
tour, just two weeks ago. She had hired a car in Braunschweig and driven to Bad Harzburg and then on the Harz
Highway to Braunlage. She had been in Braunlage once as
a child, right after the war, but in the meantime it had grown
much bigger and was now full of new apartment buildings
and spacious white hotels. She had parked her car in Braunlage and gone up to the mountaintop in the cable-car. The
landscape up there was exactly the same as here, she told
them, the same soil, the same forest, the same insects and
birds, the same smell. From the hut on the summit she had
gone down in a northerly direction alongside the track of
the ski-jump. At a crossroads there, there too, were signboards with the notice *Caution Zone Border* and behind them
a high wire fence painted grey. She had clearly distinguished
two concrete watch-towers with glass domes. She had
walked on to the right, following the wire fence, until there
was an uninterrupted view of the place in which they now
were. She had stood and looked down. For how long she
couldn't remember. It was a fine day, sunshine, a sky with
shreds of cloud and not much wind. Through the meshes of
the fence she saw red-tiled roofs. She would clearly make
out the hotel they were now staying in. She looked at the individual windows and wondered behind which of them she
would soon be living, since she had already arranged this
holiday. The border guards had soon noticed her. Signals
were exchanged, binoculars were trained on her from the
watch-towers and a two-man patrol with dogs had suddenly
appeared among the trees. She wondered what would happen
if she took out her dark-blue passport and waved it, but she
didn't do so because it seemed to her an eccentric and quite

pointless thing to do. Instead she turned round and walked back up to the top of the mountain, where she took the shaking, creaking cable-car down into the other valley, where her car was parked. Several times, as she stood up there, she was overcome by a sense of confusion. It was a melancholy, a disquieting sight, she said. To someone like her it was rather an exciting situation. She said no more. Stefan looked out of the big dining-room window at the mountain top, whose silhouette in the evening sky was beginning to turn brown and fade away. He tried—and perhaps his sister Sibylle was doing the same—to picture his mother standing on a height that was so close and yet so hopelessly far away.

Another day Stefan and his father left the hotel on their own with the dog. Although it was against the law in these parts, they let the dog off the leash. It ran towards the grey boulders, hunting about among wet blueberry bushes. The day was colder than usual and misty. "Stefan," said his father, "there's something I want to talk to you about. Your mother and I"—as he said this he stared fixedly to one side through his spectacles—"have decided to separate. We shall get a divorce." After saying this, he spoke somewhat faster. It sounded as though he had rehearsed the next sentences, to make them sound natural. "You won't be pleased to hear this. I imagine. But don't think we're glad about it. We simply don't see any other solution. In fact, there isn't one. I could tell you all the reasons. But I'm not sure you would understand them, Stefan. In any case, not understanding wouldn't change anything. You're sixteen and Sibylle is almost thirteen; you're no longer children. We don't have to worry about your accident and its after-affects any more. Your mother wants to keep her children with her. If you like, if Billa likes, you can express a different wish. Perhaps we could fall in with it."

The dog was barking shrilly as it chased a squirrel. His heart didn't beat any differently, Stefan noticed incredulously; he didn't feel numb, not even dizzy. His father filled his pipe. His left thumb, with which he was pressing down the tobacco, trembled a bit; a trembling thumb tamping down tobacco was a funny sight. Stefan moved his eyes up from his father's thumb and hand to his face. He had taken this face so much for granted that he now noted with amazement individual features which, under the pressure of everyday living, of daily contact, had remained unknown, unnoticed. But from now on the friendly face with the black moustache would no longer be available to him as a matter of course. Should he worry about that? Only the side of his body weakened by paralysis suddenly reacted with fatigue. And he had a hollow feeling behind the bridge of his nose, as though he had been punched. As far as his limp was concerned, he thought, no one could possibly notice it in their hotel where so many old people were staying who walked slowly, bent, many of them on crutches, when they came in to meals. At dinner Natasha Roth glanced at Stefan's father, a glance that expressed an unspoken question. Stefan's father nodded, almost imperceptibly, but Stefan perceived it. It obviously had to do with the conversation between him and his father about the divorce. This silent understanding by familiar signals, this practised way of reaching an agreement over matters affecting a joint life that was soon to be joint no more, seemed to Stefan crazy, and the craziest thing of all was that outward events remained unchanged. Bills were paid, chairs slid back, coats taken from the cloak-room, doors opened and closed. That evening, as every evening, the television was switched on in his parents' room. Among other things the news reported that the poet Arnold Bodakov had, surprisingly, been given permission by the GDR authorities to accept in person a literary prize recently awarded him in the Federal Republic. For several years Bodakov had been forbidden to travel abroad. His latest book had so far appeared only in the Federal Republic.

When the week at the hotel was over, when Billa too had been informed of the imminent change and had asked her brother childish, imprudent questions, Stefan was asked by his father to come to the museum on a particular day after school. Stefan appeared. The attendants knew him. He greeted them and they nodded. He went to his father's office and knocked on the door. His father opened it. The room in which his father worked was full of old furniture, none of it genuine, all of it reproduction antique, as his father had once told him and now repeated, perhaps because he liked saying it. He laughed as he said it. Stefan saw a young woman who was not blond, but had dark hair. She had freckles and a narrow gap between her upper front teeth. She was pretty. His father said this was the woman he was going to marry. Stefan obediently said how do you do, stretching out his right hand. He answered questions and asked none. This woman was not like the fair-haired one he had once seen in the company of his father at the streetcar stop in the Kirchstrasse. So perhaps the blonde existed too. Or the man he had seen wasn't his father at all. He was much amused by the idea that he had related to his father an incident which, although it must have been a case of mistaken identity, was in another sense perfectly true. He would really have liked to talk to his father about it. But this was obviously not the right moment. Later he forgot about it. There were far more important matters. Everything had to be very carefully thought over. His visit to the Köpenick Museum had given a visual force to what had previously been only a verbal communication by his father. As though the words had had no validity, but the evidence of his eyes made everything real, he suddenly felt nothing but dejection, coldness, sorrow. There was no one he could talk to about it, not Billa, who was still too childish and too silly, not his mother, certainly no stranger. His mother was working and mustn't be disturbed. She sat in her room writing until far into the night. Any inter-

ruption made her angry; at times she screamed almost hys-
terically. Ferenc Butterman returned to Berlin. He said he
had been in Bonn, then for a rest to Lake Constance and
Lake Geneva. He had two new gold teeth in his mouth and
told long, boring fishing stories. He was evidently sensitive
to atmospheres. He seemed to perceive immediately what had
happened between Stefan's parents, or he had learned from
gossip. Anyhow, he knew and now asked for confirmation.
For a week he came every day. He brought food from West
Berlin delicatessens and cooked devotedly, as though that
might change things.

On the other hand, Stefan's father stayed away. Often he
was away for several evenings and nights in a row. Billa invited friends home. This produced noise. All the life in the
house became haphazard and somehow improvised. The
first trees were shredding their leaves. The foliage of the big
oaks in the street turned brown. When you walked the
acorns crackled under your feet: a sound and a feeling, as
though you were crushing plump insects. Thus time passed.

ONE TUESDAY in November—it was late in the after- **24**
noon—the telephone rang. Natasha wasn't near the instrument and before she could react herself she heard irregular
footsteps in the hall. That meant Stefan was about to answer
the call. Soon afterwards he shouted her name twice. She
went across to the other room and lifted the receiver. Crackling electronic noises. She knew from this that the call came
from far away. The name given to her was that of the junior
partner in the West German publishing company. His voice
sounded agitated. He was in Bavaria at a conference of West

German and Austrian publishers. An agency news release had just been brought into the conference room to the effect that the GDR authorities had refused the poet Bodakov permission to re-enter the country and had deprived him of his citizenship. For the last few days Natasha Roth's thoughts had been devoted to quite different matters of great importance to her. The information she had just received was incomprehensible to her, since it belonged to a life that had once been hers but was so no longer. She said she wasn't prepared to believe this news. The publisher became even more excited; he gave a guarantee; he named the names of agencies, as though agencies had never made a mistake. He pressed her to express an opinion, which in his view could only be one of indignation such as he felt himself. He urged her to utter a sentence, several sentences, which he could write down, which he would immediately channel into the publicity machinery. A comment of this kind could only enhance Natasha Roth's prestige, there was no doubt of that. It would also enormously increase the sales of her latest book, indeed of all her books. She repeated, hesitating several times, that she was not prepared to accept the news of Arnold Bodakov's loss of citizenship without proof; she wanted to find out for herself whether the news was true. When the publisher asked if he could call her back in an hour, or next morning, she said she was not prepared to express herself publicly on this matter. She put down the receiver. She immediately went across to the living-room and switched on the radio. She heard the last few bars of a music programme, then the newsreader began to give the news, the first item of which confirmed what her publisher had just told her over the telephone. The newsreader added that Bodakov had yesterday received a literary prize in Tübingen. He seemed completely surprised by the decision of the GDR authorities. As though she were able, for a few seconds, to register her own emotions as if they were a stranger's, Natasha Roth observed that she nodded her head several times, looking—she had to look somewhere—at her son's mouth. He wouldn't make much sense of this piece of news. He didn't even know who Arnold Bodakov was. To her surprise she noted that the news seemed to have produced a change in Stefan; his forehead creased, his eyes had an expression that appeared to her like a reflection of her own. She switched the radio over to the Oberschöneweide station. Here too news was on. The news of Bodakov's deprivation of citizenship was given drily as the last item but one. It was explained that Bodakov had grossly disregarded his civil responsibilities, thereby forfeiting the right to live in the GDR. This phrase, it seemed to her, had finally given the verbal announcement an irrefutable reality; it had become a leaden truth. Now her first thought was how Rebecca would react to the step that had been taken. She went to the telephone again. At her first call, Rebecca's number was engaged. At subsequent calls no one picked up the receiver. She watched with vacant attention as her son Stefan slowly put several books in a pile, picked them up and, with the pile of books on his left arm, went out of the room and upstairs to his own room. She heard the sound of his irregular footsteps on the wooden stairs.

H E C O U L D clearly hear his mother striding up and down 25 on the floor below. Again and again a door was thrown open, then there was music or a voice on the radio; again and again the name Bodakov was uttered. He could tell from various sounds that his father had come home. The banging of doors, footsteps, voices. He tried to concentrate on certain mathematical problems which he had to solve by tomorrow morning. From the ground floor he could hear his parents' voices growing louder and louder. His mother in particular was speaking fast and very agitatedly. He heard little pinging sounds coming from the telephone, indicating that someone was trying to make a call, evidently his mother, but she seemed unable to get through. His sister came into the room; she wanted to know what had happened and who this Bodakov was. Stefan replied, and it was quite true, that he didn't know much about it, didn't want to say anything and didn't want to know. An hour later he went downstairs again with his sister. Throughout the evening the television was on. His mother, a liquor glass in her hand, kept walking to and fro across the room, stopping only when the name Bodakov was mentioned. Both the West German news programmes showed photographs of Bodakov as well as film clips, Bodakov standing on a flower-decked platform speaking into a microphone. Stefan saw a broad-shouldered man with black hair; he couldn't hear what he was saying because his voice was overlaid by a commentator's. Bodakov looked strained. Stefan couldn't have said at this moment whether he liked Bodakov. The newscaster reported that Bodakov's family was still in the GDR, in a village in Mecklenburg. At once a short film was shown: a television reporter was standing outside a timber-frame house; behind the thatched roof grew blue-green pines; the reporter said into his microphone that this was where Frau Bodakov lived with her four young children; she was in no condition to make any statement about her husband's loss of citizenship. Billa said she was hungry. The newscaster read protests against the deprivation of citizenship issued by various organizations. Stefan's father put down his pipe and went into the kitchen. Natasha Roth started wandering round the room again. In her right hand she held her liquor glass. Billa's father brought her a sandwich and she began to chew greedily. The television was switched from one channel to another, always in the expectation of news about Bodakov's deprivation of citizenship. Natasha Roth drank glass after glass of Polish vodka. She still walked straight and gave no sign of being drunk. Stefan took his sister by the shoulders and went back upstairs with her. Even when half asleep, he could still hear the voices of the newscasters. Once there was the little click in the telephone again.

Next morning both his parents looked as though they hadn't slept. It was far more noticeable in his mother than in his father. Stefan himself, when he woke up, had completely forgotten the withdrawal of citizenship from a poet whom he didn't know personally. Now he saw that his mother's agitation had not diminished; the radio was on again; almost every word that was broadcast still had to do with Bodakov's loss of citizenship. Stefan looked into his mother's face. She looked to him completely limp, apathetic, dejected, almost ill. He himself felt frightened. It was a gnawing, faint, very vague fear. It had to do with the fact that he wasn't well, that he never again would be well like other people, that he had been paralysed, that he still limped, that this made him feel more helpless than other people. He was afraid of being completely alone and completely vulnerable and unable to defend himself, because there were more of the others and this made them more powerful. Such feelings were a completely new experience for him. Or at least they had never been so persistent before. At any time during the last few weeks when he had suspected that he might fall victim to such feelings, he had been able to shake them off without difficulty, by a simple movement of the body as it were. Now he knew, he could feel, that he would never again be able to do this, so there was no point in his even trying, no matter how hard. He made an effort to put all this into words, which wasn't easy. He told his mother that before taking any steps she should first consider what consequences they would have for him, and perhaps also for Billa. She looked at him attentively as he spoke. She said she had already thought of that and she wouldn't do anything without talking it over with him first; she promised. He grew somewhat calmer after this statement. At school a normal seven-hour day of classes took place. He had to do things he did every day, open exercise books, write down words, sometimes answer a question out loud. The name "Bodakov" wasn't mentioned once, not even during the breaks between classes. Stefan was finally ready to forget him again.

 THAT MORNING Natasha Roth had watched the man she was married to leave the house, followed a little later by her two children. She drank several cups of black coffee. She wandered around the empty house. The radio was switched on and broadcast music, interspersed with the same announcements about Bodakov, about Bodakov's deprivation of citizenship, about protests against Bodakov's deprivation of citizenship. She went to the garden gate. She took the newspapers out of the mailbox. She read the report about Bodakov on page two and also a commentary. Arnold B, a well-known opponent of real Socialism, had repeatedly slandered the country in which he lived. In the course of a speech in the FRG city of Tübingen he had compared the German Democratic Republic to a Fascist dictatorship. With great verbosity the services of the GDR to anti-Fascism were extolled and the omissions of the FRG pointed out. The superiority of the Socialist camp was demonstrated.

Natasha Roth took her coat, got into her car and drove towards the inner city of Berlin. She had repeatedly tried to

imagine how Rebecca had received the news of the last fifteen hours, how Rebecca would now behave. Rebecca had
left her telephone off the hook, perhaps she wasn't in her
flat. Even the commercial broadcasts from Radio Luxembourg spoke sympathetically about Bodakov. Natasha Roth's
thoughts moved away from Bodakov again and concerned
themselves with the judicial processes of the division of property, the assessment of property, maintenance claims, en-
titlement to maintenance, divorce. Outside the gates to the
building in the Auguststrasse, in the rear of which Rebecca
had her flat, she saw several parked cars. This was striking
in a street, in a part of a street, where cars were rarely
parked.

The door to Rebecca's flat was ajar. As though a visitor
was expected, as though Rebecca had anticipated a visit from
Natasha Roth. Was this so unlikely? Rebecca looked bloated,
she staggered, she had rings round her eyes, she spoke slowly;
but she wasn't drunk, she had taken several strong tranquillizers, Rebecca said without being asked, giggling and
apologizing. Sitting in Rebecca's flat were four writers whose
presence in this place at this time Natasha Roth wouldn't
have expected. A poet, a playwright, an old novelist and a
young one. The attitude of each one of them to Rebecca indicated that they were old and intimate friends. Natasha
hadn't known about that; on the contrary, when she had
talked with Rebecca about any one of the four, she had
always had the impression that Rebecca knew them only
slightly.

The sudden discovery of this fact annoyed her. Like the
discovery of a betrayal or a conspiracy or an infidelity. And
yet Natasha Roth had nothing against any of the four, except that he was a writer. Each one of them was vain and
self-seeking in his own way. They were all considered important, even abroad. Each one of them was certainly as important as Natasha Roth, and each of them, she knew,

secretly thought himself more important than Natasha Roth. Then she forbade herself to have such thoughts; she ordered herself, rather, to regard the fact that they had all come here to see how Rebecca was standing up to Bodakov's deprivation of citizenship as a humane and comradely act. The melancholy, passionate relationship between Rebecca and Bodakov was widely known among authors. It was part of the country's unwritten literary history.

Natasha Roth saw the poet pick up a piece of paper and begin to read passages from it. The poet, a physically large, white-haired man, lived outside Berlin, near Potsdam, in a house that had belonged to his grandfather, full of historical weapons and antique furniture. The poet's grandfather had been a man who for sixty years had carried on a legal battle with his neighbour over the ownership of three nut trees and finally won, whereupon he died content. There was an autobiographical account of this event from the pen of his grandson, the poet, that was printed in the country's school textbooks as a model of literary style. The poet was considered as pugnacious as his grandfather, and what he now read out in a voice that completely contradicted the well-known sensitivity of his verses, being as gnarled as the wood of his grandfather's nut trees, was nothing else but a text defending the poet Bodakov and protesting his deprivation of citizenship. Socialism was the realm of freedom longed for in the dreams of the nations which, in the words of Lenin, could live with its contrary. Finally, like the lines of a poem, the poet read out the names of the people in the room, in alphabetical order; hence Natasha Roth's name came last.

There followed a solemn silence. Natasha Roth asked who was to receive this declaration. The older novelist said histrionically: "Those who will make it public." Natasha Roth noticed now that the younger novelist's hands were trembling. None of them was willing to modify the answer that had been given. Natasha Roth suddenly felt gripped by something like paralysis. The solemnity with which the poet had uttered one name after the other had sounded like a judgement. The young novelist didn't know what to do with his trembling hands. Natasha Roth felt sorry for him, and above and beyond this feeling, the awareness shot into her like an injection that something unusual was going on here, perhaps an act of audacity which had long since become clear to the others and to which, nevertheless, she had firmly made up her mind to hold fast. Suddenly they all started talking at once. Cigarettes were smoked and Natasha made and poured out tea, in place of the apathetic Rebecca. Odd things would be left in their memories from these hours—how many actually?—such as the way the famous poet drew a straw from a Virginia cigar. She had the impression he was pulling out a long gold needle. At one point she had the bizarre thought that this moment was witnessing the creation of the one and only effective vaccine against her fear of wordlessness.

They repeated sentences to one another, or modifications of sentences, modifications of modified sentences. Because of the repeated alterations, the agreed text, running in the end to exactly one hundred and seven words, was typed out three times in all on Rebecca's typewriter by the older novelist. Then it occurred to the young novelist that the quote they had used in the text might be from Marx, not Lenin. Fortunately, Rebecca had the necessary books in her bookcase. The quote was indeed from Marx, not Lenin. They all laughed together, relieved that they had avoided a ridiculous mistake, and the older novelist typed out the statement for the fourth time. Apart from Rebecca, who seemed to be sinking deeper and deeper into the apathy brought on by the tablets, they all felt gripped by a triumphant happiness, and on top of this Natasha Roth was also gripped by the thought that this alone had made everything worthwhile.

27 WHEN STEFAN came home from school he found his mother missing. His sister Billa, in a bad mood, was chewing a piece of bread and cheese that was too dry. She was hungry, she grumbled, and there was nothing better in the refrigerator. The dog barked and jumped up against the veranda door, a proof that no one had bothered about it that day. Stefan put the animal on the lead and took it out and, because he suddenly felt like it, walked for half an hour through various streets. When he got back, his mother was still not there. That wouldn't have been unusual on any other day. It might mean something that day. It wasn't until an hour later that she finally drove into the garden and got out of the car.

Stefan noticed an air of gaiety about her which was striking, which he had never seen before. Instead of an explanation, she held out a piece of paper with writing on it. He saw three paragraphs and perhaps a hundred individual words, which all had to do with the poet Arnold Bodakov's loss of citizenship. There was a request for its restoration. There was also a verbatim quotation from Karl Marx. Beneath the text stood six names; the name Natasha Roth came last, after Rebecca's name. His mother wanted to know what he thought about it. "I don't know," he said. "I promised I would ask you first," she said. "But it was suddenly not possible." Her gaiety so overcame her that she almost lost her voice. "So you see, we writers here are capable of acting together." But he didn't understand the whole thing; it didn't interest him; he didn't reply. Her high spirits lasted until his father came home. Stefan saw that after reading the text his father thought about it; then he shook his head and asked who would be the first to back down. "Certainly not me," said Stefan's mother. His father related that Bodakov's deprivation of citizenship had caused great excitement at the museum. The staff had discussed it and they would certainly discuss it again tomorrow, including the editorial that had appeared in the newspaper. Stefan pictured to himself a pretty, freckled woman with a narrow gap between her front teeth expressing herself excitedly concerning a poet's deprivation of citizenship. Stefan pictured to himself a young woman with fair hair expressing herself excitedly concerning a poet's deprivation of citizenship. The two women discussed it together. The two women together discussed it with his father. Each of the two women discussed it with his father separately. There were two of them, or three of them, in his father's office, which was full of reproduction antique furniture. That was how Stefan pictured it.

The West German television news at eight o'clock presented as its main item the letter of protest written by six well-known East German authors. All six names were read out, in alphabetical order. The newsreader said that the writing of this letter must be looked upon as an entirely new development. He went on to announce that the signatories had handed the letter over to a West European news agency. Bodakov's name was mentioned frequently in the course of the broadcast. The letter of protest seemed to be the most important event that evening. His mother, Stefan saw, remained cheerful. She became increasingly calm. His parents sat side by side in their armchairs. Stefan had often seen them sitting like that, especially in the past. Perhaps it's only a silly rumour, thought Stefan, that they're going to get divorced soon.

28 THE SURPRISING and, to her mind, uncanny thing was that, to begin with, nothing happened. The telephone didn't ring that evening or during the night. As a precaution, and in full agreement with her husband, she had decided not to send either of the children to school next day. Billa spent a long time playing in the garden with the dog. The radio was on; a letter of protest by a group of East German writers was frequently mentioned, and Bodakov's name cropped up even more often. The news reports stated that the disenfranchised poet would give a press conference that day. It was around noon when the telephone finally rang. The call came from a ministry. An employee in a department for artistic matters—a man she had dealt with on previous occasions, mostly in connexion with legal questions—wanted to know if he could come and see Frau Roth that same day. She said, "Of course," and a time was fixed. After this she put the dog on the lead, called Stefan and walked with him through various streets to the edge of the forest. On several occasions, people she had known personally for a long time crossed over to the other side of the street when they saw her, but so far ahead that there might have been some other reason, or it might have been chance; the most likely explanation, however, was that they wanted to avoid greeting Frau Roth in public. A woman she didn't know, whom she didn't think she had ever seen before, stopped her and asked with exaggerated kindliness after her welfare.

In the forest they met no one. It was an overcast day. Moisture clung to the pine trees. The sand on the path was soaking wet. There was a rustling and crackling in the plantations of young trees. This made the dog restless, and it began to whine; perhaps a herd of wild boar was wallowing nearby. It occurred to her that this was the first time for a long while that she had walked with Stefan like this. This would be the moment, she thought, to talk to him about certain things. It also occurred to her that outwardly Stefan had undergone a great change in this year that was gradually drawing to a close. She recalled that the accident had taken place exactly twelve months ago, and she told herself that this was when it had all begun. But what was this "all"? What details did it include? What details did she know about anyway? She had only to open her mouth now. Stefan said nothing. She didn't know how to begin. They only called to the dog and talked to it, as though there was nothing else to say. Finally they walked back again. When they got home they found a trailer parked opposite their driveway, of the kind used by building workers. Wasn't it really too late in the year for building work? But there were a lot of houses in need of repair in this street, their own among them.

Then the man from the ministry arrived. She sent Stefan into the next room. He would be able to hear everything through the communicating door, if he wanted to. She didn't mind that. The man sat down with his elbows close to his sides. He began to speak. This was a strange situation. Nothing like it had ever happened before. Therefore they had discussed the matter at great length and decided that someone would have to speak to one of the six. Thereupon he, the visitor, had raised his hand and said that he would speak to Natasha Roth, because he thought he knew her well. He knew her to be an unpredictable and frequently embarrassing author, but one thing they had so far always taken for granted: that Natasha Roth was loyal to her country. She said she still was. When she expressed her opinions through the media of the class enemy? the man asked. She had reacted publicly to a public event, she said, that was all. Hadn't she heard how the adversary was now exulting? the visitor wanted to know, and she said no, and anyhow that didn't interest her. Her country had done something terrible: it had deprived a poet of his citizenship. Deprivation of citizenship was something she knew from experience. It had happened to her father; it had happened to her. Among the first intellectuals to be disenfranchised by a German state were Heine and Marx. Whether they knew all that or not, such a decision had been irresponsible, and since this irresponsible decision had been taken a protest was called for. She only hoped the decision would now be reversed; there would be nothing shameful about that. What about the exultation of the adversary? lamented the man. Oh, this country would survive that, she said. In her opinion it was just as stable as it always claimed to be in its newspapers. The man shook his head with concern. He now asked what else they could have done with this Bodakov. Nothing at all, she said. The visitor asked for a cup of coffee, perhaps merely to create a break in the conversation. Then he presented his minister's request. If Natasha Roth wanted to communicate with the Western media again in this matter, would she please inform the minister first. She thought it over and then said quietly that she promised to do that. Then she raised her voice and said that if she found out that either of her children had suffered any sort of injustice because their mother was involved in these events, she would consider herself released from this promise. She would then defend herself with every means at her command, publicly, with no consideration for the public consequences. No, said the man, he could promise that nothing of the kind would happen; he would speak to his minister about it as soon as he got back. As though the most awkward part of his mission had been accomplished with unexpectedly good results, he now began to laugh and told funny stories from the theatrical world. He suddenly revealed himself as a kindly, as a witty person.

In the evening the West German television broadcast the press conference Bodakov had given that morning in a Stuttgart hotel. Bodakov's face looked ill; he moved his very broad shoulders clumsily; he called the country he came from a land of state-organized crimes against humanity. Asked about the letter of protest, he reacted almost evasively, as though he felt uncomfortable about it. It seemed, rather, as though he wanted to bear his hopeless, lonely martyrdom alone, an Upper Silesian seeker after God, a sectarian, a stubborn fool chasing after his Saviour carved in wood. No one had warned or advised Bodakov before he made this appearance. She saw how shocked Stefan was by Bodakov's attitude and statements. He asked her why she had taken up the cudgels for a man like that, and she replied that otherwise she would have suffocated.

Bodakov's press conference was immediately followed by an interview with a West German writer. It was the man she had spent half a day with in Giessen—how long ago was that? The writer expressed his revulsion at Bodakov's deprivation of citizenship and called upon all authors in the other German state to speak up, otherwise West German publishers would soon stop publishing the books of East German authors. That was a miserable statement. Horrified, she thought about the lack of political understanding across the frontier. All this was childish; they were behaving like children, that is to say noisily, thoughtlessly and cruelly. The writer added that in his opinion Arnold Bodakov was brilliantly gifted and a man of great moral courage.

The statements of the West German writer had their effect. The very next morning Rebecca telephoned Natasha Roth to tell her that lists were being circulated among the country's authors. Early in the afternoon this collection of signatures was mentioned on the West Berlin radio. Now she knew that all was lost. Bodakov would not get his citizenship back. Whoever was running around with these lists had struck him a mortal blow.

Now the journalists began to pour in. They came; they parked their ostentatious cars with the ostentatious blue-and-white Press stickers directly in front of her garden gate or, no less ostentatiously, two houses away. They stumbled over the piles of dead leaves and swept-up acorns by the garden fence. They took turns rattling the doorknob. At times there were four of them in the house. One of them, a plump man with black hair, the correspondent for a very influential paper, was positively trembling—it was impossible to tell whether out of fear or curiosity. With his false teeth clicking in a way that made it difficult for him to impart particularly important news, he kept assuring Natasha Roth how much he admired her courage. It was quite clear that he believed what he was saying and it was equally clear that he would believe the opposite the moment opportunity occurred. She heard herself replying; she heard herself talking; she kept saying the same thing, but by the fourth or fifth repetition she was speaking faster and faster, a sign of exhaustion drowned in too much black coffee.

Finally, when they had all left and the house stank of the cold smoke of their cigarettes, Ferenc Butterman came. He said he had already provided his fifteen Swiss, French, British and Canadian papers with reports of the affair, some of them left-wing liberal, others right-wing liberal; it was a lousy job but a gay life. He had brought a copy of *L'Humanité* with him, in which the letter of protest appeared on the front page with the names of all the signatories.

Late in the evening the phone rang. It was Grandmother Sinaida calling from Tel Aviv. Strangely, there wasn't much interference on the line. Sinaida wanted to know how things stood with Natasha, whether there was much to worry about, if she, Sinaida, hadn't better take a plane tomorrow, or at the latest the day after, from Lod to Berlin Tegel; she would so much like to see Natasha and the children. No, said Natasha Roth, Grandmother Sinaida should please not make the trip, she should please think of her health; everyone here at home was fine.

NEXT MORNING the daily papers were full of counter-declarations. People who had to do with the arts, as well as people who had nothing to do with the arts, declared their approval of their government's decision to deprive Bodakov of his citizenship. There were articles relating to Bodakov's accusation that the state was guilty of organized crimes against humanity. The authors made known their anger. Over and over again certain writers were attacked for betraying themselves to the class enemy. Then there was a piece by one of the six signatories of the letter of protest, the playwright. He wrote that he had not known the letter with which he had associated himself would be handed over to an imperialist news agency, and for this reason he was instantly withdrawing his signature with an expression of the most profound embarrassment.

His mother, Stefan saw, held the newspaper in her hands for a long time. She stared at the print and was perhaps reading the piece by the playwright several times over. Meanwhile they were all sitting at breakfast, and Stefan's father—possibly to distract his wife—repeated in a low voice a remark she had once made: "Writers are neurotic, vain, uneducated and uncomradely. Only tenors are as bad." His mother screamed that a kick in the teeth like that was all she needed. So an ugly scene developed between his parents. They yelled at each other and swore. The things they said expressed such a childish hatred it was frightening. Stefan looked at Billa. He could see that she obviously felt the same. Finally he took her by the hand, said something to comfort her and led her upstairs. His parents' quarrel was still perfectly audible, but no longer so close.

Stefan, like his sister, had now been out of school for three days. An unnatural time, stolen holidays, full of excitement and some anxiety. And yet there was a subtle enjoyment in these days too, since he was experiencing things he had never experienced before. He had been ejected from the nice warm symmetry of his day-to-day existence. No matter how much he might tremble in every limb, this trembling was sweet. Was he now becoming arrogant? He observed his sister, who, when she could think of nothing better to do, played with the dog and seemed in her dull way completely satisfied with this enforced apathy. When he went out into the street, he saw that the builders' trailer was still standing opposite their garden gate. The news broadcasts from Adlershof television station were full of long statements read by people who approved of Bodakov's deprivation of citizenship.

Next morning—it was Sunday—his mother took the dog out into the street. Stefan heard her call his name, and there was something in her voice, a kind of treble note, that disturbed him, making him run out immediately. He raced across the garden as fast as his physical weakness would allow. He found his mother by the garden gate. She was leaning against the fence staring at the path, whose pale-grey stone slabs bore a message scrawled with school chalk. Stefan read the words *Rot(h)e Judensau*, "Red Jew Sow," a play on her name.

He took his mother back into the house. His father fetched her a tranquillizer. After a few minutes she had recovered sufficiently to go to the telephone herself and call the local section of the People's Police. She said to Stefan afterwards that there were crazy people everywhere; times of trouble brought them out into the light. She forbade Stefan to tell anyone anywhere about the scrawl, saying she didn't want it to get into the papers. The People's Policeman arrived on a red motorcycle. He looked at the chalk writing. His face went as red with embarrassment as the nitrocellulose lacquer on his motorcycle. He wrote out a report. Then he asked for a wet rag and carefully wiped away the writing. Stefan

helped him. That day the newspapers contained more than
three pages of support for Bodakov's deprivation of citizenship.

Ferenc Butterman came. He came unexpectedly, as he
usually did. Stefan's mother left the room. Her eyes were red
and she apologized. Stefan had been worried by her appearance. He wondered if there was something in particular
he ought to do for her, but he couldn't think of anything. He
tried to read. He sat behind the closed door of the adjoining
room, while his father talked to Ferenc Butterman. He heard
Butterman say: "Are things that bad for her?" His father
answered almost contemptuously: "She thought she was Joan
of Arc; now she knows she behaved more like Don Quixote."
"Good," said Ferenc Butterman, "I much prefer Don
Quixote to all those bloody heroes." Stefan heard his father
laugh. "Do you still intend to get divorced?" asked Ferenc
Butterman. His father didn't answer. Stefan couldn't tell
whether his father shrugged his shoulders or shook his head,
or perhaps didn't respond at all. "Go away," said Butterman.
"Go to France. I know you won't starve. So do you. You'll
live better there than here. In six months you'll have a summer cottage in the Vosges." He heard his father say: "She
won't want that." "That's not true," said Butterman. "She is
attached to this country," said his father. "Why should she
be?" asked Butterman. "It's her home," said his father. "Or
at least, that's how she sees it. She has spent thirty years of
her life here. That means more than a summer cottage in the
Vosges." "I don't understand that," said Butterman. "No one
could understand that."

By the evening, Ferenc Butterman had left again. Stefan's
last impression of his mother that day was a swollen face with
red eyes. As though he might find an explanation there, he
went into his mother's study. He was not expecting anything in particular, but he found on her desk a piece of
paper with writing on it.

NOVEMBER

among the rulers of the country are some who were once
deprived of their citizenship. now they have decided to
take his citizenship away from the embarrassing poet
arnold b, by doing so they take away the dignity of the
land they rule.

other poets, among them ones who were once deprived
of their citizenship, raise a protest. by so doing they give
back some dignity to the land they live in.

the rulers force the poets to reverse their position. unable
to recognize what the poets have done for them as well,
they want the poets to share in the loss of dignity.

days in late autumn. people are burning leaves. the bare
trees of the land remember the poem of bertolt b, an
embarrassing poet, about silence.

His mother—he hadn't heard her coming—entered the room.
She saw him and took the sheet of paper out of his hand.
"That's nothing," she said, tearing up the paper and throwing the scraps into the wastepaper basket. "I'm no poet," she
said. "That was really nothing, forget it." She left the room.
Stefan left too. The poem had now been erased as completely
as the chalk writing that morning, at least outwardly.

30 SHE DROVE to the inner city of Berlin to visit the central
office of her professional association. Her presence in the
semi-darkness of the corridors, along which employees were

hurrying from one door to the next, caused dismay. At least, that was how it seemed to her. She entered the room of a secretary, took her dark-blue passport from her handbag and placed it on the desk at which the secretary was sitting. She said she still had a valid visa for France, but didn't think she would use it now. In view of the things that were being said publicly about her and four of her friends, she could no longer be sure that if she went to France she would be allowed back into her own country again. The secretary, an elderly man, was very upset by this pronouncement, which he said he could only take as a provocation. Naturally Bodakov's deprivation of citizenship was a unique occurrence. No one would think of equating Natasha Roth with Arnold Bodakov; Natasha Roth was intelligent enough to know that perfectly well. She countered with the same arguments she had used against the man from the ministry who had come to see her three days earlier. She added that it was very unlikely that any agreement could be reached between her and the secretary that afternoon. She walked out of the room, leaving her passport with the French visa on the secretary's desk.

Later when she thought back on this day, what she remembered best was an almost perfect understanding with herself. She went out of the building into the Friedrichstrasse, whose heterogeneous ugliness did her good. She confronted the noise and the blue fumes produced by the halting river of metal. She looked into the fat faces of the hurrying pedestrians. None of those who now passed her, jostling her with their shoulders, could know who she was. Even in the unlikely event that someone told them the name of this woman, short-sighted without her glasses, no one would stop in his tracks. No one would connect the name with anything. None of them cared a fig for the events linked with it. She saw herself sinking into this seething mass of general disinterest as if she were sinking into warm, welcoming quicksand. She would have liked to be no different from anyone else. She had always longed for everyday banality. She had wanted to be a particle of it, as indeed—looked at more closely—she had long since become. She looked at the smudged veins in the paving-stones. She was delighted by the chance pattern made by cigarette filters spat out and trodden flat. The dirty bubble of a discarded contraceptive was stuck to the edge of a patch of autumn-stiff grass. She saw people going through certain doors as into the waves of a whirlpool. The letters over the front of the fine black iron structure of Friedrichstrasse Station announced in blinking lights the dates for the fulfillment of a plan, dismal murder in the Middle East. It was an act of cruelty to herself to leave all this now and shut herself up inside her car. She drove down Friedrichstrasse to Unter den Linden, from there to the inhuman tower hotel in the lower Alexanderplatz. Then the major cross street via the Straussberger Platz and the Frankfurter Tor to Mahrzahn.

In his almost *nouveau riche* villa, which was merely his office—with a signed portrait of Groscurth, who had been murdered by the Fascists, above his head—her lawyer talked to her cautiously. Since events relating to her were now moving at such a pace. Since her immediate future could not at the moment be foreseen. Perhaps it would be better to reconsider the question of a divorce and any instructions she might want to give him, the lawyer, relating thereto. With a smile on his pink face, the lawyer advanced a surmise supported by years of professional experience: in times of great trouble something beyond saving could yet be saved. The common bond that had been completely buried could be worked clear again.

In the evening she visited Rebecca. She had telephoned her several times a day during the last few days. The flat with a

view of a backyard in the Auguststrasse, close to the old
No 4 Post Office which, Rebecca had discovered, still main-
tained its links by pneumatic post with every district of Berlin, including the West, had witnessed agitated visits similar
to those at Natasha Roth's house. Perhaps they had been even
more hectic and in any case more anguished for Rebecca,
since she lived alone and was more affected. Over the telephone, Natasha Roth had gained the impression that this had
aroused Rebecca from her apathy and left her no time to
relapse. At the moment, she showed an unnatural rush of
blood to the face. The authors of the letter of protest were
meeting again at the scene of their original gathering, which,
if the uproar of the last few days was to be believed, had
meanwhile become part of contemporary history, even outside the country's borders. By looks, grins and exclamations
they conjured up their common memories and confirmed
their unexpected success. Five instead of six, after the playwright had inexplicably broken with them (no one mentioned his name). Each one of them had received an emis-
sary from the state. All of them had been treated with
politeness.

Rebecca had bought two litre bottles of liquor at the
foreign-currency store, and put them on the table. Now, too,
the younger novelist was preoccupied with the trembling of
his hands. One wondered why. The famous poet was smoking a Virginia cigar. He pulled out the straw, broke it in
pieces and built airy constructions with them. In a voice that
creaked he told stories of his life as an emigré in Scandinavia.
His eyes were filled with the same sort of triumph as his
grandfather must have felt after legally winning three creaking nut trees. Bodakov's name was mentioned only five times
in all. Everyone in the room spoke very loud. As she listened,
Natasha Roth suspected that the emotions roused by this
gathering were somewhat inappropriate and artificial.

31 AT PRECISELY this time the exhibition of Marc Chagall's graphic works was opening in the Old Museum close to the Berlin Cathedral. Stefan's father had lent the colour lithograph that was in the family's possession; in fact a greatly enlarged version of it had been used as a poster. The selection and hanging of the prints in the Old Museum were the responsibility of friends of Stefan's father; consequently he felt obliged to be present at the opening. Stefan's mother felt unable to do so. No interest could be expected from Billa. So in the end only Stefan accompanied his father in the car. There would be no risk in the trip for him, since he was still not attending school.

This November afternoon was grey like all November days before it. On the wide steps leading to the museum entrance a frosty wind was blowing, picking up dirt from the many nearby building sites and slapping it against a row of children's drawings pinned up side by side on a long wooden fence. Inside, the rooms of the museum were crowded. Stefan's father said this was the first major exhibition of truly modern art in the city for a long time. The public had not yet had an opportunity to get used to works like this, so it would be interesting to see how they reacted. Then his father parted from him to speak to his friends who had organized the exhibition. So Stefan was left alone. He walked slowly, drifting through the rooms, from one exhibit to the next. He would have liked to ask his father for explanations. He tried to make a mental note of his questions. Later he would have forgotten them all. He saw the bouquets of flowers, the circus scenes, the human profiles, the animals, the houses, the religious ceremonies. The pictures were all similar, yet all distinct. He looked into the faces of

the visitors. Soon it became much more important for him
to observe these faces than to look at the pictures. He listened as the people tried to figure out the works with murmured questions and answers. Their eyes were hungry, their
movements gentle. All these people wanted was to look at
pictures and then go away with their impressions. He envied
them. He looked again at the lithograph which he knew so
well because it belonged to his parents. In the case of all the
other prints he was able to read, below the title and the date,
the name of the owner. In the case of their print it said
merely: "Lent by a private owner." As he thought over this
difference and sought reasons for it, be became increasingly
disquieted. He could only calm this disquiet by walking on.
Finally, he was most struck by the small etchings printed by
the young Chagall on yellow paper, depicting life in the poor
Jewish villages and ghettoes of old Russia. Tiny human
beings in front of narrow cottages. Tiny trees and animals
and wells. The world was pinched; human beings were like
dust; life was little more than a piece of yellowish paper.
Stefan would have liked to see more of these etchings.

Another, very large lithograph showed a couple in a close
embrace floating apparently quite naturally over roofs belonging either to a village or to an old town. All the areas of
colour ran into one another. The outlines were blurred. After
looking at it for a long time, Stefan suddenly had the impression that the man in the picture bore an inescapable resemblance to Ferenc Butterman, while the young woman
looked like his mother, Natasha Roth. This was a terrible discovery for him. He immediately looked away. He tried to
distract his attention by peering into the room, listening to
the murmur of the bystanders and finally staring at the toe-
caps of his own shoes, whose dark-brown leather was covered with white dust. Only hesitantly, with a great effort,
was he able to turn his eyes back to the lithograph, since it

wasn't right to be horrified by a mere piece of paper hanging on a wall. He now saw—and this enabled him to breathe more easily—that the faces in the picture bore little resemblance to the people who had come to mind. In fact, he now saw, there was no resemblance whatever. But he had been able to persuade himself there was, and what horrified him now was the fact that he had been ready to see such a likeness. Was he secretly afraid that what he had momentarily seen in this picture was, or could become, reality? Would he have this fear often? A dull feeling crept into his forehead, and a sharper, sourish taste shot into his mouth. Finally, he met his father at the agreed spot, in the big domed entrance hall right by the door. Actually Rudolf Roth had wanted to introduce his son to the organizers of the exhibition but, for reasons which Stefan did not discover, these friends were suddenly unable to be there and had to postpone the meeting till another day. Stefan left the museum with his father. Outside the strong wind was blowing, whirling up frosty dust. The dome stood out black against a shamelessly bright patch in the otherwise dark-grey sky. They walked to the car, which was standing in Clara-Zetkin Street. As they drove home, Stefan asked his father:

"Did you know that our picture didn't have our name under it?"

"No."

"Why did they do that?"

"They obviously don't think the owner's name is important."

"They think it's important in other cases."

His father said nothing. Stefan tried to see whether his father's face showed any reaction he could interpret, but it was too dark in the car. They drove on and Stefan asked:

"Are you scared?"

"Why should I be?"

"Because of Mother."

" 'Scared' isn't the right word. I'm afraid things won't be easy for her during the next few weeks."

"In what way?"

"I don't know."

"Have you no idea?"

"No."

"Would you have done the same in Mother's place?"

"No," said his father. "It wasn't sensible. But no one asked me."

Stefan asked: "Do you think things are going to be bad?"

"Your mother," said his father, "is a well-known person. I'm not directly involved myself. Besides, I've had practice in surviving."

He uttered this last sentence almost gaily. Perhaps he was referring to his own childhood as the son of the Jewish coal merchant Roth from the Prenzlauer Berg. It struck Stefan that his father spoke only about himself and his wife, not about the children.

At home they found Natasha Roth in a state of great agitation. She showed them a telegram that had been dispatched that same day, announcing that Grandmother Sinaida had died of a heart attack during the night. Grandmother Sinaida was seventy-eight, a woman who had had a colourful life, who at the end was rather lonely. "My poor love," said Rudolf Roth, "I wish I could say something to you in Hebrew, but I don't know a single word." He stroked Natasha Roth's hair. They were all worried about one another and hardly spoke. Only much later in the evening did Natasha Roth mention, as though casually, that other news had also arrived that afternoon. In a Thuringian university town several students had tried to demonstrate publicly against Bodakov's deprivation of citizenship, also referring to the writers' letter of protest. Four of the students had been arrested.

32 NEXT DAY, Billa was sent back to school, but not Stefan. Once more the newspapers were full of articles approving the withdrawal of citizenship from a poet named Arnold Bodakov. Opposite her garden gate, Natasha Roth saw, the building workers' trailer was still in place. She read the articles. They seemed to her empty. The sinister thing was the constant repetition of the same text, one line after the other, one column next to the other. Billa came home from school. She had nothing to tell; no one had talked to her about her mother; no one had asked her about a poet who had been deprived of citizenship. When the name Bodakov was mentioned once more at home, she screwed up her face and shouted that she didn't want ever to hear that name again, she was sick and tired of it. In the afternoon a black car with a red-and-white diplomatic sign on it stopped outside the garden gate. The chief of a foreign diplomatic mission entered the house, bringing with him a bouquet of roses as well as a big picture book on the life of the French poet Arthur Rimbaud, since it was generally known that the writer Natasha Roth was currently working on Rimbaud. They talked as though nothing had happened. The name Bodakov wasn't mentioned. The diplomat frequently laughed as he spoke, displaying several gold teeth. His German had a strong French accent and also contained many French words. He frequently said that he found certain things *curieuse*.

That evening, Natasha Roth and her husband had been invited to dinner with another diplomat. They drove into a foggy evening. Her husband said he felt constricted in his dark suit and his underclothes were making his skin burn. She immediately pictured his body with red, inflamed patches spreading over it and pustules full of blood and discharge. As she talked with him and thought about him, at one moment she felt merciless, at the next filled with a beseeching sorrow. She remembered how yesterday he had stroked her hair at the news of Grandmother Sinaida's death in Tel Aviv. He would have liked to say something to her in Hebrew. Hebrew, Hebrew, she mocked inwardly, and was immediately moved again by the memory of the warm dryness of the palm of his hand. She longed for nothing more desperately than a repetition. She thought of what the lawyer had said. She felt deeply humiliated, and she felt as helpless as an old woman. But these were all feelings from a second, lower level of her life, which belonged to her like someone else's life. She felt—and this was her real life—as though she were high on something. Lights thrust out beams like thin fingers and clutched at her hair and throat through the car windows. She turned on the car radio. Whining pop songs, news, the familiar political slogans, Bodakov. It seemed the name would never again be removed from the electronic waves. Sooner or later they were bound to run across it and wash it up to the surface.

The house, a forty-year-old villa, was in Karlshorst. They were received at the door by a butler. There were ten people besides themselves. Admiringly she watched the two black-clad lackeys' contortions as they held out the heavy serving dishes to the guests. She had the impression that their pelvises and spinal columns were made of plastic and could be turned and twisted in any direction. She was sitting next to an Austrian embassy counsellor and opposite a Polish woman journalist, next to whom was her husband. The journalist asserted in her harsh German that the writers' protest concerning Bodakov was an entirely Polish matter. How so? Very simple. It was modelled on the actions of the Polish authors who had been doing this kind of thing for twenty years; Bodakov was a Polish name; Bodakov came from the Polish town of Myslowicz; Natasha Roth was a blood relation of the famous Joseph Roth, who was born in Brody, in the old kingdom of Galicia and Lemberg, that's to say Poland. This was how the conversation went. On the table stood candelabra with lighted candles. Natasha Roth thought of birthdays, Christmas, churches, funerals; she had to hide a yawn. Across the table, half hidden by the flame of a candle, she saw her husband's face distorted by the hot air above the flame, so that it looked eroded. He was talking a lot and laughing a lot. At the end of the meal a man stood up, champagne glass in hand, and expressed his thanks, including his thanks for "this charming gathering." The Austrian embassy counsellor knew that Natasha Roth had lived in Vienna as a child. Could she remember other parts of Austria besides Vienna? The counsellor had been born in Styria. What Natasha Roth remembered best was a summer holiday near Grundlsee. The counsellor talked about Hallstatt. Had Natasha Roth no visual recollection of the town? The mountain slope on which the houses of Hallstatt stood was very steep. The houses grew on terraces. The streets were narrow, colourful; the cemetery was a narrow patch of earth; the dead who were buried in it had to be dug up after three years to make way for the new dead. By then the flesh was all rotted away; the skulls were placed in a charnel-house, where they could be seen by anyone, with a nameplate over the bony forehead identifying the former owner, who, even as a naked skull, was still recognizable as having once been either well-to-do or poor. Natasha Roth was seized by a childish desire to have the bodies of those present interred in the Hallstatt cemetery, so that three years later she could take their skulls, now divested of flesh, in her warm hands and place them in the charnel-house. She pictured the skull of the beautiful Polish woman. She pictured her husband's skull, which would still be recognizable even without the usual label because of the shape of the temples and cheekbones and certain peculiarities of the teeth. She would put her husband's skull next to her stepmother Sinaida's, which had had a particularly prominent nasal bone. The label attached to it would bear the Star of David, symbol of the State of Israel. The Austrians' obsession with death was not really an inheritance from the Christian baroque; it had reigned in the country since Celtic times. The severed heads of dead enemies were nailed to the gables of Celtic houses to rot and lose their flesh. Death lurked in veins of salt, in rock fissures, in underwater caves in the Alpine lakes. She, Natasha Roth, knew all this because she had been initiated into it. She belonged in secret to the sect of the Druids and Albs. Her name was only a pseudonym, her activities only a blind. Those present, if only they had been sufficiently observant, would have noticed it at once. Of course, she had deceived them all. So much the worse for them if she no longer knew who she was and instead was concentrating entirely on their trivial concerns.

THE NEXT DAY, a Tuesday, Billa had to be taken to a **33** special school competition in the district capital. Stefan had an appointment for an examination at the hospital. He was to undergo a series of tests which, henceforth, would have to be carried out at regular intervals. They all got up very early. Natasha Roth was to take her husband to the museum. Stefan, who at this time of the day had nothing else to do, would go with his parents. It was still dark when Natasha Roth started the car. On this trip Stefan sat in the back seat. Like his father, like his mother, he saw that today the guards on the turnpike were more heavily armed than usual and that the number of police at the check-point was about twice the normal. Every single car, most of them belonging to people on their way to work, was stopped. The police carefully checked out the occupants. To do so, they had to bend down slightly. The movement caused their machine-pistols to stick out to one side. After this the cars were waved on. Only their car, Stefan noticed, and his father and mother must have noticed it too, was waved on without being stopped first. Was that odd? Their car—a foreign make, painted mailbox-yellow—was striking, and moreover well known at this check-point. Similar close checks, carried out with the same thoroughness, had taken place before. Generally the cause had been a hunt for an escaped prisoner or a military deserter. His father got out of the car at the Köpenicker Schloss traffic island. He nodded to them briefly and made his way to the museum entrance. Stefan had changed places and was now sitting beside his mother. When they approached the turnpike at the city boundary and were waved across by the guard, the check was still in progress with the same thoroughness as before. Stefan hadn't expected anything else. The city boundary was always checked, most days not too thoroughly, sometimes with increased vigilance. Was today's intensification in any way connected with them? It never was in the past; why should it be so now? At home Billa had already put on her coat. She was on edge because of the competition in which she had to take part. Billa got into the car. During the drive, Stefan saw various military vehicles, mostly jeeps, and once a tank that was parked close to the crossroads. The crew must have been inside, or they had left the tank to carry out some special mission. Stefan saw only dead military-grey metal, no people. Only when he turned his head did he see, in the section of the street lit by arc lamps, two motorcycles that were following their car. On each motorcycle sat two men in uniform with fire-arms. They followed them at an unvarying distance until about halfway to the district capital. Suddenly they had vanished, without Stefan seeing where they went. Had they been following them? Wasn't it perhaps pure coincidence that they had been travelling behind them at the same speed and hence at an unvarying distance? Natasha said goodbye to Billa. Sibylle Roth, high-school pupil, particularly gifted in mathematics, would return home after the competition by public transport, that is to say by omnibus, suburban railway and streetcar. Natasha Roth, with Stefan now sitting beside her again, drove out of the district capital in the direction of Berlin, towards a November dawn that was emerging only slowly from the darkness. Trees on either side of the road, birches and pines, the birches with whitely shimmering trunks. Halfway along the road, two motorcycles again appeared behind them. Stefan saw them through the rear window. And now again the motorcycles were carrying armed men in uniform. His mother must have seen the motorcycles in the rear-view mirror, but she made no comment. In a large village, shortly before their own district, the motorcycles turned off and headed for the gates of a local barracks. Along the whole of the road home from here guards stood in couples at regular intervals. One of the men was always holding a walkie-talkie with the aerial extended. He spoke into the instrument and turned his upper body to watch Natasha Roth's car pass. Stefan could see this clearly. It had grown so light by now that anything happening at the roadside could be clearly seen. Stefan couldn't tell whether his mother had noticed the guards and their movements.

On the other side of the municipal boundary, the entrances to the hunting trails into the forest were occupied by two-man patrols without walkie-talkies. A personnel carrier belonging to the armed police was parked at the crossroads near their house. Stefan's mother parked her car by the side of the street and went into the house with Stefan, who remained silent and was limping more than usual that morning. As Stefan had expected, she went at once to the telephone. Stefan, who was standing close beside her, could clearly hear the regular tone indicating that the line was free. She dialled the automatic time check, and like his mother Stefan heard the monotonous female voice saying seven fifty-three, seven fifty-three. His mother now put the dog on the lead and went out into the street with it, accompanied by Stefan. They walked as far as the crossroads, where the personnel carrier was still waiting. An officer, leaning with legs apart against the front mudguard, threw a cigarette butt on the ground, carefully stamped it out, opened the door to the driver's cabin and climbed in. Soon afterwards the vehicle, which probably held about twenty policemen, left the crossroads and drove off towards the municipal boundary. Natasha Roth, Stefan noticed, shook her head slightly. There was an expression of relief in her face; she looked almost amused. She said in a voice so low Stefan could barely catch the words that people like her with too imagination were inclined to become hysterical. They went back into the house. A little later his mother took Stefan by car to the nearest station of the Berlin city railway. The manning of the checkpoint at the municipal boundary remained unchanged.

Stefan went to the hospital. His morning consisted of waiting and examinations. He found himself sitting in front of the woman doctor who resembled Grandmother Sinaida from Tel Aviv. Grandmother Sinaida was now dead. She had died in the shadow of lemon trees, close to harbour quays. Her death had been very lonely and sad. The doctor examined him at great length and very thoroughly. She tapped his joints with a little shiny hammer to test the speed and strength of his reflexes. She was unusually amiable this time. More than once she asked how Natasha Roth was, as though it were not Stefan who was ill but Natasha Roth. Following these examinations an encephalogram was to be taken. Stefan had to wait. He sat out in the corridor next to

a young girl his own age, the left side of whose face was
slack, unmoving, paralysed from the removal of a tumour
a long time ago, she told Stefan. She was intelligent, she
wanted to take the school-leaving examination, but because
of the operation, which was noted in her school records, because of the disfigurement caused by the facial paralysis, she
had been assessed by the education authority as too handicapped to merit intensive educational assistance. Education
was expensive and the result in her case too uncertain. This
had all been explained to her. The girl was crying. Tears
were running from her disfigured eye as from the normal
one. From the side, from her unparalysed side, she was
pretty. The girl was called in before Stefan. Now he sat
alone in the corridor. Once a trolley covered with a white
sheet was pushed out of the operating theatre. Beneath the
sheet the outlines of a human body could be seen. Stefan
heard the ceaseless crying from behind the carefully closed
doors of the children's ward, where he had spent several
weeks. He shook himself at the memory. To force his mind
in a different direction, he thought about his mother, about
the events of the morning. He suddenly had a vivid picture
of his mother: she was all alone in the house, cracks kept appearing in the walls, the roof beams were rotting, plaster was
falling from the outer walls and thudding down on the earth
of the garden, his mother was wandering around, she went to
the telephone, picked up the receiver, but instead of the expected dialling tone there was only silence this time, perhaps
interrupted by the crackling sound, a dull electronic hum
that didn't change even when she pressed the hook down
several times, so she replaced the receiver. When she looked
out of the window she saw that the police personnel carrier
had returned and that two uniformed men were walking
slowly towards the front door to arrest her and take her
away. Where to? The house was now surrounded by security
forces. How could his mother let the family know what had

happened? How could they find out what had happened to her? These images grew more and more vivid, probable, distinct, inescapable, until he began to sweat. He felt the moisture, sharp and sensual, trickling from his armpits. He underwent two further tests. He was given two sealed envelopes from the hospital to the school board, containing reports on the state of his health.

Now he was able to leave the hospital. The trip back seemed to his conscious awareness unbearably long. As he reached his district in the streetcar, once again he saw a pair of uniformed men guarding each of the exits from the hunting trails. The checks at the turnpike were still being carried out with the same thoroughness as in the morning. The short walk home from the streetcar stop exhausted him. In the end he became numb and indifferent. He was limping badly. He saw no soldiers. Since it was all over, every mission completed, there was no further need for them to be there.

Ferenc Butterman's car was parked in the garden. He found Ferenc Butterman in the house, smoking. Natasha Roth was sitting facing him. They were both drinking black coffee. Was everything all right? Everything was all right. He handed over the two envelopes. His mother put them aside. Ferenc Butterman slapped him paternally on the back. Soon afterwards Billa came home. She answered questions reluctantly. Everything was all right.

34 NEXT DAY the newspapers contained no further declarations concerning Bodakov's loss of citizenship. Bodakov's name wasn't mentioned anywhere. Natasha Roth telephoned Rebecca, who knew nothing about it, but also showed no

surprise. Her answers gave an impression of paralysis. Perhaps she was once again under the influence of tranquillizers. The famous poet lived in the house with three nut trees inherited from his grandfather, which had no telephone. Natasha called both the two novelists, but neither picked up the receiver, although she phoned them several times in the course of the morning. She heard Stefan moving about the house. Irregular footsteps. She was still keeping him away from school. Perhaps this decision was unreasonable, but in her eyes Stefan had been made particularly vulnerable because of his handicap. She didn't want to risk his suffering any additional injury. But would she be able to prevent that forever? Was the postponement of certain actions a reliable protection? She switched on the radio. During every talk programme the loudspeaker emitted countless names. The frequent repetition of certain names was to be noted, along with gradual or sudden changes in that frequency. The name Arnold Bodakov was patently mentioned less often. The name Natasha Roth was scarcely mentioned at all. It occurred to her that, for the sake of something to do, she could jot down the numerical frequency, make a note of the intervals at which names were repeated, subdivided into the frequency with which the living and the dead, politicians, economists and actors, dead politicians, living economists, dead actors, living politicians cropped up. The trailer for building workers was still standing opposite her garden gate. She had never seen any sign of life in it, except once, one afternoon, when vague outlines of arms had been visible through the small, dark-grey windows, moving limbs busy picking up playing cards or reaching for a tin coffee mug.

Then—for the first time since they had known each other—Erica Roth arrived. She parked her car opposite the builders' trailer and walked slowly up the garden path, looking observantly at bushes, garden trees, the front of the house. Natasha Roth watched her through her study window. She ran out. At least it made a change, and why ever hadn't she rung Erica long ago? She embraced her and her skin felt as cold and smooth as a lizard's.

"I wanted to come before," said Erica. "I could give you all sorts of excuses. Overwork—it's true and yet it isn't. I wasn't sure how I should find you."

"You can see."

"Yes."

When they were sitting indoors, Natasha Roth asked: "Were you surprised that I signed that letter?"

"It would have surprised me if you hadn't signed it. Nevertheless, I'm sorry you did."

"Why?"

"You're going to be obstinate. I can see that already."

"Would you have acted differently in my place?"

"I can't put myself in your place."

"You think what I did was wrong?"

"I think it's wrong for this letter to exist."

"There's a reason for it."

"There's a reason for everything. For stupidity, cleverness, frivolity, obscenity and crime. Everything exists as a consequence of something else. Reasons don't explain anything."

"Will you understand me if I tell you that our cause is at stake here?"

"Whose cause? The poets'? Who are you? Do you have your own special standards? Who do you think you are?"

"Listen," said Natasha Roth. "Our state has done something that was wrong. It happened in the domain to which I belong, to a person whom I know. If I had said nothing, it would have been as though I approved of it."

"Do you feel better now?"

"If I had done nothing, I should be feeling worse."

"All right. Now you've acted out your scene. A lot of noise and a lot of applause. People have long since started thinking of other things. Perhaps you wanted to put something right. Nothing has been put right. The ruins are all round us; we're in the middle of them. Was it worthwhile?"

"Yes."

"You'll have to explain why."

"There are things that are done simply so that they will have been done. For no other reason. There is something like a collective moral memory. I believe that I have to contribute to it and that's what I'm here for."

"That sounds very exaggerated to me," said Erica Roth. "The collective moral memory has gaps too. Do I have to give you examples?"

"Certain actions are performed," said Natasha Roth, "even if they are absurd. In any case, I demand the right to perform them."

"A right for dreamers," said Erica Roth.

"That's what we are."

"Then you shouldn't complain if you're treated like dreamers. That's to say, as unable to cope with reality. When things get very bad a guardian has to be appointed."

"You're obviously part of that now."

"Me?" said Erica Roth. "I cure people of skin diseases, of the consequences of thoughtless love. I have a husband at home who is paralysed and spends his day in a wheelchair. I long for the children I can't have."

"Erica," said Natasha Roth, "you know my life story. You know what the word 'emigration' means to me. I've written a book about it which you said you would have liked to read. With my life story, I can't sit mute in my country when a poet, who till now has lived in this country, is suddenly forced to emigrate."

"You can't tell me that Bodakov has been forced to emigrate."

"What do you call it then?"

"He is living in the country in which his books are published. He has left the country where, to his mind, there is cruelty and, as he says, state-organized crime."

"He lived in this country. He never said that he wanted to leave it of his own free will. Must we prove his criticisms right by demonstrating them on him?"

"I believe," said Erica Roth, "that there is a frontier for loyalty. Words can wound too."

"You credit us with a lot of power."

"You have a lot of power."

"Good God," said Natasha Roth. "Were we really not strong enough to live with this hundred-page book?"

"They're a hundred pages of insults. I want a reaction to them," said Erica Roth. "That too is a matter of self-respect."

"React against a dull-witted poet from Myslowicz? Who is perhaps simply a fool? A whole state against one individual?"

"He isn't just one. He is multiplying. He has an echo. That's why he is successful. He can do what he does because things are as they are. We're not just anyone anywhere. We have our own history and geography."

"Yes," said Natasha Roth. "Move by move we stumble over our own clumsiness. I can't bear to be told any more that I must remember our political geography. It makes me retch. It's always simply an excuse for cowardice and stupidity."

"Sometimes," said Erica Roth. "But political geography is a fact."

"So you agree," Natasha Roth screamed, "that in the city in which we live a poet should be deprived of his citizenship? In the very same city in which forty years ago other poets were deprived of their citizenship?"

"Symbols are impressive, of course," said Erica Roth. "But they can be put to so many uses. We can't avoid doing things we have to do just because we're afraid of a comparison."

"So as far as you're concerned, this deprivation of citizenship was right?"

"Yes."

"It was wrong," said Natasha Roth. "It was wrong."

"Even if it was, it has been done."

"It should have been reversed."

"No state does a thing like that."

"Why not?"

"Because it looks like weakness. To rule means power that is evident and beyond doubt. Power combined with weakness is self-destructive. I don't want us to be weak."

"I want us to be more just, more circumspect, more adult. I want our country to be easier to live in. A friendly place."

"Who doesn't? And so do I," said Erica Roth. "But we can't achieve that by public pressure."

Natasha Roth said: "There's something I've been afraid of for a long time. I've never spoken about it to anyone. Perhaps I'm telling you now because you happen to be here. Perhaps I'm telling you because you're a doctor. I'm afraid I may suddenly find myself without a language. I live by my language, you know, I think in it, I write it, I live by it. You can't take your language with you anywhere you go. You go away and you have your language, but when you're among people who speak a different language you gradually lose your own. We imagine that people speak. In reality it's the country that speaks. Stones and streets and the soil and cast-off rubbish and fabrics and bridges and leaves. Our country speaks its own unmistakeable language. Beyond the frontier there is always another language. It may look outwardly exactly like our own, but it's quite different. I picture to myself what it would be like no longer to have my own language. Every word a misunderstanding. My tongue kills me. I picture to myself what someone like Bodakov must be now. I had to do something. I shouted out on my own behalf. I don't know if you understand me now."

"I understand now that there is a serious split between writers and the state. You behaved rashly, like children. I know that distrust, mistakes, stupidity, perhaps brutality have come into being. Processes like that have their own logic. I'd like to help you, Natasha."

"Why do two different opinions immediately have to be a split?"

"Because majorities on both sides of the frontier have so decided."

"Erica," said Natasha Roth, "monstrous things have been done in our name, you know that. I'm talking about the past. That wouldn't have happened if someone had spoken up, perhaps someone like us. Silence is no solution, Erica, and mistakes put into words are better than silence."

"Sometimes the only alternatives we have are to be harsh, unjust if you like, or to go under. Revolution has always been cruel, but counter-revolution is crueller still."

"For me," said Natasha Roth, "every injustice committed in the name of the Revolution puts the moral justice of the Revolution in question."

"Then you're putting the Revolution in question."

"No."

"The Paris Commune," said Erica Roth, "collapsed because they thought too much about goodness and not enough about guns. The revolution in Chile was wrecked by its own gentleness."

"Those are unfair comparisons," said Natasha Roth.

"Possibly. But there's something else. I don't want to be in a position where any turning back is difficult or impossible. I don't want to have the mediocrities out in front, the shallow yes-men. I want our books to remain uncomfortable. I don't want your books, Natasha, to be questioned because of an open letter. I want your books to remain better than other people's books, because they are. But the public criteria for these things are arbitrary. They can be established by decree, and in the end people believe the decree."

"What do you expect then?" said Natasha Roth. "A retraction?"

"I'd never get that from you. Suppose you said the letter was perhaps written without due thought?"

"It was written with due thought."

"You would do it all over again?"

"Yes."

"You're obstinate, Natasha. You're risking a lot for vanity."

"It's not vanity. It's simply needing not to have to bow my head. To be able to hold it high. I would pay any price for that."

"Writers," said Erica Roth, "are not judged by the public according to their neck muscles, but according to their success."

"I'm not concerned with the judgement of the public."

"I can't force you," said Erica. "What's in your mind?"

"Who sent you?"

"No one."

They went on talking for a long time. Natasha Roth loved this young woman, who was so ill, whose logic was so icy. She embraced Erica Roth as they said goodbye, and the doctor drove off in her car, waving with her left hand through the half-open window. It was a misty, rainy, cold December day. Natasha Roth went back indoors. She thought: I love revolution because it is cruel, but my defect is that I refuse to take part in the cruelty, in spite of its beauty, because I'm a coward. Of course, these were extravagant thoughts, to be explained by the turmoil of recent days, which gave rise to particularly bizarre images. She switched the radio on again. She heard a declaration by a writer she knew, the young novelist who had helped to draft the letter of protest. The novelist stated that his name was currently being used by the class enemy for propaganda purposes and he must repudiate this. The word "retraction" was never uttered. The young novelist's statement would be regarded as a retraction. Natasha Roth opened a bottle of wine and began to get drunk. Opposite her garden gate the builders' trailer was still in place. She knew she would gradually get used to the trailer. It would become part of the image of the street, like the trunks of the oak trees, like the rust on the wire netting of the fence.

35 STEFAN WENT BACK to school. He had been away for ten days. He handed over his mother's letter of explanation. His form teacher, an absent-minded woman, took the letter, carefully felt the envelope, nodded absent-mindedly without saying anything and laid it aside as though it had suddenly become unimportant or the contents were well known to her. His classmates behaved towards him exactly as in the past. Yet he remained suspicious. Their behaviour seemed to him not so much genuinely natural as the result of a conscious effort to appear natural. He felt that he was looking into empty faces that had hastily emptied themselves on his account. Were they looking at him suspiciously? When he quickly turned his head he could never catch sight of a look directed at him. Had they foreseen the turn of his head, and turned their own eyes away in time? He didn't know. He could believe it or not believe it. Thinking about it was a strain. Once again he was limping noticeably. He was no longer like everyone else. But he had to admit to himself that

he never had been or could never have remained so. During a lesson devoted to current political events and theories, they spoke of the disenfranchisement of a writer named Bodakov. The class was invited to ask questions. Questions were asked. The teacher replied, as did pupils whose reliability in such replies had long since been tested. No objections were raised to the disenfranchisement; no undercurrent of doubt could be detected; the phrase "fouling one's own nest" cropped up several times. No mention was made of any part played by writers living in the country. Stefan was not invited to ask a question or give an answer.

It was December. Signs and comments in the world around pointed constantly towards Christmas. Through Sibylle's clumsiness a pane in the door between the two living rooms in the Roth's house had been broken. The glazier had been notified immediately. He seemed to have mislaid the order. In any case, he didn't come and no one remembered to ask him again. Only occasionally, for instance when they were all together at dinner, did they remind each other to see about this repair. No one did anything about it. These were just words, uttered so that some words were there to be heard. They could have been different words. The broken glass in the door between the two living-rooms didn't seem to bother anyone seriously. It seemed to Stefan as though a strange paralysis was gradually taking possession of everyone in the house. He himself could have asked his parents if they had finally made up their minds to separate or whether the decision had been postponed again. He couldn't think of the right words. In the end he no longer wanted to know. He much preferred talking with Thomas. At first it seemed to him incomprehensible that Thomas didn't want to know what was going on in the house of Natasha Roth. Thomas hadn't come to see him during the ten days of his absence. Thomas hadn't telephoned him once. Now he took Stefan home to his parents again, to the smell of fresh bread, to simple meals, to sitting on wooden kitchen chairs, to the two ten-watt loud-speakers with the songs of Frank Zappa and Donovan. Thomas remained the ruler over a colourful, weightless world of plastic. It was amazing how many things they could talk about, without ever talking about anything real. The name Bodakov never cropped up in the conversations between Thomas and Stefan, and Stefan tried more and more frequently to imagine how he would live if he were not he, were not handicapped, not privileged, not singled out, not his mother's son, not the bearer of this name, not the owner of this face and this body.

One afternoon there was a knock at the front door. Stefan was alone. He opened the door. Outside stood an elderly man with a red face whom Stefan didn't know. He walked into the house without a greeting, as though completely familiar with the environment. He nodded and narrowed his eyes, as though he were a long-awaited guest. He went into the living-room. He sat down in an armchair, lit a cigarette and then told Stefan he wanted to talk to Natasha Roth. Stefan replied that his mother was not at home. The man declared that he would wait until she came back. Stefan said his mother wouldn't be back until late and he himself had to leave the house in a few minutes. The man didn't answer. He merely giggled. The cigarette between his fingers, he ran his hand several times over his white hair. Stefan was uncertain how to act. Finally he said the visitor must leave the house now. He was welcome to come back another day. The old man seemed unwilling to understand. He stood up with a sigh and walked greedy-eyed along the rows of book spines. He took out individual books, opened them, leafed through them, read a few lines, then put them carelessly aside. Stefan repeated his demand. The old man looked up and asked irritably whether that meant he was being thrown out of the house. Without waiting for an answer, he stamped his foot, gesticulated with both arms and began to swear. He had wanted to talk to Natasha Roth. He had wanted to discuss things with her. He felt insulted by her actions. He wouldn't stand for opposition to the state for which he had fought all his life. He was against pampering artists who repaid their privileges with ingratitude. The old man's voice grew louder and more vehement. He went to the front door and out into the garden. There, perhaps under the influence of the cold air, the old man yelled: "Let her go where the other one is already. Writers are rats." Then he left.

Four days later, Stefan went with his mother to a town near Berlin. A newly erected public library had arranged for Natasha Roth to give a reading. His mother had agreed to do so several weeks before. Late one afternoon they drove there together, along roads lined with black fruit trees that looked as though they had been turned to charcoal. They drove through villages whose houses looked abandoned. They lost their way because they were looking for a petrol station and, confused by signposts sprouting aslant from the ground, had evidently taken a wrong turning. They reached the library only a few minutes before the reading was due to begin. They saw a white building in front of which debris still lay in heaps round the edges of an unfinished courtyard. The librarian received Natasha Roth in the entrance. There were restless movements and nervous faces. Chairs had been set out in a fairly large room on the first floor. Most of them were occupied. Stefan saw the faces of young people. He saw many uniforms. More listeners arrived, but some chairs remained empty the whole evening. Natasha Roth sat on a small dais at a table with a reading-lamp and a microphone. She read two sections from her book on the youth worker Lisbeth P, dealing with the attempt to free the child of an antisocial family from his attachments to his environment. Despite all efforts of individuals and social agencies, this attempt finally failed. The audience listened, gazing up at

Natasha Roth. This was the first time Stefan had attended a public reading by his mother. He had the impression that she read too fast, in a voice that was sometimes too monotonous. His mother seemed to him like a stranger throughout the evening. Outside the window a building machine could be heard, perhaps an excavator; the sound almost drowned his mother's voice and once she stopped and asked whether people could hear her. After the reading there was no applause. One or two people asked questions, which Natasha Roth answered. She seemed suddenly to be in a good mood; she spoke wittily and in well-constructed sentences. Stefan had the impression that people really wanted to ask quite different questions but for some incomprehensible reason couldn't find the right words. They really wanted to reproach Natasha Roth; their faces, their attitudes, were always quite different from the casual sentences they uttered. At one point he thought that the people in the room were simply waiting for a particular word of command ordering them to rise from their chairs. In a few seconds this word of command would be uttered and then they would gather in an ever-narrowing circle around their victim, his mother. Of course it didn't happen. At the very end, there was no applause either. Out in the street several young girls were waiting for Natasha Roth with books for her to sign. Ferenc Butterman was suddenly standing in the doorway. He had wanted to attend the reading, out of curiosity, and also to give her a surprise. But he had been turned away on the grounds that the room was already full to overflowing.

One evening a few days before Christmas, three young men came to the house. All three wore dark-green canvas jackets with hoods, and two of them had steel-rimmed spectacles. They had white faces. They were very embarrassed. They put down books written by Natasha Roth and asked her to sign them, but this was only an excuse. They had come to tell Natasha Roth that her resistance to Bodakov's deprivation of citizenship was something to live up to. They themselves didn't know what to do. They felt repelled by their own future. They wanted to do something that would prove unequivocally that they thought differently. They would shrink from no risk, indeed they sought risk. But they wanted at least to hear Natasha Roth's approval and perhaps some suggestions. Stefan could hear that his mother had understood only gradually what they were talking about and, once she had understood, was inwardly horrified. She spoke cautiously to the three young men. She told them to go home to their jobs and their families and not to do anything rash. His mother spoke warm-heartedly and in complicated sentences. The young men's heads hunched down between their shoulders. After this they said little, and nothing of importance. Stefan had understood them at once, and now he was aware of their disappointment, which smelled like sour sweat. His mother was perhaps right in what she had said. He felt every sentence as a humiliation. Her voice sounded warm-hearted, but he knew his mother and knew that behind this warm-heartedness there was emptiness. She regarded the three young men as confused children. Stefan knew that they were not. He would have liked to yell. He hated his mother that evening. The three young men slurped tea from their cups and nibbled the biscuits Natasha had placed before them. Later they would leave the house mute, backs bowed. They would travel back in underheated trains to the homes they had come from.

Christmas arrived. Electric candles beamed out from the fir trees in various gardens in the street where they lived, and in other streets. Christmas Eve came with jubilation and exultation from many loudspeakers and the thin peal of bells from the district's two churches. Stefan's mother got drunk on French apple brandy. His father was away from home on Christmas Eve and the first day of Christmas, but then returned and stayed for the remainder of the feast days.

36 NATASHA ROTH now lived a regular, puppet-like life; at least, that was how it appeared to her later. What she did, what happened around her, had the style of a predetermined puppet play whose dramatic action, no matter what the complexities and detours, served the single purpose of crushing Natasha Roth. Days passed to the accompaniment of the usual sounds. The footsteps of the children as they left in the morning to go to school. The abrupt emptiness of the early mornings, which could be filled with radio music and the clatter of dishes. The daily shopping expeditions. On every second morning Frau Konjetzki, who gurgled out her gloomy or dull stories. Billa's homecoming. Stefan's homecoming. A meal prepared by Frau Konjetzki. Heavy Silesian dishes full of cholesterol. Bodakov came from Myslowicz. Breaking the same bread was a sort of communion in a shared rebelliousness. The children walked through the house. A constant tapping and scratching in the hall, on the stairs, on the upper floor, the sounds of a gigantic imaginary ant trail. In the evening, coloured pictures on the television screen. The GDR had removed all check-points between its capital and the rest of its territory; all turnpikes had disappeared. All the European Common Market countries were introducing two-hundred-mile fishing zones. Teng Hsiao Ping was rehabilitated. The Palestinian leader Abu Daud had been arrested in Paris. After drinking too much she had sudden attacks of amnesia. She woke with tear-filled eyes to face the sharp white sounds of the television set. She would go to bed so as to be able to start another day tomorrow that would be the same as the one just past.

But this was only the two-dimensional background for the motions that she and her husband went through compulsively, habitual actions practised through two decades and preserved through the inability to say things that ought to have been said. He said "I won't be here tonight" instead of "I want to sleep with X." He need not have uttered either the one sentence or the other. The time he got home remained the same as ever; if he didn't come, it could be assumed that he was staying away; no one would worry. Or would she? When it did once happen, she felt disquiet seeping into her veins as though she were suffering from an infection, the Pavlovian signals resulting from a long life together, the idling biological clock of a couple's relationship. She recalled her lawyer's advice to think over her decision to get a divorce. Under the influence of recent events. He had written this suggestion, cautiously worded, under the printed New Year's greetings he had sent to the house. What events? Her participation in an open letter? Which, according to her friend Erica Roth, had been written without proper thought? Was a dangerous vanity? The news made no further mention of a writer named Bodakov. Radio reports and a coloured short on television informed the public that the presiding judge in the Baader-Meinhof trial had been replaced. In the United States the double murderer Gary Gilmore was executed. The first time the death penalty had been carried out in that country for ten years. Jimmy Carter was inducted into office. Would he pardon the Vietnam draft dodgers?

For weeks both she and her husband had avoided undressing in front of each other in the evening. They still slept in the beds that stood unmoved side by side in the same room. Before going to sleep they said goodnight with a light pressure of their hands that lay side by side. During the day she frequently telephoned Rebecca. She had given up trying to reach the older novelist, who never answered the phone. Of the younger one, she read in the paper that he had gone to Sweden to give readings from his book in various university towns. Her Leipzig publisher informed her that sales of

Days from the Life of Lisbeth P were very slow. When she stayed in Berlin, she saw copies of the familiar volume in the shop windows. The public seemed unwilling to read about conditions of misery, when the misery existed in their immediate neighbourhood. Every day she admonished herself to work on the projected biography of Arthur Rimbaud; every morning, instead of carrying out her intention, she smoked many cigarettes while postponing the decision until the next day. She wrote the famous poet a letter suggesting she might visit him in his old Brandenburg house. She received no answer. Her husband told her: "Your book is being highly praised by the museum staff." He might as well have said: "Some day I'll kill you."

She had great difficulty in obtaining permission for the urn containing her stepmother Sinaida's ashes to be brought over from Tel Aviv. She had to negotiate with state authorities and with the administration of the Jewish Cemetery in Weissensee. Her stepmother had left instructions that she should be buried in the tomb of her Berlin family. Driving into the city, Natasha Roth passed the now abandoned check-point building and the steel supports for the turnpike, which had been removed. A rotting still-life, open to spiders and centipedes. Rebecca set out on a tour of Mecklenburg. She was to perform in the church halls of both denominations. Rudolf Roth stayed out at night less and less often. He had come home in the evening ten days in a row. She thought she could see in the faces of her children that they were beginning to hope that life might go on the way they were all accustomed to. She herself, when she realized this, reacted with spasms in the abdomen. She felt childish, as though she were depriving herself of adult rights. Old age was turning her into a prostitute. The builders' trailer still stood opposite the garden gate. There was more traffic now in the street she lived in than there used to be; but this impression might be an illusion. She was in a state of mind that favoured hysteria and delusions. So far January had brought little snow.

Her husband had to take part in a conference in another city again. This time he would be going to Dresden. She took him to the East Station. Although he told her it wasn't necessary, she positively forced her company on him. She left the car in the Koppenstrasse car park. She walked with her husband into the station building and onto the platform. She enjoyed the smell under the station roof, a smell of soot, cold sausage meat, cheap tobacco; it all seemed to mean longing. Her husband was standing in the open door of the carriage when she said to him: "I have an appointment with my lawyer tomorrow. What shall I tell him?" He shrugged his shoulders, took his pipe out of his mouth and said: "Perhaps we should think it all over once more?" He might just as well have said: "The dog has to be inoculated against distemper again. Who is going to give us the serum?" She saw him standing in the doorway, bare white skin over his skull, transparent and vulnerable. He closed the door. As the train left, he raised his hand and waved to her through the filth of the window pane. She suddenly felt the need to do something unexpected. She went through the underpass to stand by one of the city railway lines. People stood waiting mechanically, just as they would perform certain movements mechanically when the train they were waiting for came in. How long was it since she had last travelled by the city railway? Her nerves were as hypersensitive as if she had taken a drug. She wondered at the patience, including her own, with which the passengers put up with being constantly bumped against their neighbours. She caught sight of a purulent pimple on a young man's neck, just above the edge of his dark-blue collar. She had to force her hand not to free the young man from his little boil. The buildings of the Alexanderplatz floated upright towards them, stopped and floated away, dragging the dark-grey stones of the Museum walls along behind them. Friedrichstrasse Station had become a bazaar, smelled of urine and disinfectant, was packed with people from the Middle East, old men with shabby suitcases and parcels wrapped in coloured paper. She walked down the Friedrichstrasse, then along Unter den Linden to the Pariser Platz. She watched the flags over the Quadriga billow and go slack against the grey sky. Thirty people swarmed out of a Dutch tourist bus, put cameras up to their faces and for hundredths of a second ingested the view of a half-walled-up triumphal arch through the shutter.

Back home she did indeed start re-reading and sorting out her notes on Rimbaud. On 10 June 1876, after receiving a bounty of 1200 francs, Rimbaud, whose full first name was Jean-Nicolas-Arthur, sailed on a Dutch ship, the *Prince of Orange*, to Batavia to serve with the forces in Java. He landed on 23 July, was assigned to the First Infantry Battalion and deserted after three weeks. For a time he lived in the jungle with the natives; then he made his way to the coast and signed on aboard a British ship, telling the captain he was an experienced seaman. The port of destination was Liverpool. Since the captain refused to put in at St Helena, Rimbaud jumped overboard with the intention of swimming to the island to show his devotion to the dead Napoleon. A dinghy was lowered and brought him back on board. For the rest of the trip he remained under arrest. Where did the late nineteenth century's admiration for South-East Asia come from? Even the most continental nerves seem finally to have succumbed to it. Jósef Koszeniowski from Berdichev insisted upon becoming a captain in the British merchant marine in order, as Joseph Conrad, to write *Lord Jim* and *Nostromo*. To clothe his erotic figures, Gustav Klimt knew nothing better than a collage of Japonoiseries. Natasha Roth saw them in front of her, a series of two-dimensional paintings in decorative colours on the second floor of the Upper Belvedere.

Outside the window were the French Garden, the domes of
the Salesian Church and St Charles's Church, glittering ver-
digris against a sky blown blue by the *föhn*. But this was
not the Vienna in which she had grown up and which alone
she had kept in her memory through the many years since
the end of her childhood. She had been back to Vienna in
1968 for the first time in almost thirty years. The pretext
had been a theatrical première, Marivaux's *Les fausses confi-
dences*. She had translated and adapted the play, and after all
the première did take place in the Burgtheater. You could be
proud of that or not.

Dorante is handsome and poor. Through the efforts of the
wealthy Araminte's servant Dubois, Dorante is taken on as
steward in her house. Araminte is a widow and beautiful.
Dubois is nothing less than a gluttonous, loutish domestic
à la Molière. Araminte's mother would like to marry off her
daughter to a count. Araminte learns through Dubois of
Dorante's love for her and thereupon reveals her own affection to Dorante, disregarding all currently accepted restraints
of rank and lineage, whereupon Dorante confesses Dubois's
machinations to Araminte. The première, the last before the
summer break, might perhaps be described as a success. No
one clapped in the Burgtheater—in any case there were never
any curtain calls at the end of a performance, in accordance
with instructions issued during the reign of the Emperor and
still obeyed out of the traditionalism typical of Vienna. Reviews ranged from friendly to non-committal. There were
twenty performances in all, of which she learned only
through her royalty statements.

Midsummer heat weighed upon the city, obviously creeping up-river every day from Pannonia's maize-covered plains,
a Balkan summer, a Wendish and Slavic summer. Tiny ticks
fell on people's heads from the birches at the foot of the
Kahlenberg, causing meningitis. The hospitals were full. She
lived in an old hotel in the Dorotheergasse. The porter wore

a moustache like the dictator Hitler and in other ways too was terrifying. Even before going into the theatre she drank her first eighth of white wine standing in the Rheinthaler Wirt opposite the hotel. The sight of an evidently upper-class lady drinking in a tavern before ten in the morning, like a depraved student or a city bum, would leave traces of her presence in the memory of the clientele for weeks or months. Similar eighths, with or without soda water, kept her going all day. It was the only way she could keep from lapsing into apathy at a temperature of 34°C in the shade. So it was the theatre canteen or the Café Landtmann, on the Ring three hundred paces from the Citadel. She could never eat until the evening. Then the city began to stink, of the urine of the cab horses, of the water from the sprinkler trucks, of the lime blossoms poisoned by petrol fumes. She crossed the Ring and went past the Town Hall to the Floriangasse. There she suddenly felt as if thin bare legs were tripping along beside her, belonging to the six-year-old girl she had once been. Against dust, white sunlight and her own exhaustion she turned into the Floriangasse. Cars screeched. The displays in the second-hand shops were dusty. Coins, old posters, stamps, newspapers and the accessories of ancient uniforms. Heads and torsos of toothless old women were held suspended in the windows of yellow shop fronts. Dog droppings were drying in the corners between plaster and wall-plinths. Tramway cables sliced up the sky. The Josefstadt government offices. She turned left into the Skodagasse, then into the Albertgasse. With every step she moved a week back into her past, fifty steps for a year. The crossing of the Albertgasse and the Pfeilgasse. She found the building immediately. It hadn't even become dirtier by comparison with the colour of the building in her memory, but it had shrivelled, a building with the usual dimensions of an 1880 tenement. In her memory it had been a labyrinthine palace, its corridors as dark as the inside of the eyelids or the mouth of an old woman. They had lived on the mezzanine. She wanted to reach for the door of their flat, but she stopped. Was it number twelve or number thirteen? She had a choice between the names Jelinek or Rohrmoser. The bygone years came rolling down behind her, the scree on a mountain slope. She left the building. Cars were parked at an angle to the pavement. She hurried as far as Lerchenfelderstrasse and then back to the Inner City. If she was now accompanied by someone it was no longer a bare-legged child, but at most death, who had bustled over officiously, joints softly creaking, from the Central Cemetery, down the long grey Simmeringer Strasse, past the barracks; he was thoroughly amiable and rather absent-minded, a Viennese death with a predilection for heavy fabrics and cheap ceremonial. He walked beside her past the Law Courts, down the Bellariastrasse and along the Volksgarten to the Michaelerplatz. They looked together into the shop windows in the Coal Market. Pastry shops, jewellers, books about the army. He crossed the Graben with her. He was distracted by the pasty faces of some young people sitting in a sidewalk café in the Petersplatz. Finally he sat down among them and began to look like them. She herself walked on, down the Rotenturmstrasse, which was suddenly seething with Jews in their best clothes, black suits, black hats, beards of grey, black and white. So the Sabbath was over. So it was Saturday evening. She walked along the Wollzeile; she had loved it as a child because of the deep, dusky shops with sweets and tea. Finally she found herself back in the narrow bend of the Schönlaterngasse, where the sound of her footsteps was gradually swallowed up in the mouldering doorways.

She had met Tibor in a veritable salon. The artistic director of the theatre, to whom she owed the invitation, told her it was the last salon in the whole of Vienna, and it was presided over by a real countess. There was a cold buffet, and countless old men in dark suits. All the rooms were papered with a green damask wallpaper with a repeat of Indonesian motifs, because the countess's family had some Dutch-Asiatic ramifications. After a talk delivered in a solemn tone by a completely insane American, who put forward some very bizarre theories about cultural life in Old Vienna, all the guests stood around and talked. The rather drunken man with the young face and white hair was the painter from whom she had bought an etching that morning in a gallery in the Corn Market for one thousand two hundred schillings. Along with a Chagall for two thousand. Later he laughed at her and tried to return the money, as though he had cheated her over the deal. When she left, he took her to the frontier in his Italian sports coupé. That was a mere six days later. In the meantime he had been with her to every one of the all-night cafés in the Inner City, always drunk and yet capable, in this state, of fantasizing like an Arabian storyteller. His pictures were just the same, that is to say unreal worlds made up of plants that were really birds composed of bands of agate, twisted into human figures playing with insects, which were nothing but skilfully arranged pieces of fabric. When he took her to the Upper Belvedere to see the pictures of Gustav Klimt, she realized from whom he had learnt his artificial style of painting. Tibor lived with his wife and five children in the Messepalast, the former royal stables of the Hofburg, a huge Theresian building in whose courtyards it was very still, with ivy growing on crumbling walls and pigeons flying in through open studio windows and being chased out again by cats. The smell of cats was even stronger than the smell of painting materials. Tibor's hand was flecked. He had burned it with phosphate, while playing with an incendiary bomb from the last war. He evidently had an uncontrollable urge to self-destruction, to which could be ascribed, among other things, his excessive consumption of alcohol. It was absolutely suicidal to travel in the coupé with Tibor driving, and of course he was completely drunk; but he insisted on driving with her into the Vienna Woods along the steepest and most winding roads beyond Hietzing. As far as she could remember, he was only sober during the two days in Baden. She felt like shouting with delight at the sight of so much preserved classicism, all of it in Schönbrunn-yellow among a luxuriant growth of trees. She even sat in the spa garden listening to the orchestra fiddling Lanner and Kálmán, while Tibor stroked her hand and the gold chain she always wore turned black when she swam in the sulphurous water. They drove on to the Neusiedler See, where Tibor conversed with an ancient Hungarian wine-grower in a place called Rust. Tibor drank gallons again; they all sat under a reed-thatch roof on hard wooden benches, between dangling chains of garlic; *báczi kösönöm*, said Tibor, and the old man sang languid Magyar songs and played a reed flute. They looked for fossils in St Margaret's quarry. They clambered over bone-coloured sandstone under the high, pale-blue flatland sky. Tibor drove with her along the autobahn to Salzburg, always in the overtaking lane, a drunken painter with the title of Professor who fancied himself a rally driver. One had to fear for his life, but he would cover the distance in a sensational time. Salzburg scared her. She couldn't remember ever having seen so many people side by side in any other city. It was as though the narrow alleys were packed solid with twitching human flesh. She slept with Tibor in a small hotel far outside the town, on a mountain slope, where water from the rocks flowed into a hollowed tree trunk, with gnats circling above it. At the station, Tibor refused to wave to her. He turned at once and walked away with hunched shoulders. He couldn't stand goodbyes, he had told her beforehand. Moreover, he was drunk again. In any case she immediately had to devote her attention to the frontier officials, who treated her passport like an unheard-of rarity, pointing it out to each other. The people waiting behind her also looked at her like a monster or a political criminal. She was glad when she was allowed to go with her luggage to the train, which came from the depths of the Balkans and was full of work-minded Greeks, Serbs and Croats. Then she travelled to Munich. She had always destested Munich.

About two months later, Tibor really did commit suicide, or he made a successful suicide attempt, which is not necessarily the same thing. First he slashed an almost finished painting measuring nine by fifteen feet with a knife, after which he took a whole packet of Veronal. The dose was fatal, of course, but if his wife had come home three-quarters of an hour later, as arranged, he could easily have been saved. But she came much later, not through her own fault, since the train on which she was travelling from the Wachau, after fetching her five children from their summer holiday, was no less than one hundred and twenty minutes late. By then it was all over. Two of the three cats were said to have been sitting on the dead Tibor's chest. This was a picturesque sight, in spite of everything. Now Tibor lay in the Vienna Central Cemetery and his name had entered into the history of modern art. His wife had remarried and was now living in Venice.

On subsequent visits to Vienna, Natasha Roth had intended to visit Tibor's grave in the Central Cemetery, but hadn't done so because she had too many things to see to, because the mendacious necrophilia of this city got on her nerves and because cemeteries disgusted her. She wondered which would be worse for her: if she could never see Vienna again or never again see Paris. Rimbaud had been in Stuttgart and there, if the evidence was to be believed, had learned astonishingly good German. It was in Stuttgart that the horrible last meeting between Rimbaud and Verlaine took place. She wondered whether Fräulein X, whose name she didn't know and whose appearance was a matter of indifference to her, should be regarded as a delayed reaction to Tibor. In that case, Fräulein X would have to take sleeping tablets in the next few weeks and commit suicide with Prussian efficiency. Natasha Roth stubbed out a cigarette and emptied an over-full ash tray. A feeling of desolation, as harsh as a hiccup. She knew that alcohol was the only remedy. She put her coat over her shoulders and walked through sleet to the corner grocery store. When she returned she met Stefan. He had the dog on the leash. She looked at him and waved as if to an almost complete stranger. She locked herself in her study. She started to drink; that calmed her down, but at the same time she was overcome by the certainty that everything she would do from now on would be completely useless. There were no solutions. There was only decline. She switched on the radio. She heard on the news that the old novelist with whom she had drafted the open letter protesting Bodakov's deprivation of citizenship had moved to Hamburg. The GDR authorities had approved his request for permission to move. He had arrived in his new home two days ago. The fact had only now been announced and the novelist did not wish to comment either on his move or on anything else.

ONLY PRESSURE from Thomas persuaded him to go to 37 an entertainment described by the now popular name "disco-thèque." It took place in his school's gymnasium. Masses of bright-coloured paper were scattered over the walls and floor. The loudspeakers that had been set up proved inade-quate to their task, as Stefan had fully expected. He stood in a corner of the large room, which always smelled of leather, sweat, dust and talcum powder, the ineradicable smell of every gymnasium. Now there were added smells of Coca-Cola, liquor that had been smuggled in and tobacco smoke seeping in from outside through all the cracks. He watched the efforts of two hundred adolescents to perform certain sequences of sensual movements among the bright lights. He knew many of the numbers that were being played. He listened to their mutilation with an expression of contempt. He felt angry at having allowed Thomas to talk him into coming and knew secretly that he was merely scared. He knew his physical weakness; he thought himself incapable of making the movements called for. He stayed leaning against the wall and began a hesitant conversation with a girl, which to begin with consisted of a few dismembered sentences. He knew her by sight. She was in a class belonging to the same year. He had never spoken to her before and she had not attracted his attention. He didn't know her name. The words they spoke to each other became numerous. They were words of the kind from which whole sentences can be constructed. The girl seemed to prefer the diversion that consisted in an exchange of sentences to the diversion of plunging back into the blissfully twitching multitude of bodies. This created a loose link between them. It was really a secret isolation, and the irrational counterweight consisted in an arrogance enjoyed in common. In any case, this word had increasingly haunted him in recent weeks. There seemed to exist a special set of words: *arrogant, separate, privileged, injured, vulnerable, élitist, helpless, arrogant.* He knew many of these words from derogatory gossip, also as a reproach against his mother, likewise as his own reproach against himself. He would never have thought that this reproach and also the pretext for it could be shared. He and the girl pointed out imperfections to each other. The scene before them seemed only to exist in order to provide an opportunity for comments at which they could then laugh. It was a synthetic laughter. It could be intensified. They could intensify it in one another. It seemed to Stefan a particularly venomous form of contempt. He enjoyed it. As they laughed he looked at the girl's teeth. They were almost too bright, almost too regular, they looked almost artificial. But obviously these were the kind of details that stood out: detached from the environment that gave birth to them, it would be hard to remember them even with the greatest effort. What else stood out? A mindless piece of rock music that he was hearing on this occasion for the first time. "You made me believe in magic." He would never get that out of his memory. Or the line running from the outer edge of the hand across the tiny bulge of the wrist bone and up the bare forearm. Very white skin. His world disintegrated into arbitrary particles. Perhaps the world had congealed out of such particles and hence was a work of completely crazy arbitrariness. Almost incredulously, he discovered in himself a tendency for his thoughts to keep returning to details like this, unless it was these details that drew his thoughts to them with an irresistible power. He discovered that he spent more time now looking at himself in the mirror, scrutinizing his face for irregularities and silently transposing his impressions of himself into value judgements. He alternated between contempt and indulgence.

He made an effort when he walked. He didn't want to limp. He tried, which was a strain, to overcome his tendency to come down lower on the right side than on the left when he walked. He had to force himself to move regularly from heel to toe on his right foot, which tended to slap down limply on the sole.

The next detail he noticed was a small cross, gold, on a chain as thin as a thread that followed the contours of the collarbone barely discernible under the skin. The cross had a tendency to get caught in fabric. Stefan had difficulty in bringing the person who came towards him with self-confident steps, and halted her running on his account, into a causal relationship with the way he was now thinking. Almost with dismay, he observed what a matter of course certain things had become, how completely they had blotted out their own cause. Before him stood a person who, it occurred to him, had a particular name, Vera; who reminded him of an evening which for quite a time had consisted only of words; the evening lay a mere forty hours in the past; these forty hours had become a mythical period.

More or less by chance—because the book was lying on the edge of a book-shelf and threatened to fall down, so that he picked it up—he leafed through the pages between the linen covers, paused, began to read, put it down and started reading again. He kept returning to these lines:

> O the nocturnal wingbeat of the soul:
> Shepherds, we once moved through twilit forests
> And the red deer, the green flowers and the murmuring
>   spring
> Followed us humbly. O ancient note of crickets,
> Blood flowering on the altar stone
> And the cry of a lonely bird above the pond's green stillness.

He had the impression that here, with priestly gestures, a landscape was being described in which death lurked, insect-like and all-powerful, in every dell, behind every knoll, under every stone and leaf. He really didn't know what death was. He had a vague knowledge of dying, but it was dying in hospital, which was shut away behind doors and remained silent, apart from the low squeak of trolleys being pushed along. The voice of the cricket. An ancient scream. Bone violins on the cross-hatching of a wing skin. Blood clings to the sacrificial stones. The wind dries it. Microbes devour it; the blood seeps injured into the earth; the sound of music

stubbornly follows death. The death agony and an embrace
call forth the same movements; the same movements bespoke
the same thing; there was no illusion there. The pool was the
grave of the drowned who had no one to put them in the
ground. Therefore:

> When we thirst
> We drink the pool's white waters,
> The sweetness of our sorrowful childhood.

Now he had the overwhelming feeling that a sediment was
dissolving in his memory and in his nerves, an incrustation
deposited long ago; it was dissolving the way a solid substance
gradually and progressively disintegrates under the effect of
acids. What was left was a gelatinous, amorphous conglomer-
ation of all feelings. He felt inexperienced. He felt useless.
He felt starved for this language steeped in so much sweet
melancholy of death, which was merely the expression of
virtually inexpressible things. He read:

> When I took your slender hands
> Gently your round eyes opened.
> That was long ago.

The words were simple, and yet they so overcame him that
he could have repeated them over and over again. He closed
the book. He would want to open it again as though it contained an opiate upon which he was dependent. Was there
such a thing? Intoxication springing from mere words? The
man who had written all this bore the name of Trakl. Stefan
found in his parents' library a book describing Trakl's life.
He saw the photograph of a young man with close-cropped
hair and a fleshy nose, who had been dead for sixty years.
Ether intoxication. Suicide phantasies, drunkenness, meta-
physical anxieties. Trakl came from an old baroque city,

Salzburg; his mother had often told him about Salzburg, though not nearly as often as about Vienna or Paris or any of the towns of France. The dispensing pharmacist Georg Trakl was deeply shattered by his war experiences in the Austro-Ruthenian landscape of Eastern Galicia. "My health is somewhat undermined and I very often lapse into an unutterable melancholy." Complete mental breakdown on a battlefield near Grodek, with groans of the dying, the sight of hanged deserters, roads ending in black putrefaction, the moon chasing terrified women from bleeding steps, the garrison hospital at Cracow and poisoning with an overdose of cocaine he had smuggled out, on 3 November 1914, buried twelve days later in the nearby cemetery of Rakovicz. On 7 October 1925 his mortal remains were transported to the Tyrol, to the cemetery of the parish of Mühlau near Innsbruck. Stefan's mother had never told him about Innsbruck. Perhaps she didn't know Innsbruck. Over our graves bends the broken forehead of night. It seemed to Stefan as though this poet had died a substitute death for him.

His own reality was simpler and perhaps healthier, at any rate more commonplace. He was seeing Vera almost every day now. Almost every day he had an opportunity to pick up the interrupted conversation again and continue it *ad infinitum*. They saw each other during the longer breaks between morning classes. They met in the long corridors or at the edge of the wire-netting-encircled schoolyard. He walked with her down from the second floor to the ground floor by the caretaker's cubicle. That was a lot of steps you could count. They stood by the fence in the open air. Behind them coke had been unloaded into a heap. As they talked, the breath came from their lips in the shape of fleetingly visible smoke. They walked down the Oberspreestrasse to the traffic island at the Grünauer Strasse crossing, on into the Grünstrasse, where the shops were small and had narrow windows with panes that were going blind. Before this, they passed the wooden bridge leading to the entrance to Köpenick Castle. This was where his father worked. He told Vera this and was glad that she had never expressed the wish to meet his father. He was glad that his father was busy with other things, that he never met Stefan and Vera, that consequently he had no reason to question Stefan in the evenings. Stefan and Vera walked through the castle garden to the banks of the Spree. In the late winter the grass in the meadows was sparse, the trees were bare; the opposite bank with its dark line of roofs, chimneys and trees was indistinct in the mist. Swans were circling in the water, fat dirty-white lumps with phallic necks. Vera and Stefan talked about a hundred different things, all inexhaustible and insignificant. They served to fill countless quarters of an hour. The street-cars on their way to Wendenschloss and Biesdorf screeched into the conversations. The damp car exhaust gases in the Old City of Köpenick threatened to dye them blue with carbon monoxide, lead and oil. They walked. They talked. They touched. Behind the Kirchstrasse lay an old district with low houses; the colour on the walls had faded; the plaster was peeling; but the houses looked as though they had been transposed unchanged from the past century into the present; as though at any moment horse-drawn cabs would drive out of the gateways and pass noisily over the uneven roadway. Stefan loved these streets.

By comparison, everything else became less important. On these evenings Stefan came home late, later than usual; no one seemed to notice this change, in any case no one spoke to him about it. In general, there was very little talking now when he was at home. No one questioned him, he asked no questions; he didn't even question Billa, who probably had her own childish excitements and was completely absorbed in them. Not a word was spoken about the events of last November. Did they really happen? Or were they perhaps merely the phantasy of a few sensitive writers hungry for headlines, or the anxiety dream of a child from a broken marriage? Of this too no one spoke any more. Since this was the way it was presented to him, he began to forget about it. Anyone entering the Roths' house would not have been able to observe any manifest change, as measured against the situation one year or three years before. Perhaps one reason Stefan stayed out so late was to avoid having to experience certain things, and he made the, for him, astonishing discovery that after a while things he didn't wish to see were no longer there to be seen. He sat with Vera in a tiny tavern in Old Köpenick. The innkeeper was a tall, emaciated woman with a deep voice and several gold teeth. They had to put up with her silly but well-meant comments. By so doing they bought the right to sit for hours at a table drinking cheap fruit juice, talking and watching day flow on into dusk outside the small windows. People came in from their shift, they made a noise, they ordered beer and whisky, they drank, the radio played, the tavern filled with clouds of cigarette smoke, Stefan and Vera looked at each other as through a filter of dirt and toxins, they laughed, they talked nonstop. Afterwards Stefan had the vulgar smell of this tavern in his clothes, intermingled with the smell of school. These smells were memory. He carried them with him when he went home in the streetcar, limp, satisfied, full of the desire to repeat on another day the commonplace experiences he had just been through and to surrender himself to them completely.

Perhaps Vera wasn't a very pretty girl. She was tall; she held herself erect; she had dark hair; her chin was rather large; she had very white skin beneath which, on the temples, the throat, the wrists, lay vulnerable blue veins. He shared with her the joys of going to the cinema together. They always went to the Forum near Köpenick Station. Or they went together to the Inner City of Berlin. They spent long, strenuous winter afternoons in the Schönhauser Allee, where relatives of hers lived, she told him; but she had no wish to

visit them with him. At the beginning of the Schönhauser
Allee there was a small Jewish cemetery, which Stefan only
recognized through a plaque by the gate. He knew that Vera
was a Catholic. She said she had been conscientiously brought
up in religious matters. Every Sunday she attended High
Mass or ordinary Mass, and it was no coincidence that the
gold pendant on the chain round her neck was a cross. They
didn't talk about it much. Once only she took Stefan with
her to St Hedwig's Cathedral, on an ordinary Thursday afternoon. He knew this church only as a silhouette, as part of
the ensemble that included the State Opera and the Crown
Prince's Palace; he now obediently ascended the broad steps
with Vera, opened a heavy, stiff metal door, entered a building with white interior walls and colourless glass. It was cold
inside. Vera crossed herself after quickly dipping her hand in
the font. She showed him chapel and crypts. She showed
him pictures; she told him Bible stories connected with the
pictures that were quite unknown to him and seemed sombre
and cruel. Then, sitting next to Vera in a pew, he tried to
imagine a God. He pictured a rather slovenly man wearing
an old-fashioned overcoat and a light-coloured felt hat sitting in the middle of a park bench between chattering
women, each of whom had a child's pram in front of her. He
scratched magic signs in the gravel with a walking-stick and
then fed crumbs to the pigeons and sparrows which were
hopping around. Or he might be even simpler, a kind of
crafty tramp with rotten teeth, a shirt with no collar, perhaps
even barefoot or at most wearing shabby sandals. Then, because he was so tired, he sat on the altar plinth, letting his
legs with their thick, dark-blue varicose veins dangle. You
could tell him all the misery of the world. There was such
an incredible amount of injustice and bitterness. He could
only wink understandingly or sometimes nod his head and
giggle. Finally he reached into his hobo knapsack and pulled
out a flat, battered liquor flask, opened it, took two or three

deep draughts, belched and wiped his mouth. But then, fired by the liquor, he would slip down from his altar plinth, spread his arms and begin mysteriously to float, gradually gaining height and losing dirt, until finally radiant and bright he vanished into the great bright dome of St Hedwig's Cathedral.

Vera often took him home with her. Vera's parents had a four-room apartment in a newly built-up area, the Salvador Allende district, situated at the edge of the Köllnische Heide in Köpenick. The buildings were long, smooth concrete constructions with tile fronts, each one like the next. The difference began inside after seeking and at last finding one of countless identical doors. The door had been a sluice-gate. It led from a world of aggressive and indifferent events into a world of warmth and gentle stupidity. No one asked where he came from. No one knew who his mother was. No one could know what intentions his parents had. This was a good Catholic home. To practising Catholics marriage was a sacrament, established by God and hence indissoluble; anyone who wantonly destroyed it was committing an offence against God. What practising Catholic would dare to do that? Vera's father, Herr Merck, was a thin man with sparse hair and a full beard. He smiled frequently. It seemed to Stefan as though Herr Merck was smiling vacantly. Was there anything to complain about in that? Ought Herr Merck to smile differently for Stefan's sake? Stefan had no complaint to make; it didn't even cross his mind. Stefan shook hands with Herr Merck, and Herr Merck's hand was soapy dry. Stefan answered Herr Merck's questions but asked none himself. Herr Merck (or was it Frau Merck?) had pinned coloured prints on the walls. They were the Bible illustrations by the Russian-French painter Marc Chagall. The Roths too had a Chagall print, but there were no Bible illustrations on their walls. Herr Merck constructed electronic appliances in a large research and development institution. In the summer Herr Merck went to Brandenburg to fly-fish on calm lakes. Frau Merck was still very young and treated Stefan very kindly. She always brought a pot of hot tea. In one of the rooms there stood a piano, dark-stained wood, and Herr Merck often opened up the lid and began to play. Herr Merck didn't play badly, perhaps somewhat mechanically was his own criticism, but technically he was rather ambitious. For example Robert Schumann's *Papillons* or Chopin's Nocturnes op. 48, the fingering of which was pretty complicated. Sometimes also Bela Bartok's *Microcosm*. This was very demanding, not so much technically as from the point of view of tonality. Stefan listened to Herr Merck playing the piano. The instrument was slightly out of tune, due to the excessively dry air. Herr Merck liked to tune the instrument himself, a key in one hand, a tuning-fork in the other. The rooms in this flat were in any case always overheated. Herr Merck smoked a pipe, like Stefan's father. He also smoked the same sweet Irish tobacco from the state foreign-currency shop. Stefan grew tired. He leaned back among a pile of rustling cushions; everything that was not in this room now seemed to him a long way away. With lethargic eyes he observed Vera's profile with the chin that was perhaps rather large. Your lids are heavy with poppy and dream softly on my brow. In this room life remained simple, commonplace, deaf and soft as a rustling cushion.

ERICA ROTH had collapsed at work. She was immediately taken to a specialist unit at the university hospital in Greifswald. Her paralysed husband, requiring continual care, was also taken there the following day. He was now quite close

38

to her, or at any rate in the same ward. Natasha Roth had learned all this when, after several unsuccessful attempts to speak to Erica Roth on her private line, she finally telephoned the dermatological clinic where she worked. Severe ulceration of the pancreas. Complete exhaustion due to overwork. Underweight. Most of the Latin expressions had been translated, explained or paraphrased for Natasha Roth as a lay person. Erica Roth would be away for several weeks. Intensive chemotherapy was unavoidable. Side effects of the therapy in the shape of allergies and eczemas must be feared, and a treatment for these effects worked out. Strict isolation. Visits were out of the question. The hospital would be glad to give further information on the patient's condition in the light of future investigations. Letters were permitted. They would be passed on to the patient or not, according to her condition at the time. Natasha wrote to her friend. She wrote by hand, wishing her a quick recovery and painting an early return to Berlin in bright colours. She indicated her own condition only in brief generalities. What exactly was Natasha Roth's condition?

She had been working for over a week on a piece describing the French adventurer Arthur Rimbaud's stay in Harrar, Ethiopia. There, as an employee of the wholesale merchant Alfred Bardey from Aden, Rimbaud buys cattle, skins, rubber, ivory and incense from the natives who make day trips to Harrar. Haggling over the prices absorbs all his energy. When the sellers have left, the goods are taken to Bardey's warehouse and locked up. Or Rimbaud fits out a caravan to transport the accumulated contents of the warehouse to Bardey in Aden. The coffee houses are still open. Armed patrols go through the streets of Harrar. After sunset the city gates are closed; the wild dogs are driven onto the ramparts, where they are supposed to chase away hyenas and panthers. Nevertheless, beasts of prey keep getting into the city and attacking sick people. The long evenings are terrible.

The dogs bark incessantly. Civilians are forbidden to be out in the streets after dark. The patrols arrest everyone on suspicion, without respect of persons. Syphilis is rampant in Harrar. Rimbaud is twenty-seven; he writes in a notebook the figures of the meagre fortune he has amassed in Ethiopia. Exactly ten years ago the Commune was set up in Paris. At that time he was a poet who, if he didn't want to revolutionize the whole of humanity, at least wanted to revolutionize its poetry. *Vrai, cette fois, j'ai pleuré plus que tous les enfants du monde.*

This time I have wept more than all the children of the world. Natasha Roth worked stubbornly for a week on fifteen pages of prose, read through what she had written and tore it up. The condition of being without a language could not be overcome by trying to describe and explain someone else's loss of language. Her incapacity threw her into a panic. She wrote a letter requesting renewal of her visa for France, which had meanwhile expired. As she wrote, she tried to picture the faces of the clerks who dealt with such requests. With arrogance and contempt, Natasha Roth had turned in a valid visa; now, two months after that strange action, she was applying for a new visa. There was no arrogance and contempt to be read between the lines she had written on her typewriter. The clerks would smile indulgently. Natasha Roth had obviously been worn down, perhaps even broken.

When she saw in her mind's eye the steady smile on the faces of the clerks, she knew that she was merely transferring to others a smile with which in truth she looked upon herself. Her panic continued. She had to exercise self-control in order not to get drunk. On West German television a cultural programme was running which showed her the cheerful poet Holger Musäus. He had published a new book, an anthology of contemporary prose, that was obviously enjoying a nice success. Now he was travelling through West German university towns, signing copies and answering questions.

The programme showed Holger Musäus talking with Marburg students. He defended the building of the wall and found the country in which he lived, all in all, fabulous. Natasha Roth couldn't help remembering her sick friend Erica Roth's remark that writers were not judged by the strength of their neck muscles, but by their success.

Rebecca had completed her tour of fifteen community halls and village churches in Mecklenburg. Now she was living in a pastor's house on the island of Usedom. No one knew for how long. One could imagine Rebecca, with her head wrapped and her coat collar turned up, standing on a stone stage gazing into whitish-green waves. Wind threw grains of sand into her face; slowly she chewed her tablets. A call came from Natasha Roth's West German publisher. The junior partner was going to be in East Berlin on such and such a day and wanted to meet his author Natasha Roth. On that day she drove as far as the shipbuilding quay. It was early evening.

The junior partner was waiting in a tavern restaurant. He came over to her with a smile as she stood in the doorway, pressed her hand for a long time and then helped her off with her coat. He had spent the whole day negotiating with GDR publishers. He was very pleased with the agreements he had reached. He said this, and you could see it from his face. There was a piano in the restaurant at which an elderly man now sat down and played songs from Viennese operettas. The junior partner said that barely three thousand copies of *Days from the Life of Lisbeth P* had been sold since it went on the market. This was a pretty meagre figure when one considered how much fuss had been made about the letter of protest. The chief beneficiary from Bodakov's deprivation of citizenship had been Bodakov himself. Sales of his latest book had meanwhile reached ninety thousand. One had to see things as they are. The market lived on current events.

Perhaps Natasha Roth should move in a new direction? He didn't want to find himself involved in a conflict between Natasha Roth and other interests. Finally the junior partner went red in the face. He found the whole subject embarrassing, and said so. There were certain roles one had to play, he said, laughing apologetically, and Natasha Roth said that was undoubtedly true.

The pianist was playing music from *The Merry Widow*. The junior partner revealed how impressed he was by all the building going on in East Berlin. Shortly before midnight Natasha Roth drove home. It had started to snow and the roads were slippery.

Next day she decided to visit the famous poet. He hadn't answered the letter she had written him, but she told herself that this was not the time to leave certain things undone because of certain external circumstances. Perhaps her letter had gone astray. She herself failed to receive letters which she knew, which she had been assured, had been mailed. She drove into Berlin and out of Berlin again, on the road to Potsdam and into the village where the poet had his house. It was a fine house, low, dark, with an enormous roof behind whose ridge the bare boughs of the famous three nut trees reached into the void, black against a water-bright sky. A dog began to bark. The door was opened by a deformed woman. Natasha Roth knew that it was the poet's daughter. The woman was holding the dog back by the collar, a naked mastiff gnashing its teeth. Inside the house it was dusky. In the hall hung ikons and old firearms.

The poet was standing in front of a fireplace into which he was in the process of throwing beech logs, so that the flames jumped up with a hiss and a shower of sparks. He was wearing a sweater of undyed wool and now turned round with a groan, extended his right hand to her, at the same time running the outspread fingers of his left through his shaggy white hair, and said instead of a greeting: "Have you come to make me change my mind?" "About what?" asked Natasha Roth. "About that letter," said the poet with hostility. "About that Bodakov. He's a wretched poet, but don't bother to try. Others have failed already." Now she understood what he took her for. Only when she reminded him that she had helped to draft the letter did he seem to realize who she was. He sat down with a grunt in a Biedermeier armchair and lit a cigar. Then he started to talk. It was a complicated account of the irritations to which he had been subjected during recent weeks, unwanted visits, embarrassing conversations, insulting or peremptory letters; he spoke in a grating voice, in complex sentences; he bewailed his lot; he poured scorn on the general conditions under which he was living and in which, if he was to be believed, he only stayed because he was old and because this was where the house stood which he had inherited from his grandfather, the house with the nut trees.

Then he talked about the past. He recalled the years as an émigré in northern Sweden, where he had lived for twenty months as a forestry labourer, until a PEN fellowship made it possible for him to write again. The story "Tree Felling in Morjäv" was as much part of the school readers in East Germany as the story of his grandfather's nut trees. Both of them examples of great, faultless narrative prose, such as only poets can write. "Tree Felling in Morjäv" was deeply moving for its vivid descriptions of misery, harshness, cruelty and mutual aid among the dispossessed. Now, in the poet's oral recollections, Morjäv turned into a lousy dump full of strong liquor and cheap whores. Everything in the poet's head seemed to be concerned solely with his own past and his own person. Once he mentioned the older novelist, who had moved to Hamburg. He called him a wretched writer. Not once did he ask how Natasha Roth was. When she uttered the word "revolution," he yelled: "In this country? That's not a revolution, that's simply insolence!" Then he started talking again about Morjäv, where he had met Anarchists. His deformed daughter brought tea and fed medicine to her grumbling father. After three hours Natasha Roth said goodbye. He turned his back on her irritably.

On the way home in the half-darkness a small child ran in front of the car. She was able to brake in time. The bumper just touched the child. It fell on the tarmac and screamed. She got out, picked up the child; it was unhurt; she carried it to the roadside. Windows in the houses were opened, people called down threateningly to her, but she didn't understand a word. She drove on for another two hundred yards; then she stopped and began to cry so uncontrollably that she almost threw up.

THE URN containing Grandmother Sinaida's ashes had arrived at last. A long and difficult journey lay behind; from Tel Aviv to Frankfurt-am-Main and from there to Berlin Tegel and finally through the wall to Weissensee. The burial was to take place at the beginning of the last week in January. Stefan had to wait at an agreed time in the courtyard of Köpenick Castle, until his father came, wearing a dark coat and black trousers and shoes. They travelled together by streetcar and then by the city railway. They got out and Stefan heard his father say it was really still far too early.

They walked slowly along the Greifswalder Strasse. Stefan had never been here before. A district of gas-works and uniform grey-brown apartment houses with small gardens in between. Then the street signs spoke of Gounod, Smetana, Rossini. They had to walk somewhat uphill, and now Stefan saw a wall of yellow bricks. They came to a gateway. There were a few cars parked close to it. His mother's car was not among them. Inside the gateway zinc buckets filled with water, perhaps for putting flowers in; there were no flowers in them now; it was late in the day, a grey afternoon with a sky as gloomy as zinc. Wasn't there a sign somewhere forbidding anyone to enter the cemetery with uncovered head? Stefan had no head covering. His father said it wasn't important. He himself was wearing his dark-blue beret; he had known about the rule.

They walked on, and after a while Stefan began to feel exposed. His father pulled his beret lower down over his forehead. It seemed as though by this gesture he meant to withdraw from Stefan. Stefan began to see his father as no more than a strange gaunt shadow beside him. It now occurred to him that this was only the third time in his life that he had walked through a cemetery; his mother, he knew, hated graves, shunned any reminder of death. Here huge trees had dropped their autumn leaves. They lay on the paths, soft and slippery, making walking dangerous. Stefan saw the gravestones coming towards him with measured tread, grey, black, very rarely porphyry-red. To begin with, he took note of remarkable names—Fajngold, Neigroszen, Perelsztajn—as though by reading them carefully he could obtain some particular information. He found many stones with Cyrillic inscriptions. "The great Eastern Jewish immigration, you know," he heard from his shadow, who bore the first name of Rudolf, an unusual name here, but who was the great-grandson of an immigrant from Vilna whose first name had been Lazar. In his father's low and ever more furtive voice Stefan heard about immigrations from Schleswig, Galicia, the Baltic, Ruthenia, from landscapes of mud, darkness and poverty; in his over-strained imagination he saw a

long column of bent, shuffling men in kaftans with long
beards and side-locks; they had harnessed themselves to their
hand-carts, on which they pulled their junk to the railway
station; there they waited among hissing locomotives, in a
cloud of grey steam from a passenger train; there were carriages with many different classes, but the very cheapest compartment would take them to the Promised Land, Germany,
Prussia, Berlin, where tolerance dwelt, where there were no
more pogroms.

They came to a memorial ground, a high wall surrounding
a rectangular area; there was a sunken space lined with stone
slabs, and access through one of four gates. This, Stefan read
from inscriptions, was a memorial to the dead of World War
One. The paving stones were all cracked. Grass grew between them. Leaf-rosettes forced the bricks apart. He heard
his father say the Fatherland had rewarded its Jewish heroes
miserably. This remark meant little to Stefan and it had to be
explained to him at great length. Another sign showed the
way to the house of prayer, which was nothing but a ruin
with empty window spaces. Inside, a metal candelabra hung
at an angle with only two of the original three or four
candles still in place. Stefan saw the six-pointed star. His
father explained to him that it was called the Star of David,
after King David, and that in the Cabbala it symbolized the
union of two different essences, which you could take to
mean whatever you liked, perhaps the Messiah, whose sign it
also was. But now it was the symbol of the State of Israel,
where Grandmother Sinaida had finally lived, where she had
died, from where the urn containing her ashes had just come.
They walked on. It seemed to Stefan that they were walking
an endless path, and here one path was like another. The
tombstones remained alike; perhaps they were the same
stones; he no longer read all the names; he merely noted the
sequences of names that seemed to appear most often: Loeb,
Löw, Loew, Loewy, Levy, Lewin, Levine, Leviné—the in-

flexional forms of a mysterious grammar. He had the feeling he had been walking here for hours. He was surprised at his father, who was usually unwilling to go for long walks, but here strode along with springy steps. They hadn't met a single person; there was nothing but tombstones, straggly bushes and leafless trees. His father was walking more and more weightlessly. He seemed suddenly to be no longer himself, but to have been reborn as an immaterial being, a real shadow, perhaps one of the ghosts from the tale of the one who set out to learn fear, in which the dead played ball with human skulls, Sabbath of the Dead, garden of the dead, Jewish garden, he was here without a head-covering, although he had read the request, he had offended against it knowingly, would a mysterious curse catch up with him and punish him for his impudence? Did his father still know the way? Was there still a way? Was his father still human, or had he turned into a delusion of revenge, spiteful trickery and melancholy Jewish myths? At least his father did know which path to follow, no matter whether it was crooked or straight. After walking for a time that could not have been measured by any clock, his father led him out of the labyrinth of old graves to an area by the high yellow-brick wall. Here there were no trees. The shrubs were still low. Here there were a few rows of fresh graves. The oldest were ten or twelve or fifteen years old. Stefan read the inscription "Moritz Samuel Roth born 1891 died 1962." A frame of light-coloured stone slabs enclosed white gravel. No flowers. He felt his father put his arm round his shoulders. As though this contact was intended to communicate an obscure message about true origins, which he owed to the person lying in this grave. Stefan suddenly shuddered. He also felt moved. He glanced surreptitiously into the face of his father, whom he didn't understand, who was so familiar, who was such a stranger that he shivered. Then he actually imagined that the soft soil was about to be torn apart, the earth crumble away, uncovering pink hands that beseechingly or imperiously clutched at him. It was an absurd fantasy. It was literary and childish. It came to him only because he felt so lost in this cemetery, and he owed that to the aversions of his mother, Natasha Roth. His father seemed to be free of such aversions as from other attachments and encumbrances. Then they walked back to the older part of the cemetery. By a grave two old women were waiting whom Stefan didn't know, whose thin old women's hands he now had to shake. Very distant relatives of Grandmother Sinaida, they had come over from West Berlin, where they lived in a Jewish old-age home. The tombstone was of dark-grey granite, as tall as a man, a tablet with five names inscribed on it and space for future names. Those who lay here had all been called Rubinowicz. It was Grandmother Sinaida's maiden name. In a corner of the grave a small hole had been dug for the urn. The two old women stood there whispering to each other and shivering with cold. An old man appeared, evidently a cemetery gardener; he was carrying bunches of flowers in both arms and would put them down somewhere. Natasha Roth had not arrived yet, but there was still plenty of time before the beginning of the funeral.

A LETTER arrived from Natasha Roth's Polish translator. **40** The translator's time in Frankfurt-am-Main was over, his fellowship at an end, and he was now looking for books and articles he could translate. He asked what new project she was now working on, whether she was near the end, whether the project was one that might interest Polish readers and whether he might negotiate a translation with Polish publishing houses. She remembered the material on naive painting which she had come across a few weeks ago. She immediately recalled the name Krystyna Borowska from a village near Gniezno, in the voivode of Poznán. It suddenly occurred to her that she might just as well write about a Polish naive painter as about a Surrealist poet from France. There were countless books on Rimbaud. Perhaps her own difficulties were due solely to the fact that in her subconscious she was dragging around a whole library of Rimbaud studies, among which her own would take its place and against which it would be judged. The longer she thought about it the more resolved she became. She was seized, as if intoxicated, with the need to burn the past behind her and embark on an entirely new undertaking. She would write about Krystyna Borowska. She became very excited. She wanted to produce something completely new, something no one expected of her, and to produce it with ease, as though from a sudden access of youth. The project immediately took clear shape. She saw before her a large book with a glossy cover in dark blue and crimson. Mentally she composed the first sentence, discarded it and found better sentences. Her excitement grew increasingly intense. Rimbaud was dead. He had died of syphilis, of gangrene and bigotry in a Marseilles infirmary, almost a hundred years ago. Krystyna Borowska had experienced revolution only at a distance, in art as in reality; she had borne six children and once these children had grown up she painted on fragile wooden panels likenesses of trees, peasants, wells and dogs. Natasha Roth telephoned her translator. It was difficult to get through to Warsaw, but just before midnight she succeeded. The translator told her that Borowska was still painting, a friend of his had bought one of her paintings, quite recently; Borowska had become famous and was getting tremendous prices. Natasha Roth said she might possibly come to Poland shortly; she said she would definitely come to Poland, very soon; she would pack her bags and leave. *Un pas de toi, c'est la leveé des nouveaux hommes et leur en-marche.* You didn't have to write about Rimbaud in order to remember his poems.

Winter remained mild and overcast. Snow fell rarely and then melted at once. The garden in front of the house was nothing but churned-up earth and yellow, rotting birch leaves.

On a day like any other she loaded the car with her luggage. Her husband raised no particular objections to the plan. Her expectations and enthusiasm had been irresistible. They drove along the autobahn to the border-crossing north of Frankfurt. They entered a concrete tract full of administrative buildings, Nissen huts, various wheel tracks, signboards, signal lamps, metal gates.

Their car was the only vehicle in the area. Between the Nissen hut at the edge of the roadway and the multi-storey administration building stood a border guard with a panting dog at his feet. When the Roths' yellow car stopped at the border, a second soldier joined the one with the dog. They both looked at the yellow car, perhaps the only civilian vehicle that had been at this point for hours. A grey day, cold, but no frost. Instead, mist and moisture. Her husband switched off the engine. He took his passport and hers, turned up the collar of his jacket because of the cold and got out. He walked in an arc round the car to the corrugated-iron clearance hut, through whose open window he thrust the travel permits. Then he had to wait. He turned sideways so that he could rest one elbow on the window sill. He took out his tobacco pouch and filled his pipe. The two border guards stood in the exact centre of the space between the administration building and the clearance hut. Now they separated. The man with the dog stayed where he was. The other threw away a lighted cigarette and hurried towards the

clearance hut, behind which he disappeared. Her husband lit
his pipe with hands cupped against the wind. The border
guard with the dog looked up at one of the windows of the
administration building, where a human figure could be seen,
possibly an officer. The two men exchanged signs. The second border guard came into view again. He ran towards the
administration building. Her husband took his pipe out of
his mouth and leaned forward into the window. She saw
him shrug his shoulders. He came back to the car. He opened
the door and said that Natasha Roth's passport was being
checked to see if it was in order. One of the guards had
voiced the suspicion that Natasha Roth's passport was a for-
gery. They would have to wait. Her husband looked worried; he wouldn't listen to her reply, but went straight back
to the clearance hut. He leaned towards the window. He
began to talk. It became gradually colder in the car, and
the glass panes clouded over from inside. She had to wipe
the glass with a cloth several times, in order to see what was
going on outside. She watched her husband light his pipe
again, shifting his weight nervously from one leg to the
other. She looked over her shoulder and saw a jeep drive into
her tyre tracks and stop. That might not mean anything. But
if she had wanted to back her car and turn, the jeep would
have made it impossible. She saw the border guard with the
dog approach the administration building. He hurriedly tied
the dog to a post and went in. The man who was perhaps an
officer was still standing at the window. He gesticulated.
Now a fleshy soldier emerged from the administration building, hands in his trouser pockets, gleaming boots; the dog
barked at him. The fleshy soldier walked slowly over to the
clearance hut. Natasha Roth could see her husband lean forward to the window again. Obviously very agitated, he
started to talk once more. The border guard to whom the
dog belonged came out of the administration building. He

untied the dog. He went back to roughly the same place as he had been standing before. She saw her husband straighten up with a shrug of the shoulders. Whatever he had said seemed to have had no effect. The man at the window of the administration building exchanged signs again with the soldier holding the dog. A winter's morning. It was not the time of year for much traffic to cross the border.

Then suddenly everything went quickly and seemingly routinely. The man who was perhaps an officer moved away from the window of the administration building. Natasha Roth could see the two passports being returned to her husband. The soldier with the dog bent down to his animal. Her husband came back to the car, opened the door and sat down behind the wheel. The stop at the border had lasted almost an hour. They drove off, and instead of the disquiet she had just been feeling she was now overcome by apathy. The landscape was empty and flat. Villages were followed by endless forests; pastures were dotted with puddles. She remembered Poznán as a dignified city, painfully tidy and all in pastel colours. In the long winter dusk it had begun to look dirty. Her hotel was outside the city centre, behind a public garden full of unnaturally white birch trees.

In the hotel lobby, her translator rose from a wide armchair. He no longer had a beard, but he had put on weight and his face was very white and rather flabby. He kissed Natasha Roth's hand. "Oh, my dear, everything is in a mess and it's a great pity." As he said this he spread out both arms and shrugged his shoulders. He told her that Krystyna Borowska, the naive painter of animals, trees and people, had died two days ago, very suddenly, at the age of sixty-eight; the translator had only learned about it that morning; he had immediately telephoned Berlin and been told by Natasha Roth's little daughter that her parents were already on their way. It was impossible now to gain access to either the home or the works of Krystyna Borowska. *Nie ma.* They had to respect that. Some time or other it would all be different. When would it all be different? Oh heavens, the estate was in dispute; there was the state; there were influential collectors and hundreds of demands. They would have to wait and see. The translator shrugged his shoulders and spread his hands wide several times as he spoke. Natasha Roth was struck by this manner of gesticulating, which she hadn't noticed during previous meetings. Perhaps such gestures were acquired through foreign fellowships, or they made up for the beard that had been shaved off. Only when she was back in her hotel room and about to unpack her suitcase did it occur to her that she might just as well take the case, go to her car and drive back to Berlin. The disappointment was like an artery being suddenly torn open; blood splashed out, leaving behind emptiness and nausea.

The translator knocked at the door and took her to dinner. He had ordered chicken pastry. He sent for a bottle of vodka. Around them sat groups of Polish-Americans, all of them old people; they had dyed hair and wore bright-coloured clothes; they laughed; they all spoke at the same time. Natasha Roth drank vodka and talked. The name "Bodakov" cropped up. The translator reacted as if he had scarcely heard this name mentioned. Perhaps he was pretending. What reason did he have for pretending? Poland had its own legends, as it had its own language; in any case, all legends grew out of language. Only in her head, in her own and private Natasha Roth world, had the name Bodakov remained important. She asked the translator about the dissident committee of Polish intellectuals. The translator smiled ambiguously and seemed unwilling to attach much importance to the committee. "A social game, you know us, Natasha, we have a natural tendency towards anarchism and megalomania." They drank a lot. The translator ordered another bottle of vodka. The Polish-Americans sang one Slavic folk song after another.

Two hours after midnight she lay in her hotel bed. She had to keep swallowing the bitter liquid that rose up out of her stomach into her mouth. From one of the rooms next to hers came a regular thumping sound. She pictured two old, cosmetically-patched-up Americans copulating, on a too-narrow mattress, under a colour photograph of the summer castle of Vilanóv. Suddenly her mouth was filled with sour slime. With her hand over her mouth, she groped her way into the bathroom, where she took away her hand and vomited into the toilet bowl until there was nothing left but threads of slime hanging from her chin. As though idiotically, she stared at the fallen strip of paper, assuring guests in three languages that the toilet bowl was free from germs. She cleaned her teeth. She left the bathroom, turned on the light in the bedroom and sat down on her husband's bed. He was lying on his back. He immediately opened his eyes.

"You're crazy," he said calmly. "You'll never succeed with anything. I always knew that. Everything you do now is done out of pigheadedness and panic. You can't face growing old. You're ruthless towards everyone. You've got no friends left. Bodakov has been forgotten. You're simply looking for an excuse to ruin yourself. That's the only reason you still cling to that letter."

"We were going to try once more together," she said slowly, slurring her consonants.

"Why should we?"

"You said so yourself."

"I don't remember a thing about it," he said. "Not a thing."

Then he turned his head away and yawned with a gasping sound. Her teeth were chattering. She switched off the light and went back to bed. Next morning her husband complained of a headache. Her translator had driven back to Warsaw three hours ago. They had breakfast among the Polish-Americans, who were again wearing their bright-coloured clothes and all talking at the same time. Natasha

Roth paid the hotel bill, then sat next to her husband in the car. This morning the sun was shining. The streets of Poznán were dry; the city itself suddenly seemed to her once more grave and touching.

They drove through the flat countryside. Over the pastures hung mist; the bare branches of beeches, and of the trees lining the roadside, were glistening. The closer they came to the Oder, the more overcast the sky. Finally rain fell, mingled with snow. The roads grew slippery. At the border they had to wait, this time because a convoy of lorries was being cleared. *A vendre: les corps, les voix, l'immense opulence inquestionable, ce qu'on ne vendra jamais.* She would have to get used once again to the fact that a poet named Arthur Rimbaud had stopped writing and that a convincing explanation for this had yet to be found. For sale: bodies, voices, the immense, unquestionable glut that will never be sold. By the time they were on the autobahn it was afternoon. Snow was now falling thickly. As they turned into their street, she saw that the builders' trailer that had been standing opposite their garden gate had gone.

41 DURING A WALK in the forest the bitch had pulled down a sick deer. Stefan had to go home and fetch a spade, with which he dug a hole in the wet sand. This was difficult because of the tree roots he kept coming up against. He buried the dead beast and stamped the earth down flat. Herr Merck, a qualified electronics engineer, was an enthusiastic angler in summer and autumn. In winter he turned into an equally enthusiastic skier. In good time, he had booked a longish stay

in the High Tatras during the two-week school holidays.
Now he had left to drive through Bohemia with his family
in their own car. He wasn't going to find much winter waiting for him. The radio related that depression reigned in all
the famous winter tourist resorts. Stefan received three picture
postcards with Slavic addresses on them. Vera went hiking.
The paths were covered in mud. During the day sunshine
alternated with rain. Stefan played gramophone records.
From time to time he woke from his apathy and made a date
with Thomas and they went to the bowling alley in the
Rathausstrasse.

Suddenly one morning Rebecca was standing in the Roths'
doorway. She was carrying a shabby canvas hold-all and her
guitar. She had come back from Usedom Island. A pipe had
burst in her flat and Rebecca had watched with amazement
as water poured from her wall. She had written a note to the
manager of the building telling him of the damage and then
left the key to the flat with neighbours. She had walked to
Friedrichstrasse Station, and here she was at the house of her
friend Natasha Roth, who had many rooms and undamaged
plumbing.

Rebecca was to live on the upper storey, right next to the
rooms of Stefan and Billa. Rebecca's room was small and
dark; Rebecca slept there, spent many hours there; she played
her guitar and sang, recording on tape anything she thought
worthwhile. This was how she wrote her songs. Strange
noises, alien to this house. In Stefan's ears they sounded stri-
dent, but he soon grew accustomed to them. He saw the
little dark-haired woman walking down the corridors with
soundless steps. She sang, was silent, talked, slept; she talked
to the dog a lot. Stefan heard her uttering incomprehensible
words: perhaps it was Serbian; the dog didn't react noticeably, it was friendly to everyone, even strangers. The songs
she sang were about animals, about hedgehogs and horses,

about moles, snakes, fish and beetles. Gypsy food, said Rebecca, gypsy animals. He heard her say the only cousins the Jews had were the gypsies, forever persecuted, forever on the run; gypsies could be understood only by gypsies, or by Jews. Why did she tell him that? Was she trying to convince him of something, and if so, why? She talked about the endless wanderings of her brothers, beginning in the Pamirs, through Persia and Asia Minor, with a detour through Egypt, which gained them the name gypsy or Pharaoh. Then along the shores of the Mediterranean, through the Balkans and the old Austro-Hungary as far as the Rhone delta, as far as Spain. Rebecca told him about green caravans, about fortune-tellers, scissors grinders, tinsmiths, bear tamers. She described the flight of the three Marys from Judea, across the Mediterranean, and Sarah, the child of the gypsy king, floated to meet the three Marys on an outspread cloth, brought them ashore and led them to the red earth of Provence, where vines, oranges and almonds grew. Rebecca's stories began to get entangled with the stories of Stefan's mother. This was strange. Rebecca said that Mary, Miriam, was the Hebrew word for resistance. Three times Jewish resistance was three times flight. Sarah was the Jewish word for princess. Sarah was the name of Abraham's wife, Isaac's mother, wife of the father of mankind, the father of the Jews; Sarah was the name of the gypsy's daughter at the foot of Mont Ventoux. No name was a coincidence. The same name meant the same person. The gypsies' caravan was the other Diaspora, describing hundreds of arabesques around the same space; the Mediterranean, that means the centre of the earth; in the green caravan sat the eternal Jew Ahasuerus, and the most brilliant bear tamer was Süss Oppenheimer, who ended up in a bear cage himself. There had always been just two races of men: persecutors and victims.

Rebecca's songs were about the great gypsy processions near Aigues-Mortes, in which walked the living, the mur-

dered, the saints, the forgotten, the unborn, the ghosts. There
is a light put out by the wind. There is a forest inn that a
drunken man leaves in the afternoon. There is a wine jug,
burned and black and full of holes, full of spiders. Trakl had
committed suicide. Was there any reason why Rebecca
should commit suicide? Trakl couldn't stand the war. In the
morning Stefan often used to see her walking along the upstairs corridor. She had a short neck and bare, white shoulders.

He often went for walks in the forest with Rebecca, always accompanied by the dog and sometimes by Billa. Dampness dripped from the pines. The ground was black. Rebecca
knew names, descriptions, stories of plants which to Stefan
were merely clumps of rotting leaves; she grubbed up roots
from the soil, sniffed them, giggled and talked about plant
magic, miracle-working plants, forest spirits, animals changed
into something else; this was magic root, also called false
mandrake, since the real one grew at the centre of the earth,
the Mediterranean, where gypsies and Jews lived. White
bryony grew in this soil only for Rebecca's sake. Mandrake
or mandragora is a magic plant, a love potion; its forked
root is like a man and it screams when torn from the soil; its
roots are curved like the sickles with which a plant is separated
from its root. The Druids, Celtic priests, carried golden
sickles. The Celts came from the east, from the Caucasus,
Colchis, went to the Balkans, the Mediterranean, like the
gypsies, like the Jews; they were slaughtered, persecuted,
destroyed, leaving only their myths behind, Arthur and the
Grail; that was on Mont Ventoux in Provence, where the
gypsy child Sarah lived.

The locality was suddenly invaded by wild boars. It was
like an answer to Rebecca's stories; perhaps she had actually
wanted it and brought it about by witchcraft. Herds of
sows, runners, tuskers and yearlings burst into the area at
dusk. They trotted along the streets. They rooted about in
the gardens. They lay down and wallowed in the public

parks. Dreadful stories were going the rounds: a tusker accidentally struck by a motorcyclist, instead of fleeing, had
attacked the machine and destroyed it; the injured driver was
in hospital in a critical condition. A dog had been ripped
open by a sow and bled to death. Rebecca related the story
of the devils which entered a herd of swine at the command of
the Messiah, whereupon the swine plunged into the water
with the infernal spirits in their bodies and drowned. This
reminded Stefan of Vera, who might have told him a similar
story. He thought of the fact that Vera was now staying where
for a long time Rebecca had had to live. This thought was
full of dark, unexpected connexions which he didn't want to
admit. But his joints trembled. Sleep-plant and dream-flower.
Rebecca devoured tablets from the palm of her hand with
greedily opened jaws as though they were sweets. "I'm
hooked, you know. I need poisons to survive. I have to drug
myself, you know. Otherwise I shall go crazy." Her little
crystals were frozen dreams. The poet Trakl from Salzburg
had been hooked. *Deep is the slumber in dark poisons, filled
with stars and the white face of the mother, the face of stone.*
He pictured himself one night, drunk with sleep, groping his
way from his room to hers. With the care of a sleep-walker
he would open her door and enter a warm smell that was
poisonous and perhaps obscene. Rebecca would have called
him inaudibly and conjured him with gypsy magic spells, so
she would be waiting for him already awake. She wouldn't
even make a sound as he entered, either of surprise or of
triumph. With unerring certainty he would find the way to
her arms. He would have her dry hands on his face. He
would let her take the fabric from his body. In astonishment
he would rub himself against her. Her skin would seem to
him too soft, too ample, her smell too penetrating, until he
was completely permeated by it, until he merely obeyed his
reflexes. He would perhaps have a sudden picture of frogs

coupling by the edge of a summer pond. The surface would
be green with duck-weed, and above it would hover dragon-
flies. Everything would be strange, sweet and also rather dis-
gusting. That was how he pictured it and he would have difficulty next day in not believing it was real.

The following evening West German television broadcast
a one-hour feature on the exiled poet Arnold Bodakov. The
programme had been well publicized, on the radio too. It
was preceded by an economics programme dealing with tax
savings and investments. Stefan's father came in late and sat
down beside Rebecca. For Stefan, the name Bodakov belonged to a past which, despite the dates in the calendar, lay
immensely far behind him. Perhaps this past wanted to catch
up with him and was now trying to do so. He knew that Rebecca had had a child by Bodakov that was stillborn.

The Bodakov broadcast started. The letters lay golden-
yellow on a black background. Stefan leaned forward, as
though being closer to the screen meant being closer to the
person shown on it. He now saw the individual lines of the
picture. He saw the moving outlines indistinctly, double, a
shower of coloured snow drifted over faces and objects. The
poet Bodakov walked down glistening, rain-wet streets. In
the background, black against the pale-brown sky, stood a
conveyor-tower. Bodakov was in a town in the Ruhr; viewers
had been told beforehand that he now lived there. Bodakov
went into a tavern; he sat down at a table with a bright-
coloured check cloth; he smoked, drank, chewed and stared
intently into space. Meanwhile, other people were standing
round the bar, chatting. The man behind the bar fiddled with
a radio. Over everything lay Bodakov's voice; all actions and
feelings were explained by it. He was bitter, said Bodakov.
He felt hate, which was, of course, unjust. Hate was always
unjust, but he felt hate. After this an express was shown stopping at the main station in Cologne. The doors opened. From

one of the open doors stepped a fair-haired woman and four children. Bodakov was standing on the platform. He embraced the woman and lifted up one of the children. Bodakov's voice said that five weeks after his expulsion his family had been allowed to join him. Stefan turned his head and looked at Rebecca, who was sitting curled up in her chair smoking. She seemed to be looking past the television set. Her eyes were wide open.

The film now showed a furniture van bearing the name Deutrans. Removal men were unloading boxes. Bodakov's voice said he wasn't looking for a comfortable life, he didn't want wealth, he wanted to remain sensitive to the injustices of this world. Then the film showed excerpts from a public reading. Bodakov was standing in a large bookshop; since he was evidently short-sighted, he was bent over close to the reading-desk. In front of him people were sitting packed tightly together; they were gripped by his reading and their faces were full of concern; from time to time they bent their heads. To Stefan, Bodakov's voice sounded very stiff. Bodakov read a story; his voice was now relayed outside the bookshop; the story concerned bad events that had happened in the GDR, but in these surroundings and in Bodakov's mouth the GDR sounded like an uninhabited area on another planet. Stefan understood the language Bodakov was speaking. He knew the words he used. None of the names that cropped up were unfamiliar to him. Nevertheless, none of this concerned him. Was he insensitive? He didn't know much about stories that could be written down. He lived wrapped up in his own particular world, made up of his illness, of the people he knew, of the strange customs in this house, of his own confused feelings, of his parents' moods. Nothing in it was like anywhere else. But where was anything the same as everywhere else? Where were yardsticks? Who applied them and sorted them out? Once Bodakov made a slip of the tongue.

Instead of immediately correcting himself, he looked up. He stuck out his chin; he looked into the faces of his audience and into the camera lens. His black eyes now seemed dull. He looked helpless. He looked hopeless, like someone who had lost all ties and all certainties, who had nothing left but fear of life, of time, of certain people and also of himself. In this moment, which lasted perhaps two seconds, Stefan began to understand Bodakov. Bodakov's fear was like Stefan's fear. Every fear resembled every other fear. Bodakov went on reading. The story ended as badly as it had started. The final shot showed Bodakov with broad shoulders and bent back walking slowly away down a night-time street. In the background once more stood the conveyor-tower. Yellow letters ran up the screen listing the credits. "He has remained a self-pitying Stalinist," Stefan heard his father say. "Rebecca will have to excuse me." His father left the room. Stefan saw that Rebecca didn't react. Her mouth didn't open, her hand didn't rise. Probably she had swallowed a lot of tablets that evening, before the film started, just in case.

Next morning she was gone. Since she had taken her guitar, one had to assume that she had gone for quite a while. Her canvas hold-alls were still standing in the room she had occupied. She must have left the house very early. Stefan looked for her telephone number in his mother's notebook. He dialled it several times, but no one picked up the receiver. There was a violent quarrel between his parents because of his father's remark about Bodakov. "You drove her away," screamed his mother. "You meant to drive her away." Stefan went into the room she had occupied, in which her bags stood and in which there was a faint smell of ether. He should have gone to her while there was still time; that would have been better than dreaming about it now. He should have risked her misunderstanding his visit, slapping his face; but perhaps she would have clung to his neck as though with steel bands and dragged him into the middle of her intoxication. He thought of the gypsy legends she had told him, of Del, the ancient god, who created the starry firmament, and Beng, who represented evil, a chestnut-brown Uriel. He thought of the temple of flesh which could be eaten, which men had eaten; since then God had wandered the earth homeless and punished his greedy children.

Next day he went to Berlin. He went to the Auguststrasse, to the house where Rebecca lived. He rang at her door. No one opened it. He rang several times more. Nobody came whom he could have asked for information. Slowly he went down the stairs again, crossed the courtyard and went out into the street. He walked down the Friedrichstrasse to the station. He took the train home again. The compartment in which he was sitting was empty, apart from two women wearing dark fur coats. On their laps stood full plastic bags, which they held with both arms. Their painted mouths moved busily. Their faces were powdered, but their changes of expression had caused cracks in the layer of powder. They looked at one another as though at mirror images. Sometimes they both spoke at once. You're dead, dead, he thought mechanically. You have no idea how unreal you are.

He clung to the word *unreal*. It explained everything. It allowed him to sleep, eat, move and utter sentences. It soothed him when news of Rebecca came. She had made an application to give up her citizenship and three days later had received permission to leave the country. She had left all her furniture behind. She had boarded an express with nothing but a bag full of books, manuscripts and official documents and had got out in Bremen. This was reported one evening in the West German television news. The canvas hold-alls still stood in the Roths' house. Stefan's father said Ferenc Butterman could take the bags across the border and then mail them. Stefan's mother sat in her room and got drunk.

I SEE THE HEAVY furniture van and trailer moving off 42
down the street. The vehicles sway on the uneven roadway.
I walk back along the path from the garden gate to the front
door, which is open and gives a view into a largely empty
building. The floor polish bears grey marks, dirt from the
soles of the removal men's shoes. I shall never enter this house
again. Its emptiness distracts me, its dirt propitiates me, only
in my children's eyes do I perceive an expression of sorrow
and helplessness, much more than of anticipation. I force
myself not to say anything consoling to them, because I'm
afraid that if I did their feelings would be communicated to
me and infect me. With feigned gruffness I push my children
into motion, so that their arms no longer hang limp and lifeless by their sides, but are bent once more or begin to swing.

We walk to the car. The doors on the right side are open,
revealing how many things (coats, bags, a transistor radio, a
camera) are piled up on the seats. The children have difficulty in finding room to sit among all this baggage. They
push things away from themselves and towards each other.
They start to quarrel about the space. They are behaving
more irritably and childishly than they should at their age.
I have to attribute these outbreaks to present circumstances.
I sit behind the wheel; the engine starts at once and at once
my children fall silent, forgetting their quarrel. The sound
of the engine tells them that the journey is about to begin
and that, if they want to imprint this house on their minds
once more, this is their last chance. I have to turn round with
my right arm over the back of the seat, in order to look out
of the rear window as I reverse the car. I see my children's
faces, turned as it were simultaneously to the house and to
some unknown place. Their pupils are large; the expression
of their mouths betrays fear. I sound the horn before driving

out of the garden into the street. I see no pedestrian and no vehicle. There was never much traffic in this street.

We drive to the crossroads. There I have to stop on account of a streetcar that is switching tracks. On the driver's platform stands a fat, red-faced woman with blond-dyed hair. I can now watch my children in the rear-view mirror. They are holding their heads still, looking at their knees and hands. I turn into the main street. The tarmac is damp. Behind the garden fences on either side bonfires are burning sluggishly, because of the damp air. Thin, blue-grey trails of smoke lie across the street; we rip them apart; for several seconds traces of their smell will remain in the car. On the office building of the market garden hangs a large sign, white letters on a black background: a sentence extolling the Petrograd revolution which, reckoned backwards from the coming autumn, took place exactly sixty years ago. Why did I never notice this sign before? Why do I notice it today? My children pay no attention to the sign nor to the sentence. Only when the market garden building is behind us do they raise their faces and look out of the window on their own side.

We drive past the abandoned check-point at the city boundary. More white ground mist lies over a patch of forest that has been ploughed but not yet planted with slips. The children point out path-openings to one another; on previous trips they have noticed deer crossing these paths. We meet another streetcar. It is swaying. Behind the windows of the two cars I see heads, sometimes hands, many of the hands are holding a newspaper; I can't explain why the sight of this streetcar should fill me with a bitter feeling of pain. I'm driving along streets I have driven along thousands of times before. In Köpenick, as always, the traffic piles up in front of the person on point-duty, a young woman; she is wearing a shiny white raincoat; her cap is pulled down low over her forehead. There is a smell of moisture, exhaust gas and burnt coffee. The children have started to talk. In a whisper, they exchange words I can't understand.

The Wuhlheide. The crossing to Karlshorst and Ober-schöneweide. The Radio Station. The Power Station. The building workers. The alternating interruptions of traffic lights and policemen on point-duty that I have known for a long time, to whose signals my reactions are like reflexes. Along the Boxhagener Strasse to the Frankfurter Allee, with a detour via the Bersarinstrasse because it is illegal to turn off earlier. Before turning at the Frankfurter Tor, I switch on the radio. It is tuned to the American Forces Network in West Berlin. I switch over to the local station and an emotional female voice is detailing the grandeur, planning, dimensions and technology of the new municipality to be built at Marzahn. We drive towards the television tower. The sky is greyish-yellow. At various crossroads along the Frank-furter Allee the traffic lights are out of action. The children have fallen silent. Their eyes are attentive. Their faces are frightened. I switch the radio on again. My hands are damp. I feel a pressure from the thyroid constricting my oesoph-agus; obviously my blood pressure is up; I feel pressure in my ears, it's as though I had suddenly gone deaf. The Alexanderplatz. I must get into the left-hand lane. I have to wait a long time for the green light. Out of nervousness I switch the radio on again. Again the American Forces Net-work. Piano music. I call out to my children that I've always preferred Unter den Linden; my children don't answer; I realize that I have made a remark that is inappropriate under the circumstances; it occurs to me that I haven't uttered a single sentence apart from this one during the whole journey so far. I turn right into the Friedrichstrasse. Psychologically I am now in a state on the borderline between absolute agita-tion and total indifference. I try in vain to read the neon letters on the railway bridge off Friedrichstrasse Station. Instead, I have to concentrate on maintaining the right speed for the pedestrian crossing between the two station entrances. The Weidendamm Bridge. The Hannoversche Strasse. The whitish-grey building of the West German mission. At the next traffic light I turn left into the Invalidenstrasse. On the left I see the grey building of the Natural History Museum. I always meant to go to this museum with my daughter. She asked me to take her several times; I never could or would; now she is kind enough not to remind me of it. The pianist on the radio plays *These Foolish Things*. The secret of trivial songs is that they are painfully right in all situations. I see the building site at the Robert-Koch-Platz. I switch the radio off again.

I stop at the first turnpike. A border guard, a dejected face above a thick overcoat, walks round our car. He takes the passports I hand him through the open window, opens them, reads them. I look back at my children. They are gazing with wide-open eyes that express nothing but curiosity at the plump little border guard leafing through the pale-blue pages. I wonder what would happen if I took back the passports but then, instead of crossing the border, turned the car, drove back to the Alexanderplatz, stopped at the Ministry of the Interior and informed them that I had changed my mind, that I didn't want to emigrate, that I wished to apply for restitution of citizenship—weren't they familiar with the crazy ideas the writer N.R. sometimes got into her head? Beside me, on the right front seat, the yellow document releasing me from GDR citizenship lies within reach. The border guard doesn't want to see this document. He returns the passports. He presses a switch. The turnpike opens. The border guard puts his hand to his cap in salute. I drive the car in front of the customs building. Knowing what will happen now, I release the bonnet catch. I get out and open

the boot. I tell my children to get out too. In front of us
a white limousine belonging to a small, bald-headed man in a
pale-yellow coat is being examined. He has difficulty in
getting the rear seat back into place after the customs officer
has lifted it up; his bald head goes red with the effort. I can
see my children draw each other's attention to this sight.
They giggle. A young customs officer comes over to us. He
looks at our passports; seeing all the coats, he does not raise
the rear seat, merely pressing on the upholstery several times
with outspread hands. He slips a mirror under the chassis.
My children, especially my son, follow these actions with
great interest. The customs officer returns the passports. I
close the bonnet. I close the boot. I tell my children to get
in. Our passports are stamped by a border guard who knows
me. He is an elderly man. On previous occasions he always
greeted me by name as I crossed the border. This time he
doesn't. He seems to have known in advance why we are
crossing. He brings our passports back quickly. He too
salutes by putting his right hand to his cap. I drive around
the two long concrete obstacles. My children hold their heads
to one side. The last turnpike is opened. We are still driving
on the Invalidenstrasse, on the other section; we are driving
in the other section of this city; we are driving in the other
section of this world. We shall never be able to return again.
Nevermore. The point of no return. Is there a pop song with
this title that could be played by a pianist on the American
Forces Network? I wonder whether to switch the radio on
again, but don't do so.

I drive down the Invalidenstrasse to Alt-Moabit. From
there to the Grosser Stern, to the Reuterplatz, down the Her-
denbergstrasse to the Zoo Station. I turn into the Joachimsthaler Strasse, then the Kurfürstendamm, then into the
Meineckestrasse. This route too I am not driving for the first
time today. In the rear-view mirror I can see that my chil-

dren are beginning to realize what has happened to them. Their faces have gone white. Their eyes have gone black. Almost scared, they are looking at the stream of shiny, bright-coloured cars, the seething groups of Anatolians, at exotically shaped concrete, at monuments and scenes which hitherto have been merely photographs and stories, that is to say, unreal. Have they now become more real, more tangible? In the Parkhaus there is a smell of urine. My children look at the passers-by with their different movements, their different faces, their different laughter, their different cruelty. I spot two phone booths just where the Meineckestrasse runs into the Kurfürstendamm. I have to force myself not to go to them. I can imagine myself putting two ten-pfennig pieces in the slot and then, after dialling 0–372, calling my own number. No one would answer. I was tempted to obey a pointless reflex. Nevertheless, I feel as though I have just suffered a particularly painful loss; this feeling upsets me so much that I go with my children into a tavern I know in this street. It is dark inside; there is a smell of tobacco, of alcohol, of pork, of exuded vigorous petty-bourgeois contentment. A waiter comes to our table. He leans forward slightly. He is wearing a green waistcoat. I order orange juice for my children, beer and vodka for myself. Sadly, with secret despair, I see the fatigue in the white faces of my children. There are some compulsions that can only be escaped if you go through them in your imagination, step by step, from one detail to the next. For Natasha Roth the possibility of her Exodus had been one of these. Now she was finally set free from it.

THE WINTER HOLIDAYS were over; school was beginning; Stefan would see Vera again. He told himself he didn't
need to feel uncomfortable about it; he didn't feel guilty,
just as before he hadn't felt innocent. When he took her
hand, it was as if he were taking hold of a smooth animal.
He heard himself laugh; he heard the false laughter of a
stranger, who for this mendacious instant had assumed his
body and his face. He uttered the same words and sentences
as in the past. He walked with her along the same streets,
stopped at the same places and sat on the same chairs as in
the past. Everything had become in a paralysing way futile.
He no longer felt the need for any special conversations or
special actions. Incomprehensible that things could completely change in such a short time. But what was time? How
was the length or shortness of time to be measured? He acted
in every situation under the same pressure of habit under
which he brushed his hair in the morning and washed his
feet in the evening. He drank the tea which she made, which
her mother made, which Herr Merck, the engineer, told
him was the very best Orange Pekoe, bought in Prague, in
St Wenceslas Square, where you could get such things, unlike here. Herr Merck opened the piano to play, Schumann,
Chopin, empty finger exercises, music that had become superficial for a world grown superficial, in which people ran
around each other like insects.

Once more Ferenc Butterman was a frequent visitor at the
Roths'. He was working on a series of articles on the up-
keep of the old city centres in this country. He asked Stefan's
father for information, details, examples, oversights; rather
casually he added that he was shortly going to close his
agency office in the GDR and move to Hong Kong. Hong
Kong, he said, was in many ways an ideal city for him. It was

43

so restricted in space that every kind of movement, especially on foot, was impossible. Stefan's father had just bought a car of his own, a compact, thereby at last making himself independent of the yellow car, which was now only driven by Natasha Roth.

Then one evening the radio news reported that four students had been arrested by the GDR authorities for trying to stage a demonstration in favour of the expelled author Bodakov; after being released without legal proceedings, they had left at their own wish for West Germany. Stefan saw that at this news his mother nodded with a look of relief. He couldn't figure out what cause for relief there was here. He didn't have much time to think about it. His friend Thomas attempted suicide by jumping into the street from the second floor of the school building.

It had happened during school hours, at the beginning of the third class of the day, immediately after a long break. The window was usually closed. First Thomas had to get the key from the caretaker; he must have thought up some excuse and the excuse must have been convincing. Thomas was convincing in everything he did; he was a quiet, adroit lad with a soft voice. The class from which Thomas had been missing was a mathematics class. There was to be a written test in this class. Everyone, Stefan included, thought Thomas had stayed away because he was afraid of this test. It was odd that he didn't return when this class was over.

Then word went round that someone had been found outside the school, unconscious, evidently suffering from internal injuries but still alive. For the moment Thomas was forgotten. Everyone saw the ambulance driving off with its blue light, siren and fluttering Red Cross flag. People were gathered at the side of the street. Apparently, the injured person had lain there for half an hour. People must have passed, but no one bothered about him; perhaps they took him for a drunk. It never occurred to anyone that the injured person and Thomas were one and the same.

This information was given to the class by a teacher. No one could understand it. It might have been merely a ridiculous accident. But it wasn't an accident, said the teacher. All faces were now turned towards Stefan, who suddenly felt as though he were partially to blame for this event. And yet he knew nothing, nothing; Thomas had behaved towards him exactly the same that day as on other days; he hadn't seemed worried; he hadn't shown the slightest sign of any disturbance. How did someone behave who planned to step out of life in an hour? *Frost and smoke. A white shirt of stars burns the shoulders that wear it and God's vultures rend your metallic heart.* How had Trakl behaved before he swallowed his deadly dose of cocaine? Trakl's suicide had succeeded; Thomas lay in the observation ward at Köpenick Hospital.

The teachers announced that no one would be allowed to see Thomas for the present; there was no point in going to the hospital at the moment. Stefan went to the house in which Thomas's parents lived. He rang the bell. No one opened the door. He could picture Thomas's parents anxiously holding each other's hand, sitting on two plastic chairs in a hospital corridor; there was a smell of iodoform; they looked fearfully into the face of every passing ward sister; they waited for news of their son. A person could end his life simply because it seemed called for, out of weariness, on account of some sudden, groundless idea, living was exasperating, death a beautiful, final freedom. As soon as the first shock had worn off, Stefan felt secretly, admiringly proud of Thomas. He alone could understand Thomas, his secretly beloved brother.

Then all sorts of rumours began to spread. Reasons for the suicide attempt were given. Confused, commonplace, totally incomprehensible pretexts which Stefan had heard nothing about and which he resolutely refused to believe. According to these rumours, Thomas had belonged to a group of young people who met regularly in an old house near Jannowitz-brücke Station, in Berlin. In this group he had met a girl. She was not yet fourteen, which Thomas may or may not have known. The girl was the daughter of a high-ranking army officer. She had become pregnant by Thomas. For an abortion, she needed her parents' consent, but she didn't dare tell her parents because of her age and also because she was afraid for Thomas, so that the time for an abortion had slipped past. Now Thomas and the girl suddenly had the desperate idea of going to Sweden, or to England, Austria, Italy, Hamburg. Thomas had made inquiries at foreign embassies. He had sat in taverns in the Friedrichstrasse, the Alexanderplatz, the Schönhauser Allee, trying to make contact with people who, for money, would smuggle others out of the country; perhaps he had actually made such contacts. One day a summons arrived ordering Thomas to report to the police station. He was at once convinced that everything he had done, and everything he planned to do, had been discovered. He was at his wits' end. Actually, the summons merely concerned a traffic violation. The police simply intended to warn Thomas.

Stefan found this story miserable, pathetic; he laughed when the details were presented to him; utter rubbish, he cried with a laugh, dismissing all doubt with a wave of the hand; but he knew that he was simply trying to save a legend that was beyond saving. He, Stefan, had known, had suspected, nothing, because Thomas had told him nothing. The two of them had walked side by side and each deceived the other. *A black covering is our silence and out of it from time to time steps a gentle beast and slowly lowers its heavy lids.* "Damn Trakl, damn friendship," he yelled into the void. The effort made itching tears rise into the inner corners of his eyes. He saw before him a sick-bed with Thomas lying in it, his skull bandaged, and beside the bed, at peace, Thomas's parents, also an army general with golden epaulettes, also a long-haired girl whose six-month belly bulged beneath her skirt. They would all be contentedly smiling. They would all confess that there were worse things. Something very bad had just, just barely, been avoided. The baby would be carried to term. It would grow up in secure conditions. The under-age parents would put engagement rings on their fingers. Thomas would take his school-leaving certificate. Thomas would marry, study, grow fat, the satisfied, contented father of an infant that crawled about the floor crowing.

During one break, Vera told him she wouldn't be able to see him as often as before. At most, at school during the breaks, when it couldn't be avoided, not outside any more, not at home. Her father had forbidden her. He had only just found out that Stefan was Natasha Roth's son. He apologized for not having looked into it before; the truth was that Vera couldn't afford to be close friends with the son of such a person. The Mercks were practising Catholics. Under the circumstances of the country they lived in, that was encumbrance enough; Vera couldn't assume any additional burden; therefore he forbade her to see Stefan. Vera had to admit he was right. Of course, she very much regretted this end to their friendship; in a way, it had all been very nice. She smiled sincerely as she said this.

Strangely enough, it was only afterwards that it occurred to him he might have raised objections. But what could you say to someone who had herself offered no resistance to such an order? The longer he thought about it, the more pointless every conceivable action appeared. He should have reacted at once, and what really bothered him the most was that he had been incapable of doing so. Gradually, apart from an all-embracing humiliation, he also felt something like relief. He was suddenly freed from all imaginable conflict. He didn't have to yield to the gradual petrifaction of feeling and then himself humiliate someone. There was even enjoyment, satisfaction, in the fact that he could suffer injustice and yet remain outwardly unmoved. He would read no more poetry. He would sure as hell never run the risk of writing poetry himself. He would burn Trakl's book. He would get drunk on his mother's liquor until his stomach turned over and he watched dully, almost unconscious, as vomit poured from his mouth and onto his clothes. He would steal two West German bank-notes from his mother's desk and, with a cigarette in the corner of his mouth, pick up a tart in the foreign-currency area of the Hotel Stadt Berlin, go with her to a dark corner of the City Station and fuck her till bloody slime ran down into the backs of her knees. He discovered, and this simply made him feel sad, that he was far more hurt than he wanted to admit. He carried out none of his senseless, undiscriminating projects. He sat in his room and listened to gramophone records. When he discovered how contrived and superficial Mick Jagger's vocalizing of his sexuality was, for example, he grinned and was pleased by the acuity with which he saw through so many things. He kept telling himself: she has a much too fleshy chin. She isn't beautiful at all. Every contact with her skin caused him a fleeting, painful shudder. In recollection much more than in reality. He had to admit that perhaps Herr Merck's arguments were completely sound.

Two days later, the first signs of spring suddenly appeared. When he walked in the forest with his mother, the leafless trees looked naked, hostile and dirty. They let the dog off the leash. The animal ran down the sandy path with its tail low, a big brownish-white patch behind which the dirt flew up in lumps. The dog turned off to one side and vanished among the larch trees. Stefan playfully tore off a branch as he walked past; he smelled it, then it occurred to him that this was a Thomas action or a Rebecca action. His mother and he had so far not uttered a word. This absence of words became as irritating to Stefan as an itch; he felt his brain positively swelling under the pressure of associations connected with words like love, death, future, life, disgust.

He asked: "Has anything actually changed for you?"

"What do you mean?"

"Oh," he said. "During the last few months. Because of what happened."

"No," she said.

"Are you proud of what you did?"

"No."

He heard so much weariness behind her replies that he suddenly felt an almost overwhelming tenderness and warmth for this person who was walking with him on this churned-up sandy path and who was his mother. He wondered how he could translate his feelings into an adequate and unambiguous action, instead of any words. His mother said: "Have the last few weeks been difficult for you too?" She didn't wait for his answer, but supplied it herself. "You can't have noticed anything. You're still children. Thank God." At this, he kicked a stone ahead of them with his toe. So that at least he could make some violent movement. He hoped the dog would come back from among the trees with a bleeding rabbit between its jaws. Or they would find the worm-eaten corpse of a bird, stinking, rotten, with encrusted feathers. These were just fantasies. The dog found nothing. It came back without being called and stayed at heel the rest of the way. They didn't talk any more.

In the evening he drove with his father to Köpenick Castle. An exhibition was to be opened there, organized by his

father and showing the works of a Chilean painter called
Vicente León. In the car park, Stefan saw Ferenc Butterman's car. There were about eighty people in the exhibition
rooms. Ferenc Butterman approached Stefan with heavy
steps; Stefan drew in his head, but this didn't stop Ferenc
Butterman from stroking his hair. There were three short
speeches, the last one delivered by Stefan's father. The
eighty people walked slowly around, came to a stop and
looked at pictures, drawings, woodcuts, oils on cardboard.
The subjects were Indians, cocks, doves, flutes, guitars, trees.
The faces in the pictures resembled those on pre-Columbian
monuments in Latin America. The painter explained in halting German that in his pictures he was trying to tell the story
of his homeland, in the metaphorical language of the Indians.
He was a small man, still young, with a round head and long
black hair; the skin on his face, neck and hands was yellow.
An hour later, fifteen of the original eighty people were
sitting in Stefan's father's office. They sat on the chairs that
looked old and valuable, but which Stefan knew from his
father were only imitations. The painter wiped his forehead
and throat several times with a checked cloth. He was laughing now; he seemed relieved. The fact that he was sweating
was perhaps a sign that he had been under a strain. Ferenc
Butterman rose, a glass in his hand, stood beside the painter
and started a conversation with him. Stefan recognized the
woman he knew his father had wanted to marry. She was
pouring tea and hot water into a large can. A lot of cigarettes were being smoked. The woman avoided looking at
Stefan, as though she didn't know him. His father was sitting
on the edge of his desk, sucking at his pipe, obviously pleased
with the evening. The painter began to tell the story of his
life. He was the son of a lawyer from Santiago. His uncle
had been a well-known figure in the police force, a Socialist
and a personal friend of Allende. The painter said that in

those days he hadn't bothered with politics, but after the takeover by the generals he had immediately lost his position as a teacher at the College of Art in Santiago. He became a sailor on a North American fishing boat. He didn't want to remain unemployed and perhaps in the end starve. A dull job. Catching spider crabs for California delicatessens. After four-teen months he left the ship and came to Europe with the money he had saved, Rome, Vienna, Munich, Frankfurt-am-Main and finally Berlin. He now had a teaching post in Weissensee. This was his first one-man show. "How do you feel in this city?" Ferenc Butterman asked him. "Fine," said the painter, "great." "No problems?" asked Butterman. "No," said the painter. "Doesn't it bother you that you don't find any ideal freedoms in this country?" "What are ideal free-doms?" said the painter. "I couldn't live in Chile any more. I can live here." Butterman said: "Here you fit into the gen-eral landscape; you're the nephew of a well-known Socialist." "I'm a painter," said León. "Here I can paint pictures; here I can get an exhibition for my pictures." Ferenc Butterman said: "You consider this country perfect?" "I don't know any perfect country," said the painter. "Perfection is terrible. It means there's nothing left to do."

Ferenc Butterman laughed and drank from his vodka glass. Stefan's eyes were smarting. He would have liked to spit on the floor, just for something to do. He saw his father's con-tented face through the tobacco smoke. He heard Ferenc Butterman and Vicente León talking now about painting. As they drove home together, his father told him the divorce would take place in May.

44 Dear Verlaine, I am dictating this letter with a half-paralysed tongue to my sister Isabelle, who has become a Sister of Mercy to me. She has selflessly sacrificed to me the fading remnant of her youth, and the only way in which I could express my gratitude was to become converted. This happened in the same manner as your own conversion, that is to say unexpectedly and with the likelihood of not lasting very long. I put an end to yours; mine will be ended by a great journey. To rocks in which sun is stored, or into the paradises of angelic poppies, or into that fire through which my spirit has already passed once at the price of ink on paper.

Will my voice still reach you? I am lying at the moment in the Hospital of the Immaculate Conception. I remember how all your life you had a horror of hospitals, exceeded only by your horror of prisons. It will be a triumph for you to learn the state I am now in: one leg was amputated over three months ago, just below the groin. This was the last resort, after my knee had swollen to the size of a pumpkin and I was screaming with pain. I spent the summer in Roche, on my grandparents' farm, limping from one field to another on crutches. When the pony wasn't being used for anything else, I was able to drive around in a wooden cart, like a leper; only the rattle was missing.

People tell me that at the moment you're hiding out with a whore. They say you're rotten with absinthe, tearful, cowardly—but that's the way you always were. They say you've done good business with my poems in Paris. This news, I confess, affected me deeply. In my thirty-seventh year I have become as greedy for money as an old peasant. And I look like one too, for my skin is like leather, my hair is grey and my hands are cracked.

I believe I shall die soon. Most of the time I swim in a sea of opium—not at all out of the arrogant recklessness of a dandy, like my former demigod Baudelaire. I do so out of the most pressing necessity. Otherwise I should be racked by pain. But like this I am peaceful. The poison bears me in an ivory litter past all the ikons of my life. On some of them I see the gentle face of my beloved Yami from Ogaden, on others yours.

I know I ruined you. You fired on me; I beat you up on the banks of the Neckar. So we both carried away our scars. You merely inwardly, but you too have been marked since then as forever an outcast. We foundered on one another, since we were both destined to founder. If you wish to ex-culpate yourself before your God, you had better not call upon me as a witness, since I was merely a messenger of Fate. Even without me, you would have become a drunken, filthy queer.

Twenty years ago I wrote that the two great passions of my life were love and art. Today I know better: the two passions of my life have been revolution and poetry. When I gave up one, I had to give up the other. I became a vaga-bond, a tramp, a hashish-eater, a trickster, a trader, a peasant, a derelict. I know things have gone pretty much the same for you as for me, only here too, as in everything else, you are half-hearted for the reason that all half-hearted people choose to be so: they live rather longer. The Revolution, Verlaine. For you it was an excuse to be drunk most of the time. What a good thing that when bread began to be short in besieged Paris, the Commune's supply of wine remained inexhaustible. But at the same time that you were falling belching and stinking into the arms of Mlle Mathilde Mauthé, I see myself fleeing from Charleville to Paris. The Rimbaud of sixteen. I paid for my railway ticket with money I got from selling a watch. I am penniless as I board the train. It is the fifteenth of February; it is cold. I go to André Gill, the artist, in whose abandoned studio I lie down to sleep, until Gill appears, wakes me and gives me ten francs for the journey home. But I haven't come to Paris in order to go straight back home again. So I roam the streets, past the booksellers' displays; soon I am living entirely on scraps picked out of dustbins. I spend the night in the arms of prostitutes and sleep in boats on the Seine. I take cover beneath the cast-iron bridges with a pederast's limp prick in my mouth. On 26 February I see forty thousand people demonstrating against Thiers in the most splendid street of the city. Forty thousand! It is the beginning of the Revolution. It grows. It is like a radiant insect. It bursts its cocoon and unfolds its damp wings. The season of young grasses. Then I am back in Charleville again, but in spirit I am in Paris. Am I not also there in body? People claim to have seen me in Paris at the end of April. I am among the defenders of the last barricade at the crossroads between Rue de Tourtille and Rue Rampanneau. I am among the convicted in La Roquette Prison. I am going to be shot. A furniture van will carry away my corpse, while my illumined spirit is still able to pour out several thousand lines of unhoped-for words, before entering into the body of a yokel from the Ardennes, whom it thereby turns into a vagabond and idler.

When I realized that my poetry was merely the echo of the long-vanished Commune, I wrote *Une Saison en Enfer* and then nothing more. I followed my bodily reflexes, threw myself into earning money, swindled, and in Harrar, Ethiopia, caught syphilis.

The Paris Commune, Verlaine, foundered on the gentleness with which it can be reproached. I can imagine that future revolutions will be reproached with the harshness with which they remain victorious. But I dream now of an embrace, of a coupling of the two; I believe in the non-violent Utopia of a justice that overturns everything and roots out misery. But since this divinity I have just described will seem too pagan to my sister Isabelle, I fear she will burn this letter if I die in time. You will never read these lines, you miserable wretch. They are really only intended to remind you that we met each other exactly twenty years ago, in November 1871.

A RADIO TAXI stopped in the street; the driver sounded his horn. This signal from the garden gate sent Stefan's mother running through the house. She was looking for some object she had almost forgotten and then remembered at the last moment. Then two cases and a bag had to be picked up. The front door had to be locked. Stefan walked with his mother past the whining of the dog, which for two hours would remain the sole occupant of these rooms, down the garden path to the street. Catching sight of them, the driver got out of the car and opened the boot to stow away the luggage. After this, they drove down the street. The driver asked if he could take the route through Hoppegarten; traffic was moving very slowly through Köpenick. Stefan saw his mother shrug her shoulders. They drove through a miasma drifting out over the road from a pig farm; they drove past hothouses. His mother had received a new visa for France; now she was on her way to Paris; by this evening it would be possible to reach her by telephone at her stepmother Jeanne's number. The first three figures had been changed: 887–01–24. Stefan and his mother discussed this in an undertone, but they couldn't prevent the taxi driver from hearing where Natasha Roth was going. At the name Paris he drew in his head. The folds on his neck, a fine network, grew

45

deeper and blacker. They drove through Alt-Beisdorf; then the car had to wind its way through the many detours to the building sites at Marzahn and the widening of the Lichtenberg Bridge. Natasha Roth opened her handbag and took out a handkerchief. Stefan caught sight, in the handbag, of the dark-blue passport with the yellow census-card and the white customs declaration. Would his mother want to see Rebecca again? It seemed unlikely; it seemed impossible; they hadn't talked about it and they didn't talk about it now. Two days ago there had been a film about Rebecca on West German television, from which they had learned that she was about to move into a house in the old artists' colony of Worpswede, north of Bremen. The car drove fast through Lichtenberg, down the Karl Marx Allee to the Alexanderplatz. The driver had suddenly started to talk. In clipped sentences he railed against the number and the stock of the foreign-currency stores. He described a case of corruption known to him, caused by the universal greed for West European currencies. "People like us aren't privileged," he growled. *Not privileged*. The driver lapsed into a hostile silence. He turned down the Friedrichstrasse. Directly behind the station he turned to the left and came to a stop by the glass entrance.

Natasha Roth paid. The driver lifted the luggage out of the boot. Stefan walked up the steps beside his mother; then he put down the three pieces of luggage. His mother seemed to him excited, outwardly gay; she had red patches on her face. People passed unceasingly through the swing doors of the entrance, most of them old, many of them walking unsteadily with the aid of a stick. Every time the swing door opened Stefan was able to see into the station hall, where wide steps led down to the luggage bays. Now his mother took his head between her hands. He could feel that her palms were damp. She reminded him not to forget certain things, to stick to certain agreed rules; but all he heard was the sound of her harsh voice; he didn't take in what she was saying. His mother picked up her luggage. She walked, her shoulders uneven, through the swing door. He stayed where he was. As the door swung open again he saw her going down the wide steps. She didn't turn her head. The old people were crowding round the luggage bays. The door swung shut again. Now he had a fleeting vision of his mother against the picture-postcard background of Notre-Dame Cathedral, among the green trees of the Ile de la Cité. The door swung open again. He could no longer see his mother anywhere. He walked away. Later, he thought, he would do everything differently. At the same time, still standing at his old place by the swing door, he watched himself walk away: a skinny sixteen-year-old boy who limped across the forecourt and off into the distance.

This translation is for Lotte Bullock,
née Schneller,
1918–1980

A Note About the Author

ROLF SCHNEIDER was born in 1932 in
Chemnitz (now Karl-Marx-Stadt), in what
is now East Germany. From 1955 to 1958 he
edited the literary monthly *Aufbau*, and
then became a full-time writer. His novels
and his plays for stage, television, and radio
have won him international recognition and
a number of major literary prizes, and his
works have been translated into many
languages. *November* is his third work of
fiction, and his first to be published in the
United States. He is married, with two
children, and lives in East Berlin.

A Note on the Type

THIS BOOK was set on the Linotype in Janson, a recutting made direct from type cast from matrices long thought to have been by the Dutchman Anton Janson, who was a practicing type founder in Leipzig during the years 1668–87. However, it has been conclusively demonstrated that these types are actually the work of Nicholas Kis (1650–1702), a Hungarian, who most probably learned his trade from the master Dutch type founder Dirk Voskens. The type is an excellent example of the influential and sturdy Dutch types that prevailed in England up to the time William Caslon developed his own incomparable designs from them.

This book was composed by Maryland Linotype Composition Company, Inc., Baltimore, Maryland. It was printed and bound by The Haddon Craftsmen, Scranton, Pennsylvania.

Book design by Margaret M. Wagner